10/20

THE
Penny Pinchers
CLUB

**Center Point
Large Print**

Also by Sarah Strohmeyer
Available from Center Point Large Print:

Sweet Love
The Sleeping Beauty Proposal
Bubbles All the Way
The Cinderella Pact
The Secret Lives of Fortunate Wives

**This Large Print Book carries the
Seal of Approval of N.A.V.H.**

THE
Penny Pinchers
CLUB

SARAH STROHMEYER

CENTER POINT PUBLISHING
THORNDIKE, MAINE

This Center Point Large Print edition
is published in the year 2009 by arrangement with
Dutton, a member of Penguin Group (USA), Inc.

The text of this Large Print edition is unabridged.
In other aspects, this book may vary
from the original edition.
Printed in the United States of America.
Set in 16-point Times New Roman type.

ISBN: 978-1-60285-514-4

Library of Congress Cataloging-in-Publication Data

Strohmeyer, Sarah.
  The penny pinchers club / Sarah Strohmeyer.
    p. cm.
  ISBN 978-1-60285-514-4 (library binding : alk. paper)
  1. Married women--Fiction. 2. Home economics--Fiction. 3. New Jersey--Fiction
    4. Domestic fiction. 5. Large type books. I. Title.

PS3569.T6972P46 2009b
813'.54--dc22

2009010665

For Rita,
who can pinch a penny 'til it screams.
Thank you.

"Gather up the fragments left over, that nothing may be lost."

JESUS, IN JOHN 6:12

"But lo! Men have become the tools of their tools."

HENRY DAVID THOREAU, *WALDEN*

"I always say shopping is cheaper than a psychiatrist."

TAMMY FAYE BAKKER

PROLOGUE

ENGAGEMENT RING: $7,340

WEDDING AND RECEPTION: $23,000

RAISING ONE KID FOR EIGHTEEN YEARS:
$250,000

HOUSE IN JERSEY SUBURB: $462,000

TWO MINT TINGLE TROJAN
CONDOM WRAPPERS FOUND IN YOUR
HUSBAND'S POCKETS: $1.40

BEING FINANCIALLY READY WHEN YOUR
HUSBAND ANNOUNCES HE'S LEAVING TO BE
WITH HIS ASSISTANT: PRICELESS

*I*t was the cruel law of Murphy that Mary Ellen Bartholomew chose the one time I'd been arrested to pick up the police permits for the Project Graduation yard sale and fund-raiser. Now it would be all over town that she saw Kat Griffiths in the Rocky River Police Department wearing a bloodied sweatshirt and, almost worse, a pair of Keds.

Of course, the handcuffs wouldn't have been

necessary if the FBI hadn't gotten involved. But the shackles were totally absurd. Did these federal agents honestly believe I, a forty-something mother who could barely jog three miles, would make a run for it?

It was simply embarrassing any way you cut it. Especially since I'd been the Project Graduation committee member designated to get the permits and forgot.

"Kat?" Mary Ellen squinted hard in an attempt to mask her shock. "Are you okay?"

"Sorry about dropping the ball." I hid my hands by burrowing them in the folds of my skirt. "I figured we had until Friday seeing as how the sale's not until next weekend. By the way, Donna Andrews dropped off a whole slew of American Girl dolls and clothes yesterday in mint condition. That should be big. You know how popular they are now."

My attempt at distraction proved futile. Mary Ellen shifted her gaze from me to the handsome guy in his thirties by my side. Wade Rothschild III had the kind of angular jaw and flinty WASPishness one was more likely to find on the cover of the Brooks Brothers spring catalog sporting silk and cotton seersucker than in a faded yellow T-shirt and khaki shorts, his strong, tanned legs ending in a pair of ripped leather Docksiders.

"Mrs. Griffiths?" Officer Ramone—the nice one

with the potbelly and warm brown eyes—appeared at the door of a gray-painted cinder block room where he and the FBI had been holed up for a half hour. "We're ready for you now."

I got up, teetered slightly because of the shackles, and was righted by Wade's knee.

"Keep 'em guessing," he said, loving this. I'd come to like Wade, but he lived in a yurt in his mother's backyard by himself with no dependents, not even goldfish, so he had nothing to lose. One might call him footloose and fancy free except, in light of his bound ankles, not so much with the footloose.

"What about Griff?" Mary Ellen stole another curious glance at Wade.

I'd been purposely trying not to think about how my law-abiding husband would react when he found out I'd been busted kissing another man in a high-security trash bin. We were dealing with enough marital problems without having to cope with rumors of my infidelity.

"He's out of town."

She filed this away along with hunky Wade and the handcuffs. *Kat didn't even want me calling her husband!* "A lawyer, then? Stan Levinson is the best, and he's a friend. His son and Devon are on the same soccer team."

Stan Levinson charged an outrageous $250 an hour. I wouldn't have thought twice about that before joining the Penny Pinchers Club, but these days I was such a skinflint the very notion of more bills made me nauseated. "Thanks, but I have nothing to hide. Searching a Dumpster is hardly a felony."

Not so, according to Officer Ramone. He said there was an exception when the Dumpster belonged to E. W. Drummond, an accounting firm that did the books of a major international defense contractor—as if I was supposed to have been privy to that. It wasn't like I raided other people's trash routinely, for heaven's sake.

In fact, up until my arrest that morning, the only crime I'd committed was the one of paying too much for retail. By the way, that's kind of a pet punch line among the Penny Pinchers. Cracks us up every time.

Most people get the wrong idea when I tell them I'm a member of the Rocky River Penny Pinchers Club. They assume I'm naturally frugal, that all my life I've carefully balanced my checkbook and flicked off lights around the house, clipped coupons and saved leftovers, that I keep the thermostat at sixty degrees in the winter and let my family broil in the summer.

Oh, if they only knew.

Being a Penny Pincher is more akin to being a member of AA, I think. What I've discovered since joining the group and meeting Wade the Wall Street dropout, Opal the Earth Mother, Velma the elderly woman with a mysterious past, Steve the widowed security guard/cop, and Sherise the former debutante is that, like alcoholic individuals with nothing in common except being one drink away from disaster, we are one Visa charge away from bankruptcy. Though, instead of calling up old friends to make amends, we have to call up credit card companies to negotiate reduced balances. It's amazing how far you can get simply by refusing to hang up the phone.

That's how I explained it to Officer Ramone and Agent Wasko, the unsmiling bureaucrat from the FBI. But he didn't care.

Wasko was determined to link my innocent quest for authentic eighteenth-century tchotchkes to a much larger conspiracy. From his line of questioning, I could tell he was trying to pigeonhole me as a peacenik bent on bringing down the international defense contractor, maybe, or a disgruntled homeowner with a defaulted subprime mortgage since, apparently, the accountancy firm also did some work for Countrywide.

"The market crash made us all crazy," he said, as if this news flash would earn my undying friendship. "I, personally, lost forty percent of my IRA."

Ramone let out a whistle.

"So, it's understandable how a frustrated housewife such as yourself might have gone over the edge and taken matters into her own hands, especially when you lost all the savings in your daughter's college fund."

I wanted to tell him that no one calls me a housewife. Not my mother. Not my daughter. Certainly not the FBI. As for losing our shirts in the Wall Street bust? Hah! Griff and I had already drained that account years before, and we had the tax penalty payments to prove it. Don't even ask about our so-called college savings plan. Those leather couches I bought before I became a Penny Pincher didn't pay for themselves.

"It wasn't revenge," I began, pausing to observe that my plastic handcuffs resembled the zip ties on oven bags (cooked goose?). "How I ended up in the Dumpster of E. W. Drummond has far less to do with the market crash and much more to do with what you might call domestic issues. In short, I was simply on the hunt for a sweet deal."

Ramone cracked his gum dubiously. Wasko tapped a pencil.

"Nothing wrong with trying to find a bargain," he said. "But trespassing onto private property at the crack of dawn, ignoring warning signs threatening prosecution, sneaking past electric gates, ducking security cameras, and breaking into a locked repository just for an old rocker or whatever strikes me as fairly implausible, especially considering the sensitive material that might have been found on E. W. Drummond's premises. National security information and whatnot. If you're found guilty, you know, you could be looking at ten years in a federal pen."

He was pulling my leg. No one got ten years for sifting through trash.

Wasko linked his thin, pale fingers. "Then again, I might be more inclined to believe your story if not for your accomplice."

"Wade? The guy lives with his mother."

"I have a hunch there's a lot you don't know about Wade Rothschild III, Mrs. Griffiths. And I have my doubts about the real purpose of this so-called Penny Pinchers group of yours. Too bad you'll learn the truth after it's too late, when you're convicted of economic espionage for stealing corporate secrets."

That was absurd. "I promise, I wasn't in there trying to steal corporate secrets." Nevertheless, a bead of sweat balled at the base of my neck as it dawned on me I really was in serious trouble. This wasn't a parking ticket. This wasn't forgetting to get permits for a yard sale. This was ten years in the federal pen.

"Then why *were* you there?" Agent Wasko had stopped trying to be my friend. "What would motivate a suburban housewife with a nice house, a husband, a kid, a dog, and a job to risk it all by looking for a free chair?"

They leaned forward. I debated whether to tell them the truth. Was it worth it? Could confessing my most intimate secret save me from having to spend my days at a federal prison camp, as Martha Stewart had, wearing ugly brown ponchos?

I took a deep breath and exhaled. "Because I'm saving up for a divorce."

CHAPTER ONE

*T*he reason I'm lousy with money is because I was born and raised in the great state of New Jersey. In Jersey, we drive, we shop, we charge, we throw away. We do not save.

True, ours was the first state in the country to mandate recycling, but after a while we figured screw it. Let those J.Crew preppies in Connecticut separate their Paul Newman salad bottles. We had more important stuff to do, like buy more junk.

As a native of South River, I was particularly afflicted because South River is Jersey concentrate, an enclave of tidy, single-family homes straight from the backdrop of Springsteen's "My Hometown." Lots of bleached sidewalks and chain-link fences surrounding patchy lawns littered with Doritos and McDonald's bags. I grew up with a Knights of Columbus right downtown, a five-and-dime around the corner, and as many churches as bars coexisting under an umbrella of sulfurous yellow haze.

Depressing in some ways. But where God closes a door, he also opens a window. Or, to put it in

Jerseyese, he closes the window and turns on the air-conditioning.

For us, that relief was our town's easy access (if you consider sitting in bumper-to-bumper traffic down Route 18 easy) to ten major shopping malls—entrées to a more glamorous world of Pier I and cheap tamales.

So vital were the malls to our sense of freedom that I celebrated the passing of my driver's test by getting behind the wheel of Dad's embarrassing orange-brown Dodge Dart with my girlfriends and zipping right past Mom's reliable discount mall (Loehmann's of the awkward communal dressing room) for the upscale paradise of Menlo Park.

It was a complete rush of independence. Aerosmith wailed "Sweet Emotion" on the radio, our feathered, blow-dried hair waved in the New Jersey breeze, and we were headed to Edison, New Jersey, on the off chance of running into Jeff Doncha. Black hair, blue eyes. To die for. Hottest guy in South River hands down.

We didn't smoke. We didn't drink. We didn't do drugs. We didn't even have sex. Well, not *technically*. We shopped and gossiped and harassed the Clinique lady for makeovers (after which we bought nothing) before stopping off at a chain Mexican restaurant for virgin daiquiris. That launched our pastime, and in almost thirty years not much has changed.

Yes, we've moved up from the Dart. Most of us

drive Highlanders or Lexus SUVs, cars with bigger rear ends (like ourselves) to hold more stuff. Our hair is foiled, and Loehmann's now stocks Diesel jeans. We no longer endure the torture of seeing our pores enlarged in a Clinique magnifying mirror. But we still crank the Aerosmith and every so often treat ourselves to strawberry daiquiris that, like us, are not so virgin.

As for Jeff Doncha, last I checked he was holding his own down at his dad's salvage yard after a couple of stints in rehab and one strike short of permanent incarceration. Funny enough, the guy I ended up marrying had black hair and midnight blue eyes, too, though that was where all similarities between him and Jeff ended.

My husband and I met when I was fresh out of Rutgers, sharing an apartment near Princeton with my former college roommate Suzanne Veruki. Back then, the two of us were miserably employed at PharMax, a corporate pharmaceutical conglomerate in Bridgewater, though we'd known each other for years, having been visual design majors in college with plans to be snapped up by the hottest interior design boutiques from Manhattan to Palm Beach.

Ah, the naïveté of youth. Our mortarboards weren't yet dusty when we realized we couldn't get jobs assembling furniture at IKEA, much less redoing interiors for Jed Johnson in Manhattan. So, I got a position at PharMax schlepping a new birth control pill (OvuTerm—later found to trigger early menopause), while Suzanne hawked a new colorectal cancer test made popular by Ronald Reagan's very own presidential colon.

It was tough going, pushing drugs. Being a pharmaceutical rep meant constantly being rejected by snooty doctors' receptionists after hours of waiting patiently with a smile for "just a moment to tell you about our new product." It takes a very special person to face that kind of humiliation every day—a stripper, maybe, or a Jehovah's Witness. But without the Franklins being shoved in our panties or the promise of eternal salvation, Suzanne and I couldn't see the point. We went down in PharMax history as achieving the worst sales ever, a dishonor in which we took weird pride.

About the only good thing happening in my life back then was Liam Novak. Liam was a wunderkind on PharMax's corporate track, destined to be CEO with his Wharton degree and uncanny memory for the most mind-numbing pharmaceutical minutiae.

It helped that he was a rather sexy, Polish-Irish version of Dudley Do-Right, right down to his dimpled chin, fit physique, and blond hair that, unlike Dudley, he wore with a shock of long bangs, a style left over from his days at the all-boy Jesuit boarding school, Georgetown Prep, where he'd starred as lacrosse captain and cross-country record holder.

Lucky for me, I met Liam's ideal of a perfect potential wife, probably because I'd been raised Roman Catholic, which pleased his conservative Irish Catholic mother, and because with my own white-blond hair; fair, almost transparent, complexion; ridiculously high forehead; and pale, pale blue eyes, I resembled the living incarnation of every beatific Madonna hanging over every Polish grandmother's bed west of Warsaw. Not that that was something to be proud of, mind you. Back then I'd have much preferred to be compared with the other gap-toothed Madonna in pearls and lace bustiers—as would have most of the guys I dated.

Except for Liam. He pursued me with the same gung-ho energy he used to win over PharMax's shareholders and blitz his friends with ninety-five-mile-an-hour aces. Dinners at the upscale Princeton Inn, huge bouquets of flowers sent to my desk, shopping sprees on Fifth Avenue, and weekends at his family's beachside compound in Avalon, New Jersey, were par for the course.

This worked out well because I loved his family and they loved me. Such a boisterous bunch of mindless consumers like myself, not a deep thinker in the group. With Liam and at least two of his seven brothers and sisters, I'd spend entire days at the beach playing Frisbee or zoned out on the sand, shopping for bric-a-brac along Ninty-sixth Street in Stone Harbor and hitting the beachfront clubs afterward. No matter how late we stayed out on

Saturday nights, though, Bridget Novak (Liam's haggard mother) managed to rouse us out of bed and get us to the ten A.M. mass at Maris Stella every morning, delicate lace veils perched primly on our occasionally hungover heads.

My own smitten mother used to call them "Kennedy South," but she was wrong. Yes, like Joe Kennedy, Liam's father, Karol, had come to America and "done good," becoming the hands-down gypsum king of the tri-state area. But that was where all similarities between the Kennedys and the Novaks ended. Karol Novak had no more sense of noblesse oblige than Paris Hilton, and his politics were lever-pulling straight Republican like that of my father and so many other first-generation American Eastern Europeans.

Even with a patriarch like Karol calling the shots, though, it was easy being Liam's girlfriend because he loved me to death and also because he was gorgeous with a terrific sense of style. From his choice of automobile (BMW 3 series, nothing less) to Gucci loafers to Ray-Ban Aviators, everything Liam owned was top notch. It might sound shallow, but that made being with him all the more thrilling.

Wherever we went, Liam would be mistaken for a minor actor (on *General Hospital*?) or even a fashion model. Perfect strangers—middle-aged housewives, mostly—would stop him in the grocery store and ask if he'd been that man on the

Calvin Klein billboard, the one in the white cotton briefs that was so *obscene*. (And sexy!)

He'd win me over with his modest response, shrugging off the double takes and drinks sent to him from admirers across a crowded bar as nothing more than the benefits of fleeting youth. Liam was that rare commodity—a heterosexual American male who loved style for style's sake, whether it pertained to his car, his clothes, or—my personal passion—interior decorating.

And he loved to go shopping. Happily. Half the time it would be his idea. My roommate Suzanne used to claim I'd hit the jackpot with Liam, though that might have been because she was miserably dating a chef who spent his off-hours watching football while sharpening his knives.

That said, Liam was not perfect. For one thing, he had a tendency to automatically issue decisions without my input, like making dinner reservations and advising me what to wear. At restaurants, he'd occasionally order for me or he'd take my car in for tune-ups without asking. Once, he called up my dentist to make an appointment to have my teeth cleaned.

I'm sure he thought he was being masculine and protective, or maybe he was emulating his father, who also tended toward the dictatorial, but I found it increasingly annoying to be told what I would do and when to floss.

Then there was the day when he stepped into my

cubicle at PharMax and plunked down a purchase agreement for a classic Morrisville colonial on a shady oak-lined street with a brick fireplace, kitchen nook, and five bedrooms.

"The kids might have to double up," he said.

Kids? Just how many kids was he talking about, because if Liam was entertaining notions of me turning into another Bridget Novak, with her dropped uterus and bulging varicose veins, he had another think coming.

"Go with it," my sister Viv advised when I mentioned this over lunch. "You just know Liam's going to propose to you this spring, followed by an August wedding at Our Lady of Perpetual Pain in South River. It's the script! Then all you'll have to do is spit out babies like a royal princess while he climbs the corporate ladder. With nannies galore—what could be easier?"

I took a bite of my chicken salad and thought about the possibility of being Mrs. Liam Novak.

"In between stints in the maternity ward, you can spend your days working out and driving around in your wood-paneled station wagon from mall to mall, shopping to your heart's content. Wouldn't that be fun?"

I put myself in Viv's picture. Me with a high-lighted bob and bright pink lips, one of those little woven purses in the crook of my arm. Entire summers at the Shore making peanut butter sandwiches on Wonder bread for when the kids got back from swimming. Bright green lawns. Blue country club swimming pools and the squeaky clean perfume of chlorine in my children's hair. Perfectly appointed living rooms with fireplaces and deep shag. Whole school days devoted to choosing new drapes before the kids got home at three and I had to chaperone them to piano and catechism.

That wasn't so bad.

Besides, I loved Liam—or so my twenty-three-year-old self assumed. He was kind to me and I was kind to him. Our religious and ethnic backgrounds were comfortably similar and yet different enough to spice up the mix. My only concerns were his mother—who no doubt would be at our house every single day organizing the sock drawers—and those controlling tendencies of his that seemed to be growing stronger the closer we got to marriage.

But, heck, I could nip that in the bud, right? We were still young and flexible. It wasn't etched in stone that he had to turn into his father.

As Viv predicted, Liam did propose on Easter Sunday while we took a chilly walk on the beach in Avalon after church and brunch. We were holding hands and chatting about nothing in particular, dodging the frigid waves, when I felt something cold on my ring finger, looked down, and saw his grandmother's diamond, repositioned in a spectacular Tiffany platinum setting.

"All I can promise you," he said, gently kissing me on the forehead, "is that I'll do my best to provide us a beautiful life, Kat. A home, children, and my undying love forever. You'll never want for anything."

It was an irresistible package and there's no doubt in my mind, looking back, that had he popped the question three weeks before, I would have eagerly and gladly responded with a resounding "Yes!" Nor is there any doubt that we would have gone on to lead that beautiful life with the home, the children, and me never wanting for anything.

But something had happened in the meantime. Something unexpected and terrifying and more life altering than I'd have ever expected.

I'd fallen head over heels in love.

CHAPTER TWO

*I*t happened shortly after I began working for Chloe Sykes, having left PharMax on the advice of my supervisor, who worried, rightly so, that my romantic relationship with Liam could create issues for the corporation. No matter. I never cared much about OvuTerm—as my sales records proved—and Chloe was in dire need of an assistant when I went hunting for an interior decorating job. Sometimes, the stars are just aligned.

Chloe owned Interiors by Chloe, a boutique firm

in the heart of posh Princeton, where she tried to recast herself and her perky redone nose as a blond Presbyterian raised in New Jersey's horse country amid polo matches and white-gloved luncheons, a distant relative, naturally, of New York City's A-list Sykes.

It was all a sham.

In reality, Chloe had been born Tammy Ann Szabo, native of Manville, New Jersey, where asbestos used to roll in big white balls down Main Street like cancerous tumbleweed. Having grown up across the street from heiress Doris Duke's 2,700-acre walled estate, Duke Farms, young Chloe was the girl with her face pressed to the proverbial candy store window. She grew into adulthood with a bottomless appetite for wealth, status, and luxury.

What she got was Scotty Boy Sykes, her rich duffer of a husband some thirty years her senior. With his blue lips, liver spots, paunchy eyes, and tendency to spit while stuttering, Scotty Boy would have repulsed most women of Chloe's age and beauty. But Chloe was *that* desperate and he'd had *that* last name, although years later she would learn Sykes was merely an Ellis Island shortcut from his family's original—Siemankowski.

I think this is why Chloe hired me. Once she learned I was Katarina Popalaski from Manville's not-too-distant cousin South River, she knew she was onto something. Here, at last, was one of her people. Had our descendants not stepped onto the boat at Gdansk, both of us would have been wearing ankle socks and headscarves, gumming salted fish and cursing the apparatchik. Only, unlike Chloe, I hadn't changed my name and tried to parlay my blond hair into WASP credentials. Therefore, she assumed I was clay to mold, a novice she could impress with her late-model Range Rover and designer bags.

I *was* impressed—mostly by Chloe's determination to get out of bed every day and put on a show, arming herself with Chanel, Ferragamo, Nancy Gonzalez satchels, Bulgari shades, and constant dieting. It took so much work to fight back those Szabo genes, so much studying and brushing up on who was in and who was out in the Bedminster–Far Hills set, that being in her presence was often enervating.

Especially when she was second-guessing herself into a nervous breakdown.

That was what she was doing the fateful day beaucoup bucks client Barb Gladstone (as in Peapack Gladstone, an irrelevant detail Chloe never failed to mention) announced she was displeased. The drapes Chloe had designed for Barb's master bedroom were doing absolutely nothing about shutting out the morning sun, as she'd specifically requested. She demanded Chloe come up to Bedminster ASAP.

In the incestuous world of high-end Jersey

redecorating, this spelled disaster. Barb knew everyone who was anyone and she'd taken a chance on Chloe after she and her regular interior decorator had suffered a minor falling-out. It had been Chloe's golden opportunity to wedge her Dior sandals in the door and she'd blown it big-time.

"It's not a huge deal, don't you think? I mean, it's not as if the drapes can't be replaced or that I'm not willing to absorb every last penny of replacing them." She furiously flossed her teeth while zigzagging the Range Rover through Bedminster's winding roads, paying scant regard to nuisances like stop signs and speed limits. Or trees.

I'd only been working for Chloe two weeks, so I wasn't quite sure what to say. At the moment, I was more concerned with staying alive as I gripped the door handle and assessed the situation. It seemed to me that the cost of replacing the drapes that had averaged about $800 a panel was prohibitive. Plus, my sense was that Barb had given Chloe a simple task as a test case. If she couldn't throw up a pair of curtains, then how could Chloe be expected to redo a whole kitchen?

"I'm sure you're fine," I lied, patting her purse as a safe alternative to patting any part of her physical presence. "Barb's probably one of those grand dames who complains about everything. Look how she fired her regular decorator."

Chloe slammed on the brakes. "If Barb fires me, then I should fold up the business right now. My name will be mud."

I decided if I was going to keep my job, I had better work on my tact.

We arrived at the white stone house where Chloe, so beside herself, nearly plowed her Range Rover into the back of a truck filled with dirt and grass belonging to two landscapers hard at work resetting the Gladstone slate walkway. They leaned on their shovels and stared at Chloe, who inconsiderately left her car smack in the middle of the driveway so no one else could get around.

I shrugged in apology and trotted after her, though I had no idea what I was expected to do or say.

Inside the mansion, that role became no clearer. Barb, dressed in blue, glided down the stairs—pale from insomnia—and escorted Chloe to the bed-chamber of horrors. It was understood that I was to stay put.

Meanwhile, I conducted a self-guided tour, wandering from room to room, gradually forgetting about Chloe and the drapes while I let myself be dazzled by Barb Gladstone's artwork, including an original Picasso and a collection of intricately painted antique Chinese vases that must have been pre-eighteenth century. I took mental notes of how Barb placed the fresh flowers and chintz furniture for when Liam and I moved into the Morrisville colonial. Someday, we'd have a home just like this, sans the Picasso, of course. I could hardly wait.

It wasn't until I strolled outside, humming a tune and taking in the earthy aroma of freshly mowed spring grass, that I realized I was in deep, deep trouble. The landscapers were gone. So was Chloe's Range Rover.

Uh-oh. There was a brief moment of panic as I rapidly assessed my options. Since this was before cell phones, in the 1980s, it was impossible to call Chloe while she was on the road. But, surely, she would be back soon. Perhaps she'd been made to move her car. Or Barb had sent her on an errand.

Still, it would be a good idea to check with her office just in case. Unfortunately, despite possessing every luxury imaginable, Barb Gladstone seemed to have overlooked modern communication. There wasn't a phone anywhere. Not even in the library, where I rushed in and was stopped short at the sight of one of the landscapers going through Barb's personal belongings.

His back was toward me, his faded red T-shirt smudged with dirt, a maroon line of sweat running between his pronounced shoulder blades. Longish black wavy hair curled from perspiration at his neck, and from where I stood at the door, his metallic, musky odor of heavy physical labor mixed with the library's more distinguished aroma of fine leather and bound books. I couldn't imagine that Barb would approve of a man in his state flipping through her collection with his filthy fingers.

"Excuse me."

He plunked a finger between the pages and turned, at first seemingly annoyed by my interruption and then, seeing me in my short black shirt and white sweater with the plunging neckline, more forgiving.

"Hello." He raised a curious eyebrow. "Lost?"

"Kind of." I really was in no mood for idle chatter. This was serious. "Do you happen to know if the woman with the Range Rover—"

"Left? About a half hour ago."

A half hour ago? So it was true! Chloe had *ditched* me. Not only that, but my car was parked back in Princeton at the university since there was no room in Chloe's lot, a definite risk considering I wasn't a university student and that I'd been warned once before. . . .

"Shit!"

The landscaper approached, his head cocked slightly in interest. I noticed that his eyes, while blue, were very dark, and there was a slight scar on his forehead. Other than that scar, he was strikingly handsome, almost like a Greek statue, with a pointed chin, graceful nose, and a strong, long neck with sinews so pronounced I was tempted to reach out and trace one of them with my finger.

Not that I was interested, of course. I was almost

engaged to Liam. But Liam was completely averse to anything smacking of physical labor. That's what checks were for, he liked to say: to pay others to do what he didn't have to. *This* man, with his grime and muscles, was an intriguing, albeit slightly disgusting, fascination—like raw oysters.

He said, "I gather there's a problem."

I quickly explained about being stranded and about my car being parked illegally back at the university. I wasn't out and out asking for a ride, but as soon as I described my dilemma, I realized I'd dropped a very strong hint.

"Is this a common practice of yours?" He casually leaned against a bookshelf as if we had all the time in the world. "Using Princeton University as your personal parking lot?"

"I wouldn't have to if I weren't in hot water with the town," I said, choosing to ignore his amused smile.

"And that's because . . . ?"

"Because I owe them about three hundred dollars in unpaid parking tickets and if I so much as idle at a stoplight, they'll slap a boot on my car."

"I see." He ran a finger under his lower lip, taking me in, trying to decide if I was worth the effort. "I'll tell you what. Give me ten minutes and I'll drive you down."

It was a supremely generous offer, exactly what I needed, and I would have leaped at it immediately if it hadn't been for the fact that he was a dirty stranger. For all I knew, he could have been a rapist or a serial killer or . . . both! But before I could ask a few more prudent questions, he was gone, taking Barb's book with him.

He returned as promised, having showered and changed into clean jeans and a heavy white cotton shirt that he was buttoning up with one hand, his other holding the book and a set of keys. With his black hair wet and slicked back, his odor of filth replaced with the refreshing scent of soap, he bore only a vague resemblance to the landscaper from before.

"Come on." He nodded to a side door. "My car's out back."

"You can shower here? I mean, Barb lets you?" She seemed like such an ungenerous old woman.

"Oh, she lets me do more than that."

I'd assumed that we were going to take the landscaping truck. Instead, he opened the door to a small green MG Midget that looked barely large enough to hold my niece's Barbies.

"And along with using her shower, I gather Barb lets you drive her car, too," I said, getting in.

"No. This I let *her* drive, if she behaves herself." He closed my door and extended his hand. "By the way, I'm Griff."

I told him I was Kat, but inside I wasn't sure. My world seemed to have turned upside down like the book he'd taken from Barb's library and tossed into my lap. Nothing made sense. Why would a landscaper be showering in one of Barb's many bathrooms? Why would he be reading her books and driving an MG, walking about the house like he owned it?

I regarded his tanned bare forearm flecked with dark hair as he shifted gears and sent us zooming through Bedminster's quiet roads, the top down, my hair flying in the breeze. It was exhilarating, and, yet, I had to remember Liam. There was no point in even flirting with another man, not with all the unspoken plans for my marriage already in the works.

"Keep hold of that book." He boldly leaned over and placed my hand on top of it securely. "It's a classic."

I checked the title: *Capital Vol. 1: A Critique of Political Economy.* Modify that earlier question. Who was this sweaty landscaper with the sexy MG he drove way, way too fast who *read Karl Marx for fun*?

I didn't know. But I wanted to. Suddenly, I was possessed with an overwhelming, pressing need to know exactly who this Griff was. Unfortunately, he beat me to the punch.

"Pardon my bluntness, but I assume you do realize that racking up hundreds of dollars in parking tickets is a complete waste of money." He downshifted as we entered Princeton's city limits, where the cops were notorious for picking off speeders. "Three hundred dollars is what I pay a month in rent."

"I don't care." I tried not to think about my parking tickets. They gave me a headache. "I hate talking about money."

"Do you? That's too bad."

"Why?"

"Because I love it."

"Oh, I love money, too," I agreed. "Love to have it in my wallet. Love to spend it or, better, have other people spend it on me."

"No." He frowned. "I hate that. Money sucks."

"I thought you said . . ."

"I like studying how money influences the tide of human events, its ability to corrupt and redeem. But mostly corrupt, as he would say." He tapped the Karl Marx. "When you're looking for the source of evil, it's hard to go wrong with money."

"So you're a Marxist."

"Even Marx once said, 'I am not a Marxist.' Though he did say, 'I am only as young as the women I feel.' "

"Karl Marx was only as young as the women he felt?"

"No. That last quote was Groucho's. Different Marx. Old econ joke." He chucked me under the chin playfully, as if we'd known each other forever. "Now tell me where we can find this illegal car of yours."

We turned into the lot just in time to see the front

end of my blue Honda Civic passing by on the back of a Princeton University tow truck. I let out a whimper and Griff slammed on the brakes.

"Hold on." He killed the engine and leaped out without opening the door, dashing toward the tow truck and flagging it down. After much discussion and cajoling on Griff's part, the driver agreed to free my Honda as long as I promised never, ever to so much as idle the car within five feet of the university's gates.

"Good you know Griff," the driver said, unwinding the winch. "Otherwise, you wouldn't have been able to retrieve this vehicle until nine A.M. Monday."

He knew Griff?

"The president's spot." Griff folded his arms. "You couldn't find anywhere else to park? On this whole campus, five hundred acres, you pick in front of the president's house."

It definitely ranked as one of the more mortifying moments of my life, even if Griff seemed to find it funny.

"Now you can understand why I was kind of panicked. Look." I held out my arm. "I'm still shaking."

He took my hand and squeezed it firmly in his large one. "Don't worry, Kat. It's over. Not even a fine." He dropped my hand and headed back to the MG.

. . . And out of my life forever. No!

"I can't thank you enough." My mind raced for a reasonable excuse to keep him around. "Please. At least let me buy you dinner."

He hesitated, twirling his keys. "I bet you have a boyfriend."

"So?"

"So, what would he think about you taking out a man you just met?"

"It's not like he owns me, Griff. I am my own woman. And, besides, my offer is just common courtesy. Nothing more."

"All right. Why not?" He jumped back into the MG. "How about we meet at the A&B? There's a lane in the back where the cops never check for scofflaws like you."

The A&B was the Alchemist & Barrister, on Nassau Street, a hangout for students and tourists, which meant it was always crowded. Griff was right: The cops never patrolled the lane behind it, though that might have been why there was never any parking there. Eventually, I ended up leaving the Honda at Chloe's and hoofing the five blocks to the restaurant.

When I finally arrived, I found the most unusual sight. Griff at a table surrounded by three or four students eagerly vying for his attention. Over their heads, our gazes met and he waved me over.

"This is Kat." He openly took my hand and pulled me next to him. "These are my slack-jawed undergrads whining and whinging about their course loads. It's all they ever do."

They weren't whining, they were joshing with him, punching his arm and cracking jokes. From snippets of their conversations, I gleaned that they were in the intro to economics course Griff taught at Princeton to help pay for his PhD. Apparently, as he told me later, he did odd jobs for Barb Gladstone out of fondness for the old dame, a major benefactor of the university who took a liking to young, handsome men who followed her husband's passion.

"She insists I use her library," he said, bending close because the yelling at the table was so loud. "She claims it's because she likes to see her husband's books being read, though I suspect she just likes men. Barb was a gorgeous woman back in her day. Blond. Blue eyed. Very shapely." He took another sip of his beer. "Kind of like you."

Several plates of French fries appeared on the table, along with numerous beers. A few more students joined us and pushed me so close to Griff that he had no choice but to put his arm around the back of my seat. I didn't object. Nor did I mind as the heat of his strong thigh burned into mine or that his arm had dropped down from the seat and ended up around my shoulders. By the end of the evening, I was practically on his lap.

Tucked into him, warm and secure, I experienced a startling epiphany that my entire life had been leading up to this one point, to wandering through Barb Gladstone's house and meeting this man. *He's the guy, the one I've been waiting for*, I thought as Griff occasionally put his lips to my ears to provide a bit of context to one of the students, his breath warm against my neck.

A girl across from us eyed me with envy, and I felt myself blush.

There wasn't much of what the students were saying that I remember. What I never forgot, however, was our conversation afterward when we were alone.

We talked about how he ended up in Princeton from his native Oregon. (He'd met a girl, who promptly dumped him once they moved to the East Coast.) We talked about his love of hiking and roughing it on the trail and my love of beachside resorts with spas and swim-up bars.

We talked about both Marxes, Karl and Groucho, and about how Barb Gladstone desperately wanted him to marry her granddaughter Caroline, who was as smart as soap and just as sickening. I learned about his fascination with British cars and educated him about all things Bruce Springsteen. (To this day, I cannot believe he'd never heard of the Stone Pony.)

I couldn't help comparing him to Liam, as unfair as that was. With Liam, our conversations skipped across the surface, landing on safe topics—work, movies, what was on TV, and where we should go to dinner. With Griff, it was more of a mind meld. He engaged me, demanded details, thought about my answers, and laughed frequently. Under the table, his thigh brushed against mine, sending shivers up my entire leg. Once, he absently tucked my hair behind my ear in such a way that I feared my entire being would explode.

As the night ended and Griff walked me to my car, there was the inevitable "As for that boyfriend you mentioned. . . ." He ran a hand over my shoulders. "How serious are you two, anyway?"

I sucked in a breath, wishing briefly that Liam wasn't in the picture. "Let's just say," I began, choosing the most telling metaphor, "that a few months ago he bought a five-bedroom house in Morrisville."

Griff dropped his hand. "Ah."

My heart plummeted. Part of me had being dying to kiss him, to find out what he tasted like, what he felt like, and now, with the mention of Liam, that option was off the table. We got to my Honda and I stuck the key in the lock, determined to do the right thing. And then, before my better half could get control, I turned and it happened.

He kissed me the way I'd always dreamed, hand stroking my chin, lifting it to him, arm around my waist, slowly bringing me closer, pressing himself gently against me against my car. How long we remained like that, I had no idea. Long enough to process a million thoughts—that I shouldn't be doing this, that if Liam saw us, he'd have been heartbroken, that I wanted Griff to kiss me deeper. He did. That I wanted to wrap my whole body around him. I did. That both of us wanted desperately to go someplace where we could take off all our clothes and feel our bodies, naked, together.

We didn't.

"I guess that's it, then." He gave my hands a squeeze, as he had in the Princeton parking lot hours ago. "Considering you and . . ."

"Liam." I swallowed hard. "I guess so."

"Right." He backed up, paused, and walked off.

I got into my rescued Honda and drove to the apartment I shared with Suzanne, who was lying on our old green couch watching *St. Elmo's Fire* on our new VCR, to which she was addicted. I took one look at Andrew McCarthy making out with Ally Sheedy and promptly proceeded to pour out my heart in big heaping sobs.

"Stick with Liam," she said, rubbing my back. "This new guy is not *the one*. Liam's *the one* because he loves you slightly more than you love him and a wise woman will always marry a man who loves her more than she loves him. That's the key to a successful marriage."

She was absolutely no help. So I went to bed, and I went on with my life, working for Chloe, going out with Liam and trying to forget Griff, until that Easter on the beach when Liam proposed and it hit me that it was simply impossible to forget this man, this landscaper-cum-PhD student whose lips along my neck sent me into a state of frenzy.

There was just no ethical way I could say yes to Liam. Not that I had any assurance of being with Griff. Quite the opposite. Only, that having experienced what I suspected was true love, I knew in my bones I could not honestly spend my future with anyone else without making both of us miserable.

"I can't," was all I could say to Liam, removing the ring and pressing it in the palm of his hand. "But I know some other woman will be thrilled to have this."

He was shocked and, after a moment of speechlessness, recovered himself enough to ask, "Who is he?"

I told him the basics, tactfully leaving out my intense feelings of lust and longing and substituting them with rational thoughts about doubt, as if Griff had been nothing more than a handy touchstone at an appropriate juncture. It felt crummy.

"But I don't have doubts." Liam grabbed me by the shoulders. "Even if you do, you have to ask yourself if you will ever meet another man who will love you and take care of you as I will, who will ensure you never have a minute of financial worry, who will see to it that your happiness always, always comes before his."

Today, the concept of life without a minute of financial worry is a far more romantic fantasy than

Caribbean vacations, moonlit walks on the beach, and Venetian sunsets combined.

But when you're in your early twenties and have just found a man who can turn your legs to jelly with nothing more than a knowing glance, who can kiss you into oblivion, life without financial worries is right down there with annuities and insurance premiums. Meaningless and as boring as a mothballed gray suit.

That afternoon of the rejected marriage proposal none of the Novaks would speak to me as I packed up and left before Liam returned, having set out to walk the rest of the beach by himself.

Back home, Suzanne was aghast. ("Liam is the most generous and handsome man to walk the earth. If you don't want him, I do!") But her disappointment could not compare to that of my mother's, who acted like a child when I showed up for Easter dinner without him.

"But we were going to have a party!" She bit into a slice of *cwiebak*, the Polish comfort food of choice. "Your father even put in a bottle of *pezsgo*. Now what are we going to do with it?"

Pop! Viv held the prized Hungarian champagne over the sink to catch the foam. "I'll take care of it, Mom. Not to worry." She helped herself to a sip and smacked her lips. "Pretty good. Hey, you think if we invited this guy Griff up for a glass, he'd help us celebrate?" She ducked as my mother's *cwiebak* flew past her head.

Over Viv's laughing, my father asked who the hell Griff was.

I did not call Griff to celebrate. Nor did I call Liam to commiserate. Instead, I soldiered forward, convincing myself I'd made the right decision until word came through the PharMax grapevine that Liam had unexpectedly married in a huge church in Bedminster less than twelve weeks after we'd broken up.

Her name was Paige, and she was a professional tennis player as well as the daughter of the founder of a competing corporation, Trident Pharmaceuticals. Suzanne said word around PharMax was that Liam had tendered his resignation and was already on the corporate track at his father-in-law's company. The wedding had been attended by two hundred people, including a few celebrities and politicians, with a reception at the exclusive and elegant Fiddler's Elbow Country Club. Afterward, the newlyweds flew to the south of France for a two-week-long honeymoon.

"An elaborate shindig like that would be impossible to pull off at the last minute," Suzanne said, handing me a copy of his wedding announcement in the *New York Times*. "You don't think he had this Paige on the back burner all along, do you?"

"Not Liam. He's not the type to cheat." In his heartbreak over me, he must have impulsively asked her to marry him, and realizing he was such a catch, she'd snapped at the chance. "I'm afraid it's a rebound thing."

I studied the picture of my ex and the petite bride with short brown hair and firm tennis-pro body in her strapless white gown. His head was bent lovingly toward hers and she was looking up at him with such adoration, it eased some of the guilt I'd felt for leaving him on that Avalon beach. He'd found what he was looking for: a devoted wife. Good.

Still, I couldn't help feeling a twinge of regret. *That could have been me.*

Well, it was over, I thought. He was married and for all I knew, Griff had returned to Oregon. Suzanne and I found a larger apartment, blew our savings on new furniture, and hunkered down for the duration of what we suspected would be many, many years as single women.

A few weeks after we moved, however, I was crossing Nassau Street on a blustery fall day, trying to shield a book of wallpaper samples from a sudden shower, when Griff stepped through the gates of Princeton, smack into my path. He was in a gray T-shirt, gesticulating as he spoke to a young woman with shiny chestnut hair that she flipped absently with one hand.

My first instinct was to run, but he shouted my name and told me to "hold up." *Please,* I prayed as he jogged in my direction. *Please just say hello and good-bye.*

"Hello," he said breathlessly. "How've you been?"

"Fine, fine. Busy, busy." I tapped the book of wallpaper samples and worked on keeping an upbeat tone. "Apparently Barb didn't ruin my boss's career after all. Business is booming. I even got a raise."

"Excellent." He couldn't have cared less. "So are you . . ."

"Married?" I held up my left hand to show I wasn't.

He took one long look and, as if just understanding what I'd meant, broke into a knowing grin. "Actually, I was going to ask you to dinner since I think you got off easy with the French fries and beer at the A&B."

Horrified that I'd presumed he'd been asking about my marital state, I blurted, "Can't do it tonight."

"How about the rest of your life?"

Was he serious? "What about . . . ?" I nodded to the woman waiting patiently a block away.

He followed my gaze and said, "That's one of my students, nothing more, of course. How could I even look at another woman after kissing you?"

I didn't care if he was slightly teasing me. I was so happy that he was still interested and that we were both free, I could barely keep myself from dragging him back to my apartment then and there. "How about we start with dinner tonight and see where that takes us?"

"Okay, but you'll want to pencil me in for the rest."

"The rest of what?"

"Your life. You thought I was joking. I wasn't. Not a day's gone by since we met, Kat, when I haven't thought about you and that . . ."

The next I knew, he was kissing me at the gates of Princeton in front of his student, in front of the entire campus.

Yes, the rest-of-your-life line was corny. It was the kind of corny line nerdy econ grad students dream up while taking breaks from writing love letters to Ayn Rand. (Griff later admitted he'd started working on it the night he'd left me in Chloe's parking lot.) Which might be why it's the one our daughter has always loved the most.

I was certain that I had it all that rainy late September day. I was in love with a man who was so intellectually stimulating and masculine and sexy, the touch of his hand against mine could trigger a shiver of erotic pleasure. I had the job I wanted, and soon after, I had an adorable baby girl, Laura.

We were blessed with plenty, more than enough. No, I never moved into a huge colonial in Morrisville, nor did I join a country club and spend my days lunching and shopping and chauffeuring kids in a wood-paneled station wagon. Because money was always tight at our house, I had to go back to work when Laura was six months old and

I have never known the luxury of never worrying about bills.

If there was one regret, it was that I didn't pause in our whirlwind courtship to stop and analyze that offhand comment Griff had made about wasting money on parking tickets. How to handle money is one of those uncomfortable premarital topics that couples are supposed to discuss, along with kids and religion.

And, like most new couples, we artfully dodged it.

Maybe it was because I was so young and having too much fun and so giddily in love to ruin the magic by sitting him down and laying out a balance sheet. But more likely it was because I already sensed there was a conflict.

Griff was a saver; I was a spender. Therein lay the seeds of our destruction.

Despite that, we managed to survive our many, many fights about money intact, more together and more in love than we were on that fall day outside Princeton.

Or so I believed, until twenty years passed and I zipped open the suitcase from his trip to the West Coast to find I'd made an awful mistake. I'd married the wrong man.

CHAPTER THREE

*T*wo wrappers from Trojan Mint Tingle condoms. That's what I found in the pocket of Griff's khakis while unpacking the suitcase from his trip to San Francisco.

My first question—after the initial wave of revulsion—was what normal man would insist on a minty tingle there? Mint was for fighting gingivitis, no?

More important, what was my husband doing with two condom wrappers while on a business trip?

This was the key issue I might have completely overlooked if Viv had not been standing guard while I did the wash. "What's that!" she screeched, pointing to the shiny blue and green papers perched on a pile of lint. "Are those Griff's?"

"NO!" I said too quickly. "Griff must have found them in the . . ."

Hold on. Where must he have found them?

My mind fast-forwarded to an image of Griff naked on a king-sized bed in some San Francisco Marriott, his strong, familiar legs spread as an anonymous woman with long auburn hair and a fabulous body ripped the mint-flavored wrapper with her teeth and slowly unrolled the condom over his . . .

No! Griff? *My* Griff? Never. Yes, he had a robust

male sex drive, but he also possessed impressive self-control. More to the point, he loved me and loved his family. He wouldn't have done anything to jeopardize losing us. It was out of the question.

"Griff must have found them in the airport bathroom and stuffed them in his pocket to keep a kid from seeing . . . or something." I decided to change the conversation to a topic Viv never tired of—her love life. "So. How did it go with Henry last night? Get lucky?"

"Come on, Kat." She slid off the dryer and put her coffee on the folding table. "Is there something you'd like to tell me?" Viv checked me over her art deco half-glasses with the crazy swirls as if I were one of her lackadaisical students in American Writers lying about a late paper.

Though we were only twenty-two months apart in age, Viv always seemed much older and more together, the hair on her blond bob never out of place, her white capris neatly pressed and spotless. I attributed her personal order to the fact that she never had to deal with children or a husband, but the truth was Viv was not the type to lose sight of the ball. Other younger sisters might have found that obnoxious, but I found her steadiness reassuring. It only made me love her more.

"If I had something to tell you, you'd be the first to know." I batted my eyes. "Or not."

"Look, maybe Mom was right. Maybe he *is* a skunk. Not that I'm agreeing with her. Just that it's important to check in with reality every now and then."

I let that pass, having become accustomed to my mother's bizarre refusal to forgive me for not marrying Liam. Twenty years of Griff paying her compliments, hopping up to do the dishes, helping her plan my parents' retirement, and she still grumbled about him being a perpetual student even though he *wasn't* a perpetual student, he was a tenure-tracked professor at Emerly College.

"You and I know that deep down, she's crazy about him." I threw the khakis in the wash. "Besides, Griff wouldn't cheat on me in a million years." I added a pair of black socks to the washing machine, not bothering to straighten them out from their balls.

She raised an eyebrow. "How can you be so sure? He did seduce you away from Liam."

"*He* didn't seduce me away from Liam. I seduced myself."

Point taken, Viv moved on to the next. "Well, he's incredibly good looking for his age and he's surrounded by pretty, young, smart undergrads all day. Office hours behind closed doors, including that cute PhD assistant of his . . ."

"Bree?" Beyond ridiculous. "Not likely. She's getting married."

"When? She's been engaged for years and there's yet to be a wedding date!" Vivian waved her hand dismissively. "Anyway, you, especially,

51

know all too well that even the most decent women succumb to flings in the weeks leading up to their weddings. You think it was coincidence that you and Griff got together right before Liam proposed?"

"My meeting Griff was pure fate."

"Uh-huh." She folded her arms. "Okay, so if Griff is with Bree, I guess that would be fate, too."

Finished sorting, I slammed the door to the front-load washer and pressed power. "It's a little different, Viv. Griff and I've been married for ages. We have a daughter, a house. We have more than a lot in common."

Did we? I was never quite sure. There was our sexual compatibility, of course, and then there were the usual things married people share—love of our dog, favorite restaurants and movies, friends who liked the same movies and restaurants we did—but what about our other passions?

As much as I tried to feign interest in his theories of the Fed's role in creating the latest economic downturn, I'd long ago lost the enthusiasm I'd shown in the early stages of our relationship for Griff's academic passions. Maybe because he'd been working on a book about the Fed for so long his nonstop discussion of it had turned into white noise.

That was bad of me, I knew. But there were so many other things on my mind these days—getting

Laura into college and getting out from under Chloe's thumb being my current obsessions. I just didn't have the time to fold my arms and smile as he droned on about money supply manipulation and interest rates and whatever else it was the Fed did to keep the economy rolling when I had dinner to get on the table and laundry to fold and Chloe's letters to write.

Nor, might I add, did Griff want to hear about polished granite versus granite tiles (trendy, but easily stained) for kitchen counters. And he definitely didn't want to go shopping for them.

Viv would not drop it, though. "I'm on your side, Kat. You know that. However, when a couple has been married as long as you two have, they can get bored with each other and seek new stimulation. It's pure biology. We humans were never meant to be married for so long, you know. When this country was founded, the average life span was thirty-six. People didn't have midlife crises back then because they were dead!"

My sister had developed the most interesting theories from that continuing education course she'd taken on the Revolutionary War.

"Not that I'm saying Griff would intentionally hit on Bree, but you have to admit she does worship him. That's very flattering to a man—especially a man in his forties."

I thought back to how I, too, had hung on to Griff's every word, how I, like Bree and his students at Emerly, could have raptly listened to him talk for hours.

Slightly mad at myself for being a bad wife, at Viv for bringing up Bree, and at Griff for having condom wrappers in his pockets, I dumped a basket of clean whites onto the folding table and said definitively, "He's not having an affair. That's all there is to it. Let's move on." I started folding towels, my hands shaking slightly when I brought corner to corner.

The machine stopped and Viv opened the front door, water spilling onto the floor as she yanked the khakis out of the wash. "Then check the other pocket."

"Vivian . . ."

"If you're so sure . . ."

To prove I had absolutely no doubts, I thrust my hand into the other pocket and held up my find. Not a teal green wrapper. Hah! A damp, crumpled piece of paper.

She pinched it out of my hand. "Let me see this."

Was it instinct? A wife's sixth sense? Or maybe I was shaken from Vivian's comment about Griff and Bree. For some reason, I felt anxious.

Griff had seemed distant when he was in San Francisco, but I'd told myself that that was because he always shut off the world whenever he became immersed in a project. It had nothing to do with the fact that he and Bree were a coast away working side by side for three weeks researching his book and that she was a twenty-eight-year-old prodigy with the flexibility of a seventh-level yoga master and a body to match.

Absolutely nothing at all.

"It's a receipt from two days ago." Viv scrutinized it with FBI precision. "Wasn't that the night Laura had her accident?"

The Thursday before, Laura had suffered a fender bender with a state trooper outside the hospital where she was working for the summer. No big deal except she hit a freaking state trooper! And when I tried to call Griff about it, there was no answer at his hotel or his cell all night. His explanation the following day was that he'd turned off his phones and crashed early to hop the six A.M. back home.

"Yup." I threw the khakis back in and restarted the machine.

"So when you were trying to get hold of Griff to tell him about Laura's accident and he claimed he was tucked in bed trying to get his beauty sleep, according to this, he was at the Four Seasons Hotel running up a $236 dinner bill."

"No way."

"See for yourself."

It was my turn to snatch the receipt. Everything about what she'd said was so not Griff. It wasn't just that he never lied or dallied about with young women. It was also that he never went out for $200 dinners. He was way too careful about money to blow it on something so frivolous and expensive as a Four Seasons dinner.

Heck, I couldn't buy a $60 lamp without him grilling me as to why it was necessary. And the fifteenth of every month, when the credit card bills were paid, was like being on the witness stand, with Griff examining and cross-examining my every purchase.

Not that we were unusual in that respect. I'd once read that money is THE issue couples fight about most often (next to sex—not a problem for us). But there was no comfort in keeping miserable company while my friends seemed to be able to clean out Saks without blinking. There they were with their Marc Jacobs satchels and Lancôme lips, not a care in the world, while I was clutching a Target tote and feeling guilty.

Guilty because I was having bad thoughts about Griff, evil thoughts dripping with resentment that I knew was corroding our marriage. Green envy prodded me to ask why he couldn't have gone into business like Caroline's husband, Clark, a chinless college dropout who'd made a killing in commercial real estate. If only Griff had used his Ivy League credentials to *make* money instead of *research* money, we'd never have cause to fight.

At my very worst, I even entertained the unthinkable: *If I'd married Liam, I never would have had to worry about money.*

I tried to see it Griff's way. After all, what was

holding ME back from being the breadwinner now that Laura—our one and *easy* child—was grown? Why was it Griff's job to be the provider? And, by the way, didn't I pride myself on being part of a new generation of women who were financially independent?

It might have helped if Griff splurged now and then—a $500 tent or a $300 pair of hiking boots. But the more I spent, the more disciplined he became, like Jack Sprat.

I drove a Lexus because Chloe insisted it was necessary to assure our clients we were like them (rich), so he pushed his old Toyota way past the 150k mark. My daily addiction to triple venti lattes was the family joke, one that we could afford because Griff tolerated the burnt sludge from the economics department lounge. He even wore the same old ratty gray wool sweater so I could update my wardrobe with a cashmere twinset.

Which was why never in a million years would he have gone out for a $236 dinner. Never.

But there it was. Last Thursday at 10:03 Pacific daylight time (1:03 A.M. Central New Jersey), a bill of $236 paid with his MasterCard.

Hold on . . . *MasterCard!*

We didn't own a MasterCard. Though what did I know, really? I was oblivious when it came to our credit cards, our limits, and worst of all, our running balances. The best I could do was carry those nasty envelopes from the mailbox to the bowl by

57

the phone until Griff took them to his home office in the basement, where he calculated all the family finances, much to my mixed relief and fear.

Not having to open those envelopes and face those numbers was worth tolerating Griff's monthly third degree. Even so, I was sure he would have said something about getting a new credit card.

"What's wrong?" Viv asked, peering.

"We don't have a MasterCard."

"Really? You know how you are with things like this. Need I mention the red sofa?"

I once hid three months of credit card bills in the seat cushions of our red sofa back when I was deranged with postpartum depression—just so I wouldn't have to listen to Griff go off on how I'd spent $400 on a Peg Perego baby stroller even though at that price it was a total steal. I would not call it one of my finest moments.

"I'm almost positive."

She inhaled deeply and shifted gears into her familiar role of all-knowing big sister.

"Look, Kat, you have many fine qualities, but reading financial statements is not one of them. We need an expert to go through all your records with a fine-tooth comb and do a quick audit to see if Griff's been running up any other secret expenses."

"He has not been running up secret expenses. He's not like that. He's a tightwad."

She ignored this and made a suggestion she knew would not go over well. "We need to bring in Adele."

Ugh.

Adele was part of Viv's "single clique" of wronged women who traveled en masse to places like Orlando and Costa Rica and TGI Friday's, where they took lots of photos of themselves with their arms around one another, hoisting margaritas and pink Cosmopolitans. She was also an accountant and a stranger to Griff. I could not believe Vivian was serious about having Adele go over our personal stuff.

"I am not bringing in Adele. That's a violation of our marriage."

"Is it not more of a violation of your marriage," she said, "to be sleeping with one's young nubile research assistant?"

Viv's clear eyes, rimmed with bright aqua liner to better highlight her beautiful blue irises, were unflinching. She had taken me to my first Peter Frampton concert and had told me how to French-kiss (coincidentally, the same night!). And no one could make you feel better about having gained five pounds.

But there were times when she pushed too hard.

"You *want* Griff to be cheating on me, don't you?"

"No!" She gasped in shock. "No! All I want is to make sure you don't end up like Beth Williams."

She'd played the trump card.

Beth Williams's husband, Bernie, a lawyer, had planned his exit from their marriage with Machiavellian precision. He'd left scattered evidence of an affair around their house so brazenly that Beth was forced to ask for a divorce. Unfortunately, she made the mistake of not waiting to ask until their tenth anniversary, thereby allowing her husband to get off without a penny of alimony—as he'd planned. As a result, she was forced to take two jobs, working as a dental hygienist during the day and stocking shelves at Wegmans at night, just to be able to keep her kids in the family home.

The very mention of Beth Williams could strike terror in the hearts of Rocky River women everywhere.

"Okay." I pushed power again on the washing machine. "Do whatever you want. Call Adele. Call in Price Waterhouse, for all I care. Spend this whole beautiful late-summer day in my dark basement rifling through Griff's files and adding up figures. I know he's not having an affair."

Viv said, "You won't regret it."

I thought, *I bet I will.*

And I was right.

CHAPTER FOUR

*D*id I mention the discovery of the Mint Tingle Trojans happened the day before our twentieth wedding anniversary? It did.

That's why Griff rushed home from San Francisco: so we could celebrate—and I could throw him a surprise party. I even got Bree to plead an unexpected research glitch so he'd go to the office that day and leave me alone. Which he did with more willingness than I'd have expected.

And now I knew why. Talk about giving comfort to the enemy. I might as well have bought them a hotel room. Wives really are the last to find out.

No. I was not going to let myself turn into a shrill harpy just because Vivian had planted her seed of doubt. I had to stick to the facts and wait for Adele to find discrepancies in our credit card statements—the only valid indicators of male infidelity, according to my sister and her divorced friends.

So, while Viv was on the phone chitchatting to Adele about "poor Kat," and how I couldn't read a financial statement "if it were drawn in big red crayon letters with cartoon illustrations," I went to smear on a swath of neutral mauve lipstick and brush my hair in the downstairs bathroom in an effort to buck up.

But it was so hard to tamp down those insecurities. What if what Vivian said turned out to be true? Was our relationship really in such shambles that Griff had to go rushing into the arms of someone like Bree? Or was it . . . me?

Couldn't be. My figure hadn't gone completely to pot. Sure, my breasts weren't full and bouncy with that perky great-to-meet-you attitude they'd sported in their twenties. Nursing and an aversion to exercise will do that. But my hair was still blond(ish). And after professional bleaching by Beth Williams herself, my teeth were whiter.

I pulled back my lips and checked them like a horse up for auction. Yep. Still white.

Anyway, this was stupid. Griff and I were beyond breast shape and whether his abs had gone from six-pack to half dozen. (They hadn't, curse him.) We were a team. We were each other's confidantes who held hands in line at the movies and loved nothing more than to curl up in bed on a Sunday night and watch a PBS mystery, our toes playing tootsie, Griff every once in a while mindlessly planting a kiss on the top of my head.

Did he do that with . . . *her*?

It was beginning to eat at me from within—the creeping feeling of betrayal and disloyalty, how it acted like dry rot, ruining a perfectly fine foundation from underneath. So this was why adultery was so insidious. It wasn't just the act of Griff having sex with another woman, it was all the whispering machinations that made the adultery justifiable. His gripes to her about me. His girlfriend's strokes of consolation, having heard only his side of the story.

After all, no man starts off an affair by proclaiming his wife is his soul mate who is understanding and still outrageously sexy. An affair begins with dissatisfaction, with a complaint. So what was Griff's beef? What, exactly, had he told *her* about our private life? That I shopped too much? That I turned a deaf ear to his views on the Fed? Give me a break. There were worse crimes than growing bored with rants about Alan Greenspan.

My eyes hurt and I realized crying was inevitable. It was going to happen and it was going to be bad. Just when I needed to be strong and optimistic, my glands were turning traitor.

Halfway through a deep and wrenching sob, there was a knock on the bathroom door. I lifted my swollen red face to the mirror.

"Kat?" Vivian cooed. "Are you okay?"

"Just fine!" My shaking voice indicated quite the opposite. "I'll be out in a minute."

"Could you make it sooner? There's some kind of incident going on in the driveway."

A whiff of Basic cigarettes floated through the window and I thought—Saturday. Quarter after ten. Driveway. Jasper.

Uh-oh.

Throwing open the bathroom door, I grabbed Griff's shirts for the dry cleaner, tossed my keys in my purse, and flew outside. As I feared, my cleaning woman, Libby, in green knit shorts and a blue tank top, her anchor tattoo visible on her upper left shoulder, was leaning against her pickup truck, a smoldering cigarette in one hand, a black can of Mace in the other.

"I told you I was coming at ten," she scolded. "Why you didn't lock that beast in the basement is beyond me."

I eyed the "beast" Jasper, whose gray muzzle lay between his two arthritic paws. He arched an eyebrow in my direction, glanced at the Mace pointed at him, and sighed. Talk about misunderstood.

"He's something like ninety-two in dog years." I slipped a finger under his collar and gently brought him to his feet.

"I don't care. He hates me. If you weren't around, he'd bite off my ankle."

"No, he wouldn't. He hardly has any teeth left." But there was no point in explaining that to Libby, who'd been cleaning my house for fifteen years— about as long as we'd had Jasper. She hated all dogs, and all dogs hated her. If Vivian hadn't fetched me, she would have doused the old boy in pepper spray and probably given him a heart attack.

I put Jasper in the garage and closed the door. *Sorry*, I mouthed to him.

"By the way," she said, biting the cigarette as she fetched her mop and pail from the back of her truck, "I went shopping with my group this morning and picked up a few things on sale for your party."

By "group," Libby meant the Penny Pinchers, a bunch of super savers like her who met in the basement of the Rocky River Public Library once a week to swap coupons and trade tips. You'd have thought the Penny Pinchers were A-list celebrities the way she was forever going on about their crazy antics, recounting their great finds at yard sales and their coups at the grocery store beating the system, ticking off the store managers and filling their shopping carts with loads of free stuff.

She tried to get me to come to a couple of meetings, but so far I'd managed to duck her. It wasn't that I didn't *want* to learn how to save, it was just that I wasn't sure I *could*. My few attempts at living by a budget in the past had been utter, costly failures.

Take coupons, for example. I'd usually start off gung ho, buying a bunch of Sunday newspapers and cutting out each coupon, filing them by category in long white envelopes. Inevitably, though, I'd forget the envelopes when I went grocery shopping or I'd hold on to the coupons too long. They'd expire and fall to the bottom of my purse, where they'd become ripped or crumpled until I used them to hold spit-out gum or to pat my lipstick. Not to pun, but some of us were just not cut out for coupons.

Libby handed me a dozen used Ball jelly jars and a bag of tiny votive candles.

"Thank you," I said, grateful, if slightly confused. Along with not clipping coupons, I wasn't a canner, either.

"Lights for the patio. Very pretty with the glass quilting." She exhaled her cigarette triumphantly. "I got them at a yard sale this morning. Guess how much."

Libby loved to play the home version of *The Price Is Right*.

"Five dollars."

"For free!" She pumped her fist. "It was the end of the sale and they couldn't get rid of them, so they threw them in when I bought a towel rack for thirty-five cents. The candles were left over from Christmas last year. I picked them up at a post-holiday steal down at the drugstore for a buck a bag. Now you won't have to go out and drop a Ulysses S. Grant on lanterns."

She opened the candles and plopped one into a jar, lighting it with her cigarette. Although it was still daylight, I could see the candle's potential as the flame danced in the puckered glass.

"Hey. That's very pretty!"

"Isn't it?" She gazed at the jar with pride until her hand began to shake. "And . . . hot. *Ohmigod*."

Quickly, I snatched it from her hand and blew out the flame while Libby waved her red palm in the cooling air. "I thought they'd be insulated," she said.

"I don't think that's what quilting means."

I took the Ball jars and candles to the patio. Then I dumped Griff's shirts in the backseat of the Lexus, started the car, and headed toward Chloe's office, though it was Saturday and the day of the anniversary party. When Chloe summons, one comes.

Griff calls Rocky River "New Jersey's Brigadoon" because it's hidden between New Brunswick and Princeton, off Route 27, in the valley marked by a wooden bridge. It was love at first sight when Griff and I, house hunting, stumbled upon this community with its little shops, the hardware store and local ice-cream parlor, its white clapboard town hall and annual Fourth of July parades. Right off, I knew we'd found our home.

After picking up a triple venti latte with a blueberry scone at Starbs, I drove down to Princeton and parked my Lexus in its usual space next to Chloe's all-white Mercedes. Sitting in my car, I tried to reach Griff at his various numbers—home, office, cell—again. And *again*, I was sent directly to voice mail, just like when I attempted to reach him in San Francisco.

An inner voice whispered, *Your marriage is in trouble.*

Be quiet, you, I whispered back, tossing my phone into my purse and heading to work.

Honestly, my inner voice had no idea when to shut up. So rude!

Interiors by Chloe was on the first floor of the Stevens Building, across the hall from Arthur B. Winchester Properties, where my friend Elaine was one of two real estate agents. When she wasn't scrolling the Internet, she was lounging on Chloe's soft couches and flipping through our copies of *Town & Country*, which is exactly what she was doing when I opened the door and found her bare feet on the antique coffee table, a bag of Oreos in her lap.

"Shoot." She sat back and closed her eyes, placing a hand on her rather ample chest. "You nearly gave me a heart attack. I thought you were Chloe."

I put the Starbucks on my desk and dropped my keys. "Do you know what she would have done if she'd caught you like this?"

Elaine brushed the crumbs off the unflattering navy pantsuit Arthur B. Winchester insisted she wear and collected them on the magazine. "You know what? After what I've been through, I'm not sure I'd care." Carrying the magazine over to a wastepaper basket, she dumped in the crumbs and said, "Got a call from the cops at two A.M. this morning. Taylor was rounded up in an underage drinking party."

"You're kidding me." I slumped at my desk and popped open the Starbucks. Elaine had three sons, two of whom were star athletes and students. It was as though Taylor, the youngest, was trying to make up for the older two by skipping school, drinking, and repeatedly getting in trouble with the authorities. "What are they going to do?"

"I don't know. Gerry had a long talk with the chief of police and maybe, just maybe, they'll let him go with a warning. But you know how they like to make examples of kids, especially at the start of the school year."

"How about the coach?"

"Oh, yeah. Tay's kicked off the football team for the duration. Definitely."

Elaine and I sat in silence, she eating her Oreos and I sipping coffee, mulling over our separate worries.

"This might seem like a strange question," I ventured, "but has Gerry ever cheated on you?"

She coughed on her cookie. "Why?" She coughed again. "Do you know something I don't?" Recovered, she dove into the bag for another Oreo.

"No. I was thinking of Griff." I paused, debating only for a second whether what I was about to confide would be considered a violation of our marriage. "This morning while I was doing the wash from his trip to San Francisco, I came across two wrappers for condoms in the pockets of his khakis."

Elaine stopped mid-bite. "You're *noth therious*," she said, her mouth full.

"And, also, a receipt for a $200 dinner he had the night of Laura's accident, even though he told me he was in his hotel room, sleeping."

She thrust out the Oreos. "Take one."

"No thanks."

"I'm telling you, they help. They're like magic."

"I'm sure you're right, but I couldn't eat right now if I wanted to." I flipped through the calendar until I found last Thursday, the day Laura hit the state trooper. "I just can't believe he lied to me."

"Oh, honey." She rolled up the bag and tossed it onto the table, releasing a shower of crumbs that I prayed were gone by the time Chloe arrived. "It's probably not as bad as it looks. I can't think of a more perfect couple than you two. You put the rest of us to shame."

"Hmph." The more I thought about us, the more worried I got. Viv had been right. Married couples did drift apart and maybe Bree was giving him something I'd stopped gladly handing out long ago. Would it have hurt for me to ask him about his Fed book once in a blue moon? Not that his cheating could be justified. . . .

"I'm sure there's a rational explanation. Did you ask him?" Elaine said.

"Well, that would be the logical thing to do, wouldn't it?"

"Unless you were trying to trip him into an admission of sorts."

"Why would I do that?"

She shrugged. "I dunno. If I found condom wrappers in Gerry's pockets, I might consider laying a trap. But then, that's me. Men, I've come to see, are the enemy, whether they're husbands, bosses, or mouthy teenage sons."

That was just talk. Gerry and Elaine had a fabulous relationship. "I did try to call him, and he didn't answer, even though I know for a fact he's at the office . . . with her."

"Bree?"

I nodded.

"I personally think young women should be confined in convents until they have the permission of older women." Elaine was about to criticize the forwardness of the younger generation when the door slammed and Chloe appeared in a pale beige swing coat to match her pale beige shoes and pale beige headband. With her frosted blond hair she gave the impression of a human iced latte.

"Ladies?" She zoomed right in on those Oreos.

Elaine swiped her feet off the table and slipped them into her navy pumps. "Hey, Chloe. What's up?"

"Your feet," she said, "on my antique Queen Anne."

The only reason Chloe didn't get along with Elaine was because Elaine was, for lack of a more flattering word, zaftig, and with generations of hefty Szabos in her past, Chloe feared fat people like they were contagious diseases.

71

"I've got clients coming in twenty minutes." She adjusted the black Coach bag swinging from the crook of her arm. "It'd be nice if this place didn't look like a frat house."

She handed me her daily "to-do list" and marched across the room into her office, giving the door another slam.

Elaine stifled a giggle. "Does she know what dumps frat houses are? A frat house! I bet she's never even stepped inside one."

"If she had," I said, turning on my computer, "she wouldn't admit it."

"I swear, that's your biggest problem right there." Elaine pointed to the white door marked with a brass plaque that read CHLOE SYKES in ornately cursive lettering. "If you didn't have to focus all your energy on keeping her mentally stable, you'd be happier and so would your marriage."

Aha. "So you think my marriage isn't happy."

"Listen to me, girlfriend. I think *you're* not happy. But being a typical woman, you put on a happy face and pretend to be." She got up and picked the list out of my hand. "Look at this. Three follow-up calls, a write-up of her meeting Susan and Dick Weinstein, and—I can't believe it—a re-measure of the Andersons' kitchen. Tell me why this couldn't wait until Monday." She let the list flutter to my desk. "And you've got a party to throw tonight. That woman has no soul."

"No, but she does have my paycheck." Picking up the phone, I started to dial the Andersons to ask if I could stop by in half an hour.

Elaine yanked the telephone cord out of the wall. "Stop it." Checking over her shoulder to make sure Chloe couldn't hear, she whispered, "You need to call Madeleine Granville right now."

"Now?"

Elaine recently sold a house to a New York television producer named Madeleine Granville and, since then, had been trying to talk me into doing the redecorating for her as a way of jump-starting my own design business. A pipe dream, really, although one I couldn't quit obsessing over.

"I happen to know she's in town. This is the perfect opportunity."

"Chloe's got clients coming any minute."

"So?" Elaine rolled her eyes. "When Chloe's meeting with them, you can call Madeleine. The only reason she hasn't called yet is that she's so freaking busy, she doesn't know what day it is."

I was tempted. I really was. Only one teensy-weensy problem. Chloe possessed an unforgiving vengeful streak as hard as the diamonds on her fingers. When combined with her insistence on devout loyalty, calling Madeleine Granville was akin to career suicide.

If Chloe so much as suspected I went behind her back and sought a client on my own in an effort to take the first steps in establishing my own business, she would not only fire me, she would see to it that no one in the tri-state interior decorating network took me on, too. That I could not risk, not with Laura to send to school the following year in an economy where professional interior decorating was the first luxury to be axed from the average homeowner's budget.

"Take a chance." Elaine pulled out her BlackBerry, scrolled to Madeleine's number, and wrote it down on Chloe's to-do list. "Nothing good happens if you don't take chances."

With a last thumbs-up, Elaine grabbed the *Town & Country*, picked a few Oreo crumbs off the white carpeting, and went across the hall to her office. I was left to stare at Madeleine's number.

The door to Chloe's office flew open. "Is she gone?"

"Yup."

Chloe checked her watch. "None too soon, either. Ray and Andrea Perotta are five minutes late. Can't you do something about her? She's bringing down the property values."

"She's my friend. And she gets us clients."

"At the very least, she could make an effort. Oreos. All that saturated fat." Chloe shivered. "Have some self-respect, for god's sake."

Two minutes later, in walked the Perottas—a retired couple moving to New Jersey to be closer to their daughter and son-in-law—for the ritual of contract signing that Chloe demanded be done in her office. I never understood why she didn't do this in people's homes, like other interior decorators did, until I was searching through her desk one day and came across a mini digital recorder.

Along with vengeful and demanding, I could add paranoid to Chloe's many delightful characteristics.

I led the Perottas to Chloe's office and once I'd fetched the usual coffee and tea, went back to my desk, where Madeleine's number stared up at me like a dare.

Do it, I thought. *Do it now or you never will.*

My fingers tapped out the numbers on my cell as I applauded myself for having the decency not to use Chloe's phone. If anything, I was ethical.

"Hello?"

I didn't expect her to answer right away. But then, in worrying about this fact instead of talking, I created a pause that was so long, Madeleine had to say hello again.

Quickly, I introduced myself, throwing out Elaine's name a billion times until Madeleine eagerly said, "Oh, yes. I've been meaning to call you. This house is wonderful, but it's so . . . dark. I was just thinking how much I'd like to get it redone this winter and how I should probably get started now."

Great. We were getting somewhere. Moreover, I had done my homework on her Lambertville home (former rectory; possible historic designation;

great views of the Delaware; desperately in need of new windows, floors, and an updated kitchen) and was about to wow her with my knowledge when my phone beeped and I looked down to see—*Griff.*

"Excuse me," I apologized. "I've got another call on the line that I have to take. I'm afraid it's my family."

I didn't know if putting her on hold was something Madeleine would tolerate—Elaine described her as very harsh, very rushed, and not exactly family friendly—but at that moment, my marriage came first.

"Hi," Griff said, his usual cheerful self. "Were you trying to reach me? I forgot to turn on my cell and Janice isn't here today."

Janice was the Emerly Economics Department secretary. Her absence was a plausible excuse for why he hadn't picked up his office phone. "Good!"

"Good?" He chuckled. "You're *glad* you couldn't reach me?"

"No, it's just that I thought you were doing the avoiding-the-ball-and-chain thing."

"Why would I do that? Unless . . . oh, god." He pretended to sound devastated. "Tell me you don't want me to do a bunch of Saturday errands."

"Just one." I smiled to myself, so relieved he hadn't been avoiding me after all. All those worries about him having an affair with Bree—pure rubbish, I was sure.

"Okay," he said, "I've got my spreadsheet up.

Give me just this one errand 'cause I know it'll turn into twenty."

He was so jovial, I didn't have the heart to bring up the condom wrappers. "First, stop at Marksom's Jewelry. There's a lovely antique opal ring I've had my eye on that you might want to check out."

"Now, why would I be in the market for a ring? It's not some special occasion, is it? Wait. Is it your birthday?"

"Cute. You know what day it is tomorrow."

"Oh, *tomorrow*. See, now, that's a different day altogether. Wait. Don't tell me. I remember. It's our *dog's* birthday. But, then, shouldn't I be getting *him* the antique ring?"

I pictured Jasper with a ring on his paw and laughed. Big mistake.

In a flash, the door flew open and there was Chloe glaring like an angry gargoyle. "Do you have a price sheet on travertine? The Perottas are thinking of it for their master bath."

"Okay."

In my ear, Griff was softly singing an off-tune version of "Ding, Dong! The Witch Is Dead," from *The Wizard of Oz*.

Chloe didn't budge. "Actually, I'd like it now."

She wanted to watch me hang up the phone. She wanted to see me depress the power button and see me cringe in disappointment and embarrassment.

Instead, I said, "Hold on a minute," put down the

phone—thankful for more than one reason that Griff had stopped singing—and reached into my drawer for the file on tiles, realizing with dismay that I'd totally forgotten about Madeleine on the other line.

Chloe thrust out her hand. "I'm afraid it's a rush. The Perottas have to leave by one."

I riffled past marble and granite, ceramic, porcelain, and limestone. No travertine. Crap. I eyed my phone. If only she'd go back to her office like a normal person so I could say good-bye to Griff and ask Madeleine if I could call back later. But, no. She insisted on standing there like a prison guard, being no help whatsoever as I fumbled through flooring tiles and then wall tiles, finally finding the damned sheet on travertine when I got to countertops.

"There." I gave her the sheet.

"I need a few copies. At least three."

No you don't, I thought, pushing back my chair and turning on the copier, waiting for it to slowly warm up as my phone just lay there.

"Do you mind . . . ," I asked, my fingers walking toward it.

"Is it Griff?" She folded her arms. "He'll understand. That is . . . if it's Griff."

How did she do that? It was as though she just knew I'd been up to no good, like she had a sixth sense or something. At last the copies were done and, satisfied she'd ruined my personal fun, Chloe went back to the Perottas. This time she closed the door quietly in celebration of her subtle victory.

Griff was off. So was Madeleine, understandably. When I dialed her back she acted distracted and said she couldn't talk at the moment. Now was not a good time.

I'd blown it. And I'd been so close. Slumping back into my seat, defeated, I debated what to do and ended up sending her a quick email apologizing for putting her on hold and explaining as tactfully as possible why I hadn't been able to talk.

I also included the information about her house I'd researched, along with a rough estimate of my incredibly modest rates and various telephone numbers where she could reach me, if interested. That would put the ball in her court. If she never called, I'd just have to write off the incident to experience, as painful as that would be.

Shortly after I pressed send on the email, the Perottas emerged, followed by Chloe, a vision of sweetness and light when she introduced me as "my girl Friday."

"I don't know how I'd manage without Kat." She clasped her hands and beamed. "She's more than an assistant, really. She's like a partner and a good, trusted friend. We've been together for over twenty years."

The knife could not be twisted any deeper.

Andrea Perotta, a pleasant-faced woman with tight blond curls, said, "Aren't you lucky."

Her husband, Ray, added, "It's nice to work with people you enjoy."

I agreed that, yes, it was, adding silently that I looked forward to having that experience someday.

"Wait a minute!" Chloe punched the air as if she'd just had a brainstorm. "Isn't tomorrow your wedding anniversary? What are you doing here on your day off when you should be out getting ready for your party?"

That was so unbelievable a statement, I was speechless. I should have pointed out that I was there because she'd called me in.

"Go on." She shooed me from the desk as if I'd insisted on remaining. "Go on. The twentieth anniversary is the china one, you know. And it just so happens your favorite store is holding a fabulous sale on Bernardaud. I can't imagine why you're sitting here, in this office, when you should be out there engaging in your favorite hobby, Kat. Shopping to your heart's content."

Chloe knew me too well for my own good.

CHAPTER FIVE

*O*h, my goodness. Someone's been exercising her charging elbow," my mother exclaimed as a couple of tiki torches and a bag of French provincial melamine plates nearly fell out of the back of my Lexus onto her South River driveway.

"Watch out!" I barked, buffering the torches with my hip.

It was the clay planters of exotic beach grasses that had me concerned, though. I did not appreciate sand all over my car, especially since my father had already made a crack that I'd *bought grass*— grass I could have dug out for free.

"Don't listen to him," Mom said. "What does he know? Mr. I've Worn the Same Shirt for Thirty Years."

Dad, who was, indeed, wearing a stained and ripped green golf shirt Mom had bought for him when I was still in high school, knelt to survey the undercarriage of his broken lawn mower, smiling at the challenge of a new repair. He was used to being dismissed.

"Those planters are perfect for your patio," she went on. "I saw the exact same ones in *Country Living* and drooled. Now let me take a peek at those rooster plates. You say you got them for half off at Smith & Hawken?"

When it came to impulsive shopping, my mother was the whipped cream and cherries on the sundae of splurging—oohing and ahhing over every item and making me feel like a million bucks for spending the equivalent. That's why I'd made it a tradition to stop off at Mom's for the satisfying review and approval after my biggest shopping sprees.

She even put me at ease about the new blue

chiminea, a risky purchase since Griff found chimineas to be ugly and, as he put it, fodder for the landfill. But they were half off at YardPlus and crucial for the party, I'd decided. Weather reports predicted an unseasonably cold evening.

"Brilliant!" Mom stroked its chimney with appreciation. "It'll be perfect for tonight when it gets chilly. I've always wanted one, but your father wouldn't hear of it." She shrugged with a what-are-you-going-to-do? attitude.

I repositioned the chiminea in the car. "I'm worried what Griff will say. He gets so worked up when I come home with lots of stuff."

"He should be so lucky to have a wife who's throwing him a surprise party, that's what." Quick to be insulted if my husband dared to issue the slightest criticism, she squared her shoulders and ruffled up like a mother hen ready to peck out the eyes of a weasel after her chicks.

My mother even looked like a hen, her reddish-blond hair, restrained by a thick headband, puffed out in the back, and her highly arched, overtweezed eyebrows gave her the appearance of a startled chicken. Despite her constant dieting, however, my mother could not achieve her much desired chicken legs. No number of dressing-free salads or five-mile walks could outwit the Polish genetics that forced her to wear elastic-waist black pants and long blouses. Mom was a block of a woman. It was her life's greatest disappointment that she didn't turn out like Audrey Hepburn.

"I just don't want to get in a fight with my husband," I said. "Not on our anniversary."

Mom went *hmph*. "That's Griff's problem, if you do. Look, your father was never a spendthrift, either, but at least he knew better than to give me a hard time if I went on a spree now and then." She flashed a triumphant look at Dad, who was trying to stay out of it, pretending to preoccupy himself by cleaning the lawn mower cutting blade. "We never fought about money. Did we, Stan?"

Dad looked up, sweat beading on his red dome of a head. "What's that?"

"We never fought about money."

"Sure, we did. And then I put you on an allowance, which took care of that. Aww, would you look at this gunk." He plunged his hands into the undercarriage and removed a hunk of greasy black grass. "No wonder the damn thing wouldn't start."

Mom said coquettishly, "Here's an idea. Maybe Griff should step down from his ivory tower and try getting a *real* job in the *real* world instead of the groves of academe. Then money wouldn't be such an issue with you two."

"Mom," I said warningly. "Let's not start that again. Besides, this book Griff's writing on the Federal Reserve could take wing." Or not. Academic press publications usually garnered no

more than five-thousand-copy print runs, earning prestige and tenure more than money.

"As if being an author is any way to support a family." She sniffed. "That reminds me. I ran into Sophia the other day."

Her faded blue eyes twinkled with mischief. Sophia was Liam's sister, and if my mother said she "ran into" her, it meant she saw Sophia a half a mile away, then trailed her in the car and overtook her at the next red light.

"You didn't."

"And you'll never guess what's happened." She folded her arms. "Liam and his wife have . . . separated!"

Mom waited for my reaction, but I didn't dare show it. To see my eyes light up would only fuel her hopes that someday I'd leave Griff and reunite with Liam, as she dreamed and prayed for every Sunday.

The disturbing thing was my eyes would have lit up if she hadn't been there. It wasn't that hearing of his marriage made me feel smug. It was that a small part of me was glad that Paige hadn't been his big love. It was so confusing and weird, I pushed my feelings aside until I could analyze them later, when my mother wasn't observing my every twitch.

"That's too bad," I said.

"Maybe for her, not for him." She frowned. "Sophia said his wife was so conniving that she waited until they closed on a huge house in Saddle River to demand a divorce. Can you get over it? Already, there's another man in the picture, of course—some former tennis pro like herself."

Screwing on a bolt with his blackened hands, Dad said, "Didn't Kat used to date some boy named Liam?"

I loved how out of it my father was when it came to my personal life.

"Yes, Dad. We were almost married. But don't get Mom started."

Mom gave me a look that said it wasn't her fault I'd messed up my life. "All I can say is, thank heavens they don't have any children. Though, according to Sophia, that wasn't Liam's decision. Poor boy." She blinked into the afternoon sun. "He would have been a great father if he'd been with the right woman."

Mom was really laying it on thick. I'd have been curious to find out how long she'd been holding on to that acorn of gossip, burrowing it like a squirrel until the opportune moment arose so she could produce it for the most effect. She must have been bursting at the seams.

"Do you know that he still asks about you? Maybe you should give him a call. . . ."

"Mom!"

"What?" She threw up her hands. "I didn't say you should take him to bed, only that you should inquire if he's okay. He's a cuckolded man,

Katarina. It's at times like these when men need the reassurance and validation of other women."

Fortunately, the phone rang, and, never one to miss a call, Mom ran after it like a teenager. Thank god. I wasn't sure how much more I could take of *All My Liam*.

Dad stood creakily, arched his aching back, and wiped his fingers with a dirty blue rag. "You know, Katie, an allowance might be just the ticket for you and Griff. Could head off another fight."

He was right back to what mattered: my marriage and money.

"I don't want to go on an allowance, Dad." I removed a piece of grass from what little was left of his hair. "And I couldn't stand the idea of Griff putting me on one. It'd be humiliating and sexist."

"Now, hold on. An allowance can be very creative. Your mother used to make a game of it, spending less than I gave her every week. Eventually she built up a nice little nest egg that was all hers. Even bought stock." He righted the lawn mower and gave the choke a tug. It whimpered and stalled. "Goddamnit."

We stared at the stubborn machine. "That lawn mower has to be from the Reagan Administration, Dad. Don't you think it's time for a new one?"

"Are you kidding? It's just broken in."

Mom reappeared with the portable phone in hand. "That was Viv. She's on her way and wants you to stay put, Kat, until she gets here." Giggling, she sing-songed, "I think she has a surprise for your an-ni-ver-sa-ry!"

"A surprise?" My pulse raced as I remembered that while I'd been shopping, Viv had spent the afternoon going through our accounts with Adele. If she wanted me to stay put, it meant the news was good, that there was no evidence of Griff cheating and she wanted to tell me in person.

Or . . . perhaps it was bad and Viv couldn't bear telling me over the phone.

Dad gestured to the pile of junk on the driveway. "Katie here says it's time for a new lawn mower. I told her it's barely broken in."

Mom nodded. "You're absolutely right, Stan. It's fine." Turning to me, she whispered, "Why spend money on a new lawn mower when I can put it toward a vacation in Florida this winter?"

And she thought Liam's wife was conniving. . . .

"There's Viv!"

My sister swung her VW Passat into the driveway, nearly running over Dad, who held up his hands and told her to slow down. Getting out and slamming the door, she was all business, planting Mom and Dad with perfunctory kisses before taking me aside and murmuring so Mom wouldn't hear, "I need to see you alone."

A ball of something hard formed in my throat. "Is it bad?"

"It is what it is." She led me around back to the screened-in porch, summer home to my parents, who'd installed indoor/outdoor carpeting and even a small TV. We stepped inside and she let the screen door slam.

"Okay," I said. "Give it to me. I can take it."

Viv got right down to business. "Did you spend $663 at Eastern Mountain Sports, or was that Griff? Because while he would shop there, I don't think he'd spend that much money."

This seemed like a stupid question for her to be so worked up about that she'd have to drive up to my parents'. I thought back to EMS. Why would I have . . . oh, right. "Yup. That was me. For Griff's godson, Jack. I bought him a sleeping bag because the place where they're staying in Stone Harbor is short a bed."

Jack was Griff's favorite godson and nephew, and I refused to feel guilty for spoiling him.

"Hold on," I said. "I thought you were supposed to be finding *Griff's* malfeasance, not mine."

"That's what I'm doing." She dropped her bag on the round glass table and brought out a white legal pad on which was written a bunch of notes and numbers. "First thing, your finances, Kat, are a mess. Adele was shocked by how you buy and buy with total disregard for your income."

I went hot, embarrassed that Adele—barely an acquaintance—was "shocked" by my spending.

"A lot of the credit card charges we found were from box and mall stores, Kat. Junk. Bed, Bath and Beyond. Pottery Barn. Crate and Barrel.

Williams-Sonoma. Not one of which is under a hundred dollars."

"Everything I bought we needed. Trust me."

She looked up from the legal pad. "Build-a-Bear? What could you have ordered from there for seventy bucks?"

I tried to recall. Oh, right. "The cutest Bunny Big Ears with Build-a-Sound and a heartbeat in the most adorable wedding dress."

"For whom?"

"For Bree." I winced.

"*The* Bree?" she hissed. "*Griff's* Bree."

"I wouldn't go so far as to call her *Griff's*, but, yeah. She'd been doing such a great job helping him out with the book that, in gratitude, on a whim of generosity I decided to send her something cute. That was before all this, naturally."

Mom appeared outside the screened porch. "Is there something I can get you girls? Iced tea, perhaps? Decaf coffee?"

Viv muttered something about Mom always sticking her nose in other people's matters. "No, Ma!" she yelled. "We're fine. We got a glitch with the party, that's all."

"Oh." Mom slapped her cheek. "I hope it's nothing serious."

"Just a problem with the mini quiches. Kat and I will be right out."

Not quite buying the mini-quiche excuse, Mom tinkered in the backyard, rolling up a hose and generally keeping herself within eavesdropping distance until she finally disappeared around the corner and Viv said, "Don't freak. But Adele called Toni Feinzig for advice."

How could she have not expected me to freak? Toni Feinzig was the lawyer who represented Beth Williams's husband, Bernie, in his divorce. In fact, she was *the* premier divorce lawyer around town. "Why . . . what need would you have had to call Toni? It's not that bad, is it?"

She pulled out my mother's chaise and pushed me into it, a wise idea since my legs were beginning to feel weak. "It's that bad."

I sank further.

Sitting sideways on my father's chaise, Viv leaned forward like I was on death's bed. The expression on her face was so worried and sad, I almost felt more sorry for her than for myself.

"Griff's having his cell bills and his brand-new MasterCard bills sent to his office at Emerly."

"How did you find that out?"

She shushed me. "Quick. Let me get this out before Mom pops in with a bogus plate of cookies. That's not the worst part. You have to brace yourself. . . ."

What could have been worse than finding out that one's husband had a separate credit card and that he didn't want me to see what numbers he was calling on his cell?

"He's also got a separate banking account, Kat.

He opened it a few months ago with $10,000." Her eyes reddened, as if about to cry.

"Why would Griff have a separate bank account?" It was like the world had stopped making sense.

"Toni said that's exactly what one of her clients did and I bet it was Bernie Williams. She said this client opened a separate account a few months before he forced his wife to ask for a divorce. She said that between the MasterCard and the condom wrappers and the dinner in San Francisco Griff lied about and the cell phone records and the separate bank account, it was as if he was taking a page out of this client's playbook. Who else could it be but Bernie Williams?"

I was stunned. Griff was no Bernie Williams, because Bernie Williams was a slimeball. Griff would never have gone to such lengths to deceive me, opening a secret bank account, of all things. Even if he had wanted to do that, where would he have gotten the money? Ten thousand dollars was a lot of cash, and as far as I knew, he hadn't come into a sudden inheritance.

But it wasn't just the logistics that was bother-some, it was the logic of *us*. We were a pair who had fused our lives, promising to love, cherish, and have and hold until death us did part. We were par-ents to Laura and owners of 2116 Waldorf Hills Road. We were one.

Just this morning we'd made love as dawn

broke, Griff stroking my cheek afterward and kissing my hand as we chatted about the day ahead, about calling his nephew Jack at the Shore, inviting him up for Sunday night dinner, and trying to remember if Laura had to volunteer at the hospital and whether we'd go out to dinner to celebrate our anniversary or stay in and pop a bottle of champagne. What we had was so perfect, so comfortable, so *solid* that even through our worst fights I'd never questioned our validity.

I looked to Vivian for an objection, for her to throw back her head and tell me it was a big prank. Instead, tears were running down her cheeks. "I'm so sorry, Kat. I like Griff. Always have. And you two make a great couple and a great family. This should not be happening."

Dazed, not quite following what she was getting at, I said, "What *is* happening?"

"Can't you see? It's all there, Kat, in the black and white of your bank statements and credit card bills. Men might lie, but the numbers never do. Honey, he's leaving you."

CHAPTER SIX

*S*urprise!"
That this shout came out of my mouth while my arms went up in feigned glee was more personally repulsive than the expression of manufactured astonishment on Griff's handsome face as he

opened the French doors to the patio and dropped his jaw. His *stubbled* jaw (a nice effect), like he hadn't been expecting thirty of his closest friends and neighbors to be gathered in the backyard.

Hah! He was so obvious. Having had my eyes opened to his secret machinations, I could see what a charade he really was, right down to his old gray Emerly College T-shirt that highlighted his pecs, carefully preserved through daily push-ups, and those faded worn jeans that outlined his firm thighs. Of course, that was exactly the getup he'd have picked to pretend to be caught off guard.

Why had it taken me so long to realize the truth?

I used to think he dressed young because he hung out with students, but that wasn't the reason; it was because he wanted to impress Bree. My god, his hair! It was ridiculously longer than most men's at the party and when he ran his fingers through it, even Chloe let out a sigh of lust.

Griff waved me over. "Don't tell me *you* had anything to do with this, dear wife of mine."

Wasn't he just adorably naïve? My innocent geek of a husband so immersed in researching the Federal Reserve—and doing nothing else—he never suspected his loving wife would trick him with a surprise party. My hands involuntarily formed fists as I imagined Griff in bed with *her* in San Francisco while I frantically tried to call him about Laura's accident practically a whole continent away.

Buster Newcomb, an assistant football coach at Emerly and about as smart as pigskin, slammed his beer on the glass table so hard, foam exploded from the top. "You're in trouble now, girl. Get up there and take your punishment."

All eyes were on me as I picked my way across the patio sensing a wide range of emotions among our friends—admiration, respect, and perhaps even a smidgen of jealousy. *Who among them knows?* I thought. Who was pitying me as I smiled and played demure? Who was saying to herself, if she only had an inkling of the horrible truth, that her so-called loyal husband was bonking his research assistant?

"You never fail to surprise me." Griff took me by the shoulders and gazed at me lovingly with his midnight blue eyes.

A part of me wavered. *Look how much he adores you, Kat. Worships, even. You know he's not the type to cheat. Viv must have read the records wrong.*

But I was unable to fight a blitzkrieg of internal questions: *Where were you all day, really? Why was your cell off? Why do you have a separate credit card and checking account, and how come you lied about being asleep in San Francisco when Laura hit the state trooper? Just when are you planning on leaving me? How could you cheat on me after all we've been through?*

"And you," I managed to purr, summoning every

ounce of inner civility, "never fail to surprise me."

"That's what I'm talking about." Buster clapped his beefy mitts when Griff bent down and graced me with a stage-show kiss, soft but not too soft. No tongue. Sweet and warm with hints of hidden passion. It melted me—and, I hoped, Bree, too.

I couldn't help it. The blue eyes were bad enough, but I was an absolute sucker when it came to Griff's lips. I wrapped my arms around his neck to pull him tighter, and everyone went, "Awww."

What a schmuck I was. Absolutely no backbone at all, the way I couldn't help loving my husband. Halfway across the crowd, I could sense Viv's pity flowing toward me like the waves of heat off the chiminea.

We broke apart and thanked our guests, shaking hands and hugging, showing our appreciation for their support and love, inhaling so much patchouli in the process I nearly sprouted new leg hair.

I often teased Griff about his college colleagues, but deep down, I was aware enough to know my teasing was a poor attempt to hide my own insecurities. Unlike me, the women Griff worked with at Emerly did yoga and eschewed makeup. They developed their "inner beauty" (for what that was worth) by meditating and reading books written by authors with foreign names. To them, Botox was always *botulinum toxin*. They were politically active, Ivy educated, environmentally conscious recyclers.

No wonder they had nothing in common with *my* friends and relatives—Viv (already half tanked on chardonnay), Libby (chain-smoking by my Smith & Hawken fire pit, the strap from her green tank top halfway down her spray-tanned arm), and Chloe (poring over the day's Daily Candy sample-sale update on Elaine's iPhone).

These were *my* people—superficial, gossipy, born consumers. Of course Griff was bored by me and my ilk. One might have argued he should have been awarded a medal for tolerating my materialism for as long as he had.

Laura came around the corner still in her purple scrubs from her volunteer job at the hospital and reminded me of the one bond Griff and I would always share: her. Cheeks naturally pink, her hair in frizzed brown braids, she came off as far more childish than her seventeen years. She was a treasure.

Laura had never given us five minutes of worry. She was a cheerful, easygoing kid who knew exactly what she wanted out of life: to go to NYU, become a doctor, marry her boyfriend, Todd, and move to France.

"Wash and wear," Griff called her. "As easy as they make 'em."

She gave us a pinkie wave and wafted her top. *Gotta get out of these clothes*, she mouthed, slipping through the crowd and inching right past the infamous Bree.

My body turned to ice.

I guess I'd never studied this home wrecker before, how her sweetheart face and bouncy brunette hair created the misimpression of a vapid Texas debutante—until she opened her plump red lips and in a sultry Houston drawl explained why the Fed's tampering with the interest rate undermined a Keynesian view of market forces.

Bree was that intoxicating Southern combination of self-deprecating humility, sweetness, sexiness, and smarts. Of course she was having a premarital fling with my husband. She had way too much on the ball for her fiancé, Dewitt.

"That Bree's one in a million," Griff had said one night while straightening the forks and knives in his geeky way. "They didn't make women like that when I was young, I swear."

At the time, I'd passed off his comment as nothing more than an endearing fatherly attitude toward his much younger assistant. Though there must have been something disturbing about his words since they remained with me. Perhaps my subconscious realized what my ego at the time could not: that Griff wasn't being protective. He was being jealous.

Bree swished our way and casually placed a hand on Griff's forearm. "You two are just the most darling lovebirds. I can only hope that after twenty years Dewitt and I will be the same way."

Out of the corner of my eye I could tell Griff was

struggling to bite his tongue. "I don't know," he said, carefully extricating his arm. "Kat and I got damned lucky, didn't we?"

"Mmm," was all I could manage.

The two of them exchanged meaningful looks—in the open, right in front of me!—before Bree sauntered off, her A-line skirt hanging provocatively.

Once she was out of earshot, Griff murmured something about wishing "that asshole Dewitt would drop off the face of the earth."

"I just bet you do," I said. "That would make you *sooo* happy, to have her all to yourself."

"What's that supposed to mean?" His voice was edged with irritation.

The last thing I wanted was to have a fight in front of all these people at our anniversary party, so I said, "I'm sorry. It was nothing. I wasn't even thinking."

"Yes, you were. You've been frosty to me ever since I got here, and you were almost rude to Bree. What's going on?"

Like most men of his ilk, Griff rarely asked about our relationship or how we were doing, but on the few occasions when he did, he refused to drop it until he was satisfied. We needed to talk—alone—before we ruined our own party.

Taking him by the hand, I said, "Come with me," before leading him to the house on claims there was an emergency with the grilled lime shrimp. As

I passed Viv, I asked her to keep the party going and to maybe turn up the volume on the music.

She opened her eyes wide and whispered, "Good luck! I love you."

We made it to the kitchen, where Griff closed the swinging door and blocked it, his tanned arms folded across his broad chest. Did he have to be so sexy?

"It must be pretty bad if you dragged me into the kitchen," he said. "What's the matter?"

Okay, Kat. Keep your cool. Don't let him put you on the defensive. "Well, for starters, you weren't exactly surprised out there, were you?"

"Is that what's got you upset? That I wasn't surprised?" He acted incredulous. "So what? Would it have been better if I'd told everyone I already knew and that they could go home?"

"No. It would have been better if you'd been surprised. Who told you . . . Bree?"

"Bree?" He rolled his eyes and moved from the door to the counter littered with open cracker boxes, bunches of washed green grapes, and cheese rinds. "Why Bree?" He popped a Wheat Thin in his mouth and crunched once, then twice, then stopped. "Geesh! Look at you with your arms on your hips and that sour puss. You're envious!"

For the record, I did *not* have a sour puss, though I gave him points for being extremely perceptive. "Envious? No!" I scoffed. "Of Bree?" Then, in what I thought was a very clever turnabout, I said, "This has nothing to do with Bree. All I wanted to know was how you found out about the party."

He dove his hand into the Wheat Thins box again. "You wanna know?"

"I do."

"Really?"

"Try me."

"Visa called." He crunched down. "Now it's your turn to be surprised."

Shit. Next to Griff running off with Bree, any encounter with a credit card company was my worst nightmare. "Why? I didn't reach the credit limit, did I?"

"I should hope not. Just how much did you spend on this party, anyway?"

The rough estimate—because I couldn't bear to sit down and actually add the numbers—would have been high enough to send him into outer orbit. "Not that much."

"Five hundred?"

As if! This wasn't one of Laura's baby birthday parties. We weren't serving pizza and ice-cream cake. There was smoked salmon and champagne on those tables. "Yeah. About right." *Multiplied by four.*

"Whew. I thought it might have been twice that. Which wouldn't have been good, considering our current bank balance."

The familiar feelings of regret and dread briefly

washed over me as I cursed myself for ever opening the door of Smith & Hawken.

"So, if I didn't reach the credit limit, why did they call?"

"Just a routine fraud alert, one of those things the computer generates randomly."

Like when your wife is racking up thousands of dollars in merchandise over a three-hour period, I thought, fighting a renewed spike of anxiety.

Hold on!

"How come Visa was able to call you at work and I wasn't? I thought Janice was off."

"They left a message." Griff cocked his head. "Did *you* leave a message?"

"No." I hadn't, come to think of it.

"Let me get this straight. You tried me all day at work and instead of leaving a message and waiting for me to call back, you got all upset about where I was, is that right? I mean, I called you on my cell. What more did you want?"

He sliced off a piece of Swiss and let it fall to the cutting board as I weighed what to say next. Toni Feinzig's advice to Viv was that I should avoid confronting him until I'd met with her, but that was a bit drastic. This was my husband, after all.

"The reason I didn't leave a message," I said, gripping the oven handle for support, "was because of what I found when I unpacked your suitcase from San Francisco today."

He placed the slice of cheese on top of the cracker, completely unperturbed. "And that was . . . ?"

I took a big breath and let it spill. "Two condom wrappers in the pocket of your khakis and a bill for $236 at a restaurant on the night I was trying to reach you about Laura's accident. How could you, Griff? How could you be having an affair with . . . Bree?"

There. Done. Out in the open. Suddenly, I felt dizzy.

He carefully put down the cracker and stared at the rooster timer by the sink. This was vintage Griff—mature, steady, unflappable—and I hated him for it. "You mean to tell me you seriously think I've been having an affair with Bree."

I remained silent. Years of fighting had taught me that if I answered, I'd be caught in his powerful rhetorical vortex in which he'd suck out all the meaning of my words and trivialize my concerns.

"Bree," he said, "who's getting married."

Again, I stayed mum.

"All because you found a couple of condom wrappers in my pants and the receipt from my dinner with Walter Maddox, head of economic research at the Federal Reserve in San Francisco and definitely not my type."

Walter Maddox? "But last Thursday when I tried to reach you and couldn't, you claimed you were asleep."

"I was. On *Thursday* night. However, I believe if

you check the receipt you'll see that dinner happened the night before. In your eagerness to prove me an adulterer, you must have forgotten to consult your calendar."

I counted back the days and then thought about the receipt. Today was the twentieth. Friday was the nineteenth. Thursday was the eighteenth. Wednesday was the . . .

Curse that Viv. Never trust an English teacher with even the simplest numbers.

"Don't you remember me telling you about the dinner with Walter to thank him for giving us so much help?"

Flames of red shot up my neck. He was too clever by far. I would have to change course in order to set a new trap. "Okay, so maybe I was off about the dinner, but where *did* you get those condom wrappers?"

"From underneath the seat of our car, darling. Your Lexus, in fact." He turned and frowned. "Sorry. I was trying to spare you."

"Our car?" That was shocking. "Why would there be condom wrappers in our car?"

"Our daughter. She drives the Lexus more than you these days."

Laura? But she was so . . . perfect. "She told me she wasn't having sex." And with *Todd Wilner*? He with the pet tarantula and Guitar Hero collection? Why in a million years would she have lost her virginity to *him*? "She promised she'd wait."

"Come on, Kat. Don't be like that." He pulled me to him, pressing my head to his warm chest. "She's almost graduated from high school and she's a big girl now. Let her go."

I would not let her go, not Laura. Laura, who, just yesterday, I'd wrapped in a pink blanket and played "little piggy" on her teensy-weensy toes to make her chortle and laugh. Laura, who used to build fairy gardens in the backyard with moss and acorn hats.

"You should be proud of her for being smart enough to protect herself." He kissed the top of my head, and, reluctantly, I returned his gesture with a hug. It was so comforting to have him hold me at a time like this that I didn't care about the money stuff. I needed my husband. I needed the father of our daughter to assure me everything was okay, that we would get through this together.

He bent down and kissed away my tears, pushing back my hair and tilting my chin so he could have my full attention. "Don't cry, Kat. We've done a good job. Laura's a great woman who will go on to do great things and you know you will always be her mother no matter how much sex she has." A smile played at the corner of his mouth.

That was the annoying thing about Griff: He knew exactly the right thing to say. Even more than his eyes or those sexy lips, it was this quality about him that I found most alluring.

"As for whatever insanity I inadvertently put you through earlier today by the crime of not answering my office phone, don't be silly," he said simply. "From the first moment you wandered into Barb Gladstone's stuffy library, I have always loved you and I always will. No cute assistant will ever change that. Well—" he grinned—"depending on how cute. . . ."

He laughed, and I punched him gently on the chest. "How cute my ass."

"Yes. I like that, too." To drive the point home, so to speak, he reached around and playfully squeezed my butt, bringing me to him as hard as he could, his lips trailing down my neck and sparking an unexpected urgent craving.

There was a party outside, but it was impossible for us to go back to it when we'd headed down this path. We'd been together long enough to recognize the signs, the signals, even the smells of unstoppable passion. "The laundry room," I gasped. It was our old safe haven, where we used to flee when Laura was small and we were hit with sudden bouts of lust.

"But," he tried to protest as I kissed his rough neck, "we've got . . ."

"Now!"

Wordlessly, Griff lifted me and, with the strength of a man half his age, carried me across the kitchen to the door. Kicking it open, he gently set me on the folding table and closed the white shutters to the outside window as I madly yanked the shirt over his head.

"Lock," I whispered, sliding out of my underwear and fumbling at the zipper on my dress.

"No time." He meant the dress, not the lock, as he undid his jeans, the hardness of him unmistakable under his boxers.

Please, I begged, crazed as usual by the overwhelming physical madness he could inspire, the almost animalistic urge to have him inside me. He pulled up my dress and, kissing me softly, slid himself in, pumping with masterful, determined strokes. Our mutual explosion was almost instantaneous and immediately cleared my head—a leaden accumulation of worry and fear rapidly dissipating into nothing.

Of course he loved me, I decided calmly. How could I have ever thought otherwise?

"Wow." He pretended to be embarrassed, clearing his throat as he zipped up his jeans. "I'm very sorry, Mrs. Griffiths. I have no idea what came over me."

I playfully tapped him on the nose. "Oh, I think I know what came over you."

He rearranged my dress and kissed me once more. "Happy anniversary, my love."

"Ditto."

We composed ourselves as best we could, careful to return to the party from separate entrances. I stalled by going to the bathroom to finger-comb my hair and carefully redo my lips in the emergency Pink Plum lipstick I kept in the downstairs medicine cabinet, trying not to laugh at how spot-on Buster had been about the room rocking.

When I was through, I looked matronly, not at all like I'd been banging my husband on the laundry folding table minutes before. Viv would know, though. She always did.

Done, ready to face the party, I opened the door to find a very small, very strange woman with jet-black hair and cat-eye glasses tapping a foot impatiently. "Oh," I said, searching to place her. Perhaps someone's new girlfriend. "I had no idea you were waiting. Sorry."

She reached in her purse and pulled out a business card. "I was waiting for *you*, not the bathroom. I saw your husband outside and thought this might be my chance to introduce myself."

I glanced at the business card.

TONI FEINZIG, ATTORNEY
SPECIALIZING IN MATRIMONIAL
  AND FAMILY LAW
"I FIGHT SO YOU DON'T HAVE TO!"

So this was the famous Toni Feinzig.

"Actually," I began, embarrassed that Viv had been so bold as to invite her to the party, "I don't think I'll be needing your services after all. My husband and I are fine."

"I thought you might say that. It's hardly usual for these matters to proceed in a linear direction. However, if circumstances should change, my cell is on the back of my card. Don't hesitate to call me at any time of day or night." She glanced at the laundry room. "I find it so pathetic, the extremes some men will go in order to buy themselves more time, their superficial attempts to fool the women they no longer love with presents, jewelry, extra attention." She narrowed her eyes with suspicion. "Sex."

I forced myself not to blink.

"Of course, I expect you're too smart to fall for those tricks. After twenty years you'd know when your husband is being manipulative, wouldn't you?"

It was definitely a trick question. There was no way to answer it. All I could do was shrug.

"Interesting." She smiled thinly and tapped the card in the palm of my hand. "Just remember, don't say anything to him until you talk to me. Better not to shoot yourself in the foot at the start of the race."

CHAPTER SEVEN

*Y*es, what Toni had said was haunting. *She* was haunting with her drastic red suit and those rhinestone cat-eye glasses and jet-black hair— Kelly Osbourne meets the Wicked Witch of the

West. As she minced away in her stiletto heels, I ripped up her business card and tossed it into the wastepaper basket, vigorously washing my hands afterward to remove the poison.

It was Adele's fault for jumping the gun and impulsively contacting that awful, awful ambulance chaser. Or, rather, in the case of divorce, *moving van* chaser. I hoped Toni wouldn't continue to bug me with spot visits. I wasn't exactly sure how these divorce lawyers worked, but I'd heard stories that they could be ruthless in their quest to beat out the competition and drum up business—following women to the ladies' room and such.

Shaking off Toni's bad vibes, I returned to the party, where the tiki torches were flickering and our guests were enjoying themselves in the cool late-summer night. For once I'd thrown a decent gathering, I thought with pride, snatching a flute of bubbling champagne and drinking in the heady elixir of perfume and forbidden cigarette smoke.

Over the glass rim, I caught Griff smiling at me from across the patio and I went all squishy. Too bad Bree wasn't around to witness us in top form. Then she'd back off—she and her tiny A-line skirt.

Turned out, the only drawback to the evening was Viv, who, tipsy on chardonnay and erroneously believing I'd confronted my husband about having an affair, stuck out her lower lip and offered her services as amateur psychologist/confidante.

"How are you holding up?" She darted her eyes at Griff with new loathing. "You wanna go someplace and talk? That's what sisters are for, you know, to lean on. You don't have to put on a brave face with me."

I gently removed her hand from where it was stroking my hair. "Thanks, Viv. But nothing happened. It's over."

"Don't say that. You and Griff can get counseling and . . ."

"My marriage isn't over. I mean . . . this misunderstanding." Elaine and her husband, Gerry, were getting ready to go, providing a welcomed escape from Viv's hovering. "Excuse me. I have to thank Elaine."

But my older sister would not be so easily dissuaded. Lingering in the kitchen until the last straggler had left, she handed me a cup of decaffeinated coffee, put her arm around my waist, and said, "Finally, we have some girl time. Let's talk."

It was past midnight and I was so tired of talking. Period. It had been a stressful day, what with finding the condom wrappers and then dealing with Chloe, shopping, being told that my husband had a secret bank account and MasterCard, throwing a party. All I wanted was to fall in bed and slip into the deep, dark abyss of blissful unconsciousness.

"Tell you in the morning." I took her cup of

coffee and gave her a hug. "I promise I'll tell you everything in the morning."

She hesitated. "At least tell me what you two were discussing here in the kitchen."

"I can't." I willed my lips not to smile.

"Why not?"

"Because we weren't exactly . . . *discussing*."

She snapped her hand off the kitchen counter as if it had been contaminated. "Oh, no, Kat, you didn't."

"We did, and I'm glad. I have absolutely no doubts about Griff now." That wasn't completely true. I had plenty.

"That explains why you two were so lovey-dovey later. And here I assumed you were putting on a noble act." She hooked her purse over her shoulder and regarded me with grave disappointment. "That's only going to make it worse, you know, in the long run."

"He's my husband. I love him."

"I know. That's why I despise him, because he knows that and he's using your unquestioning love for him to take advantage of you by sleeping with that hottie assistant of his."

"Shhh." I did not want Griff overhearing.

She held up a finger. "Remember, men might lie, but the numbers never do." Clearly, Viv was proud of that line because it was the second or third time she'd said it that day.

"Who sang that, Mary Chapin Carpenter?"

"No." She acted hurt that I hadn't recognized her genius. "Me . . . I think."

"Good-bye, sister dear," I said, practically pushing her down the hall to the front door.

"Mark my words." Miffed, she tromped to a waiting Jaguar, where a teetotaling Adele was behind the wheel to take her home.

But the damage had been done.

After a brief sleep, I tossed and turned, unsatisfied, anxious, and incredibly thirsty. I drank two full glasses of water and returned to bed wide awake, staring at Griff's bare, broad back, torturing myself by imagining Bree stroking her hands along his wing muscles, moving lower, the two of them buck naked on his hand-carved Honduran mahogany desk.

Then, for some bizarre reason, I thought of Liam and wondered if he'd been through this exact same hell when he'd learned his wife was having an affair. Miles and years apart and yet we were connected by a common heartbreak of infidelity.

Maybe Mom was right; maybe I should give him a call. For old times' sake, of course, nothing more.

Griff rolled over and flung an arm around my waist, pulling me into the C of his naked, warm body. "Love you," he murmured. "Great party."

That's what he thought. But what about when he woke up and opened the Visa bill and found that I hadn't spent $500 on the party but $2,000? Then what? What if Viv was correct in her assessment that our finances were a serious mess and we had no money left and I'd blown our last line of credit on crab cakes, cheese puffs, and champagne?

Geesh. Laura was going to college next year. What if we couldn't afford to send her and no one would give us a loan because our credit was crap and Laura would have to join Todd at the community college, where he majored in Call of Duty 101, forever resenting that her mother had ruined her dreams of becoming a French doctor by buying towels and sheets and pillows and leather couches and . . . party stuff?

All of a sudden, I felt out of control, as if the condom wrappers and the receipt were simply the first symptoms of a larger disease, the spots before the fever of chicken pox. Griff and I were cooked, and no amount of laundry room sex was going to change that.

Somehow in this turbulent sea of anxiety, I fell asleep and woke up, groggy, to a bright dawn. Griff, who never slept in, bounced out of bed and suggested we go for a run to start our twenty-first year as husband and wife. I did (only because Bree would have) and, after a mile of whining and complaining and practically falling on my knees begging for coffee, I loosened up and managed to put one foot in front of the other.

We went through the neighborhood and I waved to Mrs. Demorts, who was putting her garden to bed for the year. Seeing me, she slowly stood and waddled over to gossip, brushing dirt off her knees along the way. Mrs. Demorts could talk you to death about such minutiae as where the trash collectors leave her garbage cans, which was why Griff begged off, saying he was going to sprint ahead "to get the sweat going."

Chicken.

Fifteen minutes later, I turned the corner and found Griff dry as a bone, checking his iPhone, the one I bought him over his protests that it was nothing more than a fad and another one of my expensive impulsive purchases. His addiction to it was my own sweet vindication.

"What's up?" I bent over to catch my breath, though I'd gone barely a half mile.

"Not much." He clicked it off and shoved it into the pocket of his running shorts. "Let's go. I'm starved."

At home, I took a shower while Griff cut up fruit and flipped a few omelets that we took to the patio table where he read the Week in Review of the Sunday *New York Times* and I read the Style section. Every five minutes behind his paper he checked something in his lap.

"Breaking news?" I gestured with my fork to the iPhone.

"Just waiting for word on whether we snagged an interview with Hunter Christiansen."

Ah, yes, the elusive Hunter Christiansen, the

Fed's most charismatic and secretive former chairman, the man who most economists—aside from Griff—claimed was single-handedly responsible for failing to recognize the need for the regulation of Wall Street, thereby leading to the biggest crash since the Great Depression. Which might have been why Christiansen had retired in disgrace and fled to some remote outpost eschewing all interviews and demurring from the time-honored tradition of selling the rights to his memoirs for a million plus.

An exclusive meeting with Christiansen would transform Griff's book from an obscure academic treatise by a small university press into a non-fiction best seller. It would be read by every economist, politician, stock broker, venture capitalist, businessman, and small-town banker searching for secrets to the Fed's inner workings. Not to mention it would definitely get him tenure.

The odds were Griff didn't have a shot in hell of talking to Christiansen. The old codger had already sent final word through his people that he wasn't interested in participating in any book having to do with the Federal Reserve. So how come Griff was on tenterhooks, checking his iPhone every three seconds to see if Christiansen had changed his mind?

"Good luck with that," I said.

He said, "You never know."

So true.

As it turned out, the big call did come. Not for Griff, but for me.

"I'm so sorry to bother you at home. It wasn't until after I dialed that I remembered it was a Sunday and that you might have other plans besides work," an earnest voice prattled.

Madeleine Granville. She must have read the email I sent on Friday and reconsidered. "No. I'm the one who must apologize," I jumped in. "I'm not in the habit of putting clients on hold, and someday when we're old friends, I'll be able to tell you the truth of what happened."

She laughed. "I have an idea, from Elaine. Would it have anything to do with your boss?"

"Of course not. My boss is a lovely woman." Who was I to burn bridges?

"Good for you, keeping it on the up and up. But even with the best boss it's not easy breaking out on your own, is it?"

This question seemed more profound than it probably was in light of yesterday's revelations. Madeleine was right. It wasn't easy breaking out on one's own. It required drive, planning, and, most of all, money.

The thing was, I could list a thousand reasons why I needed to break free from Chloe. What was the one reason Griff needed to break free from me?

Anyway, as it was not the time to drift off into an existential analysis, I snapped to and focused on reassuring her that I could do wonders for her house, and inexpensively, too. She'd appreciated the ideas in my email, which made my pitch easier. All we had to do was meet.

"The directions are rather complicated," she said as I rustled through the bowl by the phone for a pen and paper. "Being a city girl, I don't have a driver's license, so the best I can do is tell you how to get to my house from the Princeton Junction train station." At last, I found one of Laura's eye liners and a thin envelope from Franklin Savings with an ominous OPEN IMMEDIATLY/TIMED MATERIAL stamped on top.

Uh-oh. I must have missed it in yesterday's mail. Tentatively sliding my finger under the flap, I didn't need to read the opening paragraph to realize it was a notice that on Friday our checking account had gone into overdraft by $64.

Griff was going to have a fit.

As Madeleine went into a lengthy description of lefts and rights and turning at the second light—or was it the third?—I crumpled the letter into a ball, my mind racing for a possible way to fix this. It was Sunday, the bank was closed, what could I do?

A car door slammed and I peeked out the window to see our godson Jack's beaten-up Toyota in the driveway. True sport and loving kid that he was, he'd driven up from Stone Harbor for our anniversary. Or perhaps . . . to use our washing machine.

Done with Madeleine, I hung up and rushed outside to tell Griff, not only about Jack, but about my first bona fide client. Forget the overdraft, Madeleine's call was so much more important and reminded me of one of the great perks of marriage—having someone with whom to share not only the bad news, but also the good.

My excitement quickly vanished when I found Griff bent over his iPhone again, his thumbs working back and forth, a huge smile on his face.

"Did Christiansen say yes?"

He lifted his head abruptly and, I swear, tried to hide what he'd been typing. "Pardon?"

"Christiansen. Did he say yes?"

He frowned, lost in a shadow of confusion. "Er, no. Did I just hear a car pull up? Is that Jack? He said he might come up."

What was making him so happy if it wasn't Christiansen? I debated whether to push the iPhone issue further but, hearing Jack call, "Hello!" I decided to drop it. "Yep. Jack's here."

"Great. Let me finish this memo and then I'll be out to see him." And he went back to that damned phone.

Deflated, I left the patio to meet Jack in the driveway. He must have grown a foot since I saw him three weeks before, so tall and blond and . . . red. The boy had skin like a lobster.

"Didn't you ever hear of sunblock?" I reached up to kiss him on the cheek.

"Yes, Aunt Kat. I know all about sunblock. It's

not my fault; blame global warming." He hugged me tightly before handing me a present—a pillow-case packed with laundry. It reeked of old, mildewed sneakers, like he hadn't done a wash since he'd left. Which he hadn't.

Laura shuffled out in a pair of light flannel pj bottoms and a tank top and, without saying so much as hi, began to tease her cousin about his surfer hair and bronzed skin. Again, I found myself glancing off, unable to think of her alone with Todd in *that* way. Well, I would just have to learn to deal with it. She couldn't stay my little girl forever.

We whittled away the rest of the day in pleasant family togetherness. Jack did his laundry and helped his uncle fix the backyard fence. The four of us played a couple of halfhearted games of bad-minton before a few of Laura's friends—alerted that a strapping, blond lifeguard was on the prem-ises—stopped by to clean us out of chips, crackers, cheese, and hors d'oeuvres left over from the party.

Griff, ever the professor, gravitated to the kids, plying them with questions and abstract bits of random economics theory having to do with the purchasing power of their meager after-school earnings.

Any other middle-aged man explaining the "income effect of a price increase on demand" would have driven off the most polite teenagers. But Laura's friends didn't mind. In fact, they seemed to get a kick out Griff's mini lecture, needling him about being mind-numbingly boring, pretending to commit hara-kiri or keel over dead as, playing to their jokes, he proceeded to use a tortilla chip to draw a price curve in the bowl of salsa.

It reminded me of our first unofficial date at the Alchemist & Barrister when he was hanging out with the Princeton students and I realized my whole life had been leading up to our meeting. It wasn't merely that he was still handsome, that, with his longish, dark hair and jeans he stood apart from these girls' staid fathers. It was—as always—his energy, his enthusiasm, his interest in others.

I must remember to think of him like this, I thought, confused by my shifting feelings of suspicion, anger, doubt, and intense love. If I only knew for certain he wasn't cheating on me—or if he was—it would be far easier on my psyche than hovering in this limbo. At least I could take the appropriate action and move forward.

But, as the saying goes, be careful what you ask for.

It happened completely by accident. I was *not* snooping (no matter what Viv claims). I was simply going downstairs to get the last bottle of champagne to accompany our anniversary dinner of steaks and the last of the summer's corn to put on the grill.

If Griff, or Laura or Jack, had fetched the champagne, if I hadn't accidentally bumped his desk and jolted the computer out of sleep thereby revealing the outbox for Griff's online iPhone email account, there was a good chance Griff and I would never have stepped on the road to divorce.

But I *did* bump the computer and I *did* see the emails he'd sent that morning when I'd been on the phone with Madeleine, and once I read them, I knew Toni Feinzig was right: His passion for me in the laundry room had only been a pathetic ploy to buy time.

CHAPTER EIGHT

*Y*ou did the right thing," Toni said, pushing a box of aloe vera Kleenex in my direction, "by coming to me first."

She sounded more like Tony Soprano than Toni Feinzig, I thought, blowing my nose and rethinking my decision to see a lawyer so soon. I didn't want to ruin Griff or leave him destitute, far from it. I didn't even want a divorce.

"I want him to, to . . . to love me."

"Absolutely. Of course." Toni's voice was scripted sympathetic. As a veteran divorce attorney who specifically sought women clients in her yellow page ads, she'd been in this position many a time before.

"I can't believe I . . ." Oh, god. Here came the tears again. ". . . love a man who's lying to me,

who's planning to leave me for his assistant. . . ."
My chest tightened, the crushing words of Griff's
email hitting as hard as they did the first time I'd
read them. ". . . as soon as Laura graduates from
high school."

Another tsunami of self-pity crashed and I
broke down in waves of sobs. Viv brought her
arm around my shoulders and squeezed tightly.
"It's okay," she murmured. "Try to forget about
the SOB and concentrate on what you need to
do."

Thank god for Viv, that she was always there
for me when the chips were down. It was true
that on the night of the party I'd been so annoyed
by her nosiness I'd literally pushed her out the
door.

And yet, within twenty-four hours, there I was
in the master bath on the phone to her, breaking
down about the emails as she clucked in sympathy
just like she used to when I was thirteen and
couldn't stand the utter heartbreak of learning that
Justin Danyhew had been passing me love notes
in class only to get to my best friend Francine
Bracchia, the prettiest girl at South River Junior
High.

Sisters were gifts from heaven, even if they
borrowed your jewelry without asking and
snitched to your parents behind your back.

"Take a deep breath and drink some water,"
she'd urged during my master-bath breakdown as

I robotically followed her order, putting my mouth to the bathroom faucet like Laura used to when she was little. "Now start from the beginning. You found the emails on Griff's computer. Then what?"

With difficulty, as if it had been years, not hours, after discovering them, I tried to re-create the chain of events:

When I'd read enough, I shut down the computer to preserve what was left of my self-esteem, sat back, and tried to breathe. I almost couldn't. Two thoughts: A) My marriage was over, and B) What the heck was I doing in this dark basement?

Oh, right. Champagne. To celebrate.

Because I am a woman and a mother, I made the definitive choice to say nothing about what I'd read so as not to ruin what otherwise might have been a perfect day for Laura and Jack. Instead, I brought up the champagne and toasted our family, chatted with the children as we did the dishes, and even, later that night, succumbed to sex with my husband. (I know! Awful!) Numb, stunned, I kissed him good night and somehow managed to look, talk, and act like a functioning human the next morning despite the black hollow rotting me from within.

It wasn't until the house was empty that I let myself unravel in a deep, hot bath, crying forcefully as I reread Griff's emails I'd printed out that morning.

TO: b.robeson@emerly.edu (Bree!)
FROM: d.griffiths@emerly.edu
RE: last night

you're right. . . . it'd be a burden off our backs if we could tell Kat now, especially, as you point out, the fight she and I had last night indicates there's good reason to think that if she doesn't know already . . . then she suspects.

. . . still, I want to stick with my plan to break it to her after Laura graduates. like I said, that'll give Kat a summer to adjust. Change is hard enough . . . but, in this case, she'll not only have to cope with change but also the fact that I've been—let's face it—lying to her for months. She's been my wife for 20 yrs, bree. She's going to be devastated.

And then, another email to Bree, at the bottom of which was . . .

—I guess it goes back to what you said—my age. I'm a few years away from fifty and it's either now or never. And if you and I don't do this now, I'm sure I'll regret it for the rest of my life.

I just hope I can keep it together until June. I dunno. Kat's smart and I dread to think what she'll do when she finds out. But if we tell her now, I can guarantee the first thing she'll do is drain the account and leave us high and dry and that, my dear, would be the end of our future. ☺

Bottom line? We have to be more careful in what we say, etc. . . .

Until Monday . . .

G

"Interestingly enough," I told Viv, "his inbox had been cleaned out sometime either in the night or the morning after I got the champagne. I can only imagine Bree's emails to him."

Viv was silent for a while. "Well, I guess we have our confirmation."

I sniffled back a few tears as I shivered in the cooling water. "I guess so."

"Kind of supports what I said earlier, about couples not being designed to stay together for fifty years. I gotta say, Kat, from that line you read about him turning fifty, this is a guy going through a classic middle-age crisis."

I checked the mirror and was horrified by my

reflection, puffy, red-rimmed eyes. "Why couldn't he have just bought a Miata?"

"Indeed." In the background, the school bell rang, indicating her free period was up and she needed to get ready for her next class. "There's only one thing to do. We gotta go see Toni."

"But I don't want a divorce. What I want is for my husband to love me."

"And, as your older sister, I want you to be protected. You can't just sit around until Laura's graduation and hope he changes his mind only to have him hand you a set of divorce papers."

"I can't?" Seemed like a fairly reasonable course of action to me, provided I had enough chocolate . . . and didn't have to get out of bed. Could humans hibernate?

"Think of Beth Williams. Do you want to end up like her, stocking shelves at Wegmans? At least you have the advantage of a heads-up, so let's use it. I'm calling."

Which she did. Which was how I ended up in Toni's office.

"Earth to Kat." Toni's piercing voice snapped me to attention. "I know you're grieving, but now is not the moment to drift into the sea of pity. I need you here, present, thinking not like a wronged woman, but like a wronged man."

Viv, her arm firmly around my shoulders, said, "Don't you have that backward?"

"Absolutely not. In other words, I want you to

grow a pair. Look, when it comes to divorce, most of my jilted clients . . ."

I bristled and, sensing this, Viv cleared her throat in warning. "She's a bit more than a wall-flower stood up at the prom, Toni. Though, I should add, right now she's about as fragile."

"The point I'm trying to make," Toni said, soft-ening her tone, "is that, when faced with marital dissolution, women tend to think with their hearts whereas men think with their bank accounts. Which is why nine times out of ten, women get screwed financially in divorces."

The "D" word again. I wished everyone would stop using it.

"How do you think with a bank account?" Viv used her practical teacher's voice. "Bank accounts don't have brains."

"Neither do other parts of male anatomy and yet I've found they drive most thoughts of the male population."

Harsh.

"What I'm trying to press upon you, Kat, is that if you confront your husband now with virtually no assets to your name besides the ones you two hold mutually, you will only be hurting yourself in the long run since there is a very strong possibility that he'll call your bluff and declare immediately that he's leaving you, at which point you will be on your own. Think of his email—this is a man with one foot already out the door. Do you understand?"

I told her I did, but she went on, anyway, to relate the story of another local woman—not, for once, the infamously abandoned and unwise Beth Williams—who, upon finding her husband had been conducting an affair with a colleague at work, packed up and took the children to her mother's house.

"This is categorically the worst move a woman can make. In so doing, she robbed herself of her own home, the one she'd maintained, simply because she left the domicile first. At least you didn't do that."

Though it had crossed my mind, as had several other dramatic scenarios:

Fantasy #1—After finding those emails, my first impulse was to run to my bedroom, gather my stuff, throw it in the back of the car, and head west. I wanted to never see Griff again. At which point, he'd find himself missing me so much he'd pledge to never rest until he held me in his arms, promising his undying love forever.

Fantasy #2—Not nearly as romantic, but still inspiring in a Thelma and Louise kind of way, was to print Griff's emails and lay them out on the marital bed, followed by packing up, stepping on the gas, and heading west, yadda, yadda, yadda. When he came home and realized what horror he'd wrought, he'd read my succinct note—something about how I was sorry to have burdened him for twenty years—after which he'd get down on his knees and curse himself for not appreciating me when he had the chance.

Toni was right. Both scenarios ended with Griff apologizing and begging my forgiveness. I couldn't think of the alternate ending—him leaving. It simply did not compute.

Toni regarded me with her fishy eyes. "I'm assuming the situation is not abusive."

"Of course not!" The idea of Griff hitting me or even raising his voice was preposterous. "My husband has never been anything but considerate."

"She's right," Viv added. "He wouldn't hurt a fly."

Toni bit her lip, as though Griff's placidity were regrettable. "Then here's my suggestion, and bear with me. It might be rather hard to take initially."

Kick him out. Change the locks. Serve him with papers. Demand a divorce and circle for-rent ads in the classifieds. Take Laura aside and tell her the truth. Get yourself into daily psychotherapy with antidepressants. Change back to your maiden name. Burn the socks he scatters around the bedroom floor. Pour yourself a shot of tequila. I held my breath, anxiously awaiting which dramatic step she'd have me take.

"Shut up and stay with him, so if—and when—he asks for a divorce, you'll be prepared financially."

What? Anticipation popped like a balloon. "How am I supposed to do that?"

Viv said, "You have to admit, Toni, that would be kind of hard, to live with a man, have *sex* with him, just to save money."

"Nonsense. Women stay with their husbands for financial reasons all the time, have for ages. In Kat's situation, it's the only sensible strategy."

Screw strategy. This was my heart, my soul, my very sanity at stake here.

"I'm not asking you to stay with your husband forever like they used to in your mother's generation."

Viv and I flashed each other questioning looks. *How did she know?*

"I'm saying use this window until June to photocopy all your records, clear up your credit rating, get a better job, and open your own bank account with enough money to keep you afloat after he leaves. Prior planning prevents piss-poor performance, and all that."

"I can't." I wiggled out of Viv's grasp. "No way. I've barely been able to endure the past few days without going out of my mind. A minute more of living with him and not admitting what I've discovered would be torture."

"Ah, ah, ah." Toni wagged her finger. "You're thinking with your heart instead of your bank account, Kat. What did I say about that?"

Viv, more focused than I, said, "Speaking of thinking like a man, let me ask how much you *think* this divorce will cost my sister."

It was the question my very female brain wanted to pose since I'd first stepped into Toni's plush office with its pewter-colored walls and thick oriental rugs, built-in bookshelves, cushy leather furniture, and expensively framed, expensively obtained diplomas. But somewhere between crying about the end of my marriage and reeling from the shock of Toni's advice to stay with Griff, I'd forgotten about money.

Then again, I always forgot about money. Hence, my problems.

"My usual retainer is $15,000."

Holy crap! In home designer currency, that could buy a French Godin stove *and* hood.

Viv and I were speechless. Fifteen grand was my annual starting salary when I'd first started working for Chloe. Fifteen grand had bought Viv her used Passat.

"Fifteen thousand is reasonable for this area," Toni said. "Go to New York and it can be $10,000 more. Keep in mind that's just my retainer, too. The actual divorce could end up costing much more, depending on complications, not to mention the additional expenses of moving, renting, insurance, your own food, health care, et cetera."

The prospect of coming up with all that money was overwhelming. It was impossible. Even $3,000—more in the ballpark of what I'd expected to pay—would have been a hardship. Fifteen thousand dollars was out of the question.

Now I could see why women in my mother's generation stuck with their inattentive, cruel, obnoxious slobs of husbands who snored and swore and cheated and yelled. They didn't have the wherewithal to leave.

Toni motioned for her assistant to find a file. "Don't worry, ladies. I've got a solution, that is, if you've got the discipline."

I certainly didn't like the sound of that.

Opening the file, she pulled out a paper and said, "Here's a handy divorce preparation check-list that might help you. I'll go over the highlights and give you a copy to take home."

Yippee.

"First thing, obviously, is you need a job." Toni glanced at me over her half-glasses. "You do have that, right?"

"I do."

Viv added, "But she doesn't make very much, and her boss treats her like an indentured servant."

Toni asked, "Does your job have health insurance? A 401(k)?"

"I don't know." It was embarrassing how little interest I took in my employment benefits. "I never had to ask because I'm on Griff's policy at Emerly." This was so dull, not at all the fiery rants and threats of vengeance I'd expected from a hot-dog divorce lawyer who drove a Jaguar and sported bloodred nails.

Toni made a mark on the sheet with her pencil. "Okay, so that's something you need to follow up on, your benefits, since once you're divorced you can't go on Griff's health plan. Onto personal finance. How much money would you estimate the two of you have saved for retirement? More than $100,000? More than $300,000?"

Viv brought her hand to her mouth and snickered. I gave her a dirty look.

"Sorry," she said, biting her lip. "It's just that, when Toni asked that . . . the idea of you having over a hundred grand in savings. You gotta admit, it's pretty funny."

Toni, again over her half-glasses, asked, "Is there a problem? Kat's in her forties. I should hope she has that much."

Viv said, "She should hope, too. *Hope* she's got. Savings, not so much. If there's one thing you should know about my sister, Toni, is that she can't save worth squat."

I punched her arm. "That's a nice thing to tell my lawyer."

"Well, it's true!"

"Your sister's right. It's better that I'm apprised of these issues in the beginning." Whipping off her glasses, Toni bit an end and scrutinized me. "No savings at all, eh?"

I shifted in my seat, uncomfortable. Wasn't it bad enough my husband was planning to leave me? Did I have to be subjected to the third degree about my spending habits, too? "See, I'm not quite sure my sister is right about that."

"I'm right about that. Trust me."

"*Because,*" I continued, "I haven't had the opportunity to sit down and go over our accounts myself. Therefore, I don't know how much we have in an IRA."

I could feel Viv roll her eyes.

"You gotta understand something, Toni." Viv patted my knee, like she would take care of the talking from now on. "My baby sister's a great person. Loving. Kind. Smart. Last summer she rescued a clutch of baby rabbits who were drowning in their hole and stayed up all night feeding them with droppers of milk and keeping them warm with a heat lamp."

"They died anyway," I said. Where was Viv going with this?

"But she's horrible with money. Even as a kid, she was the first one to smash open her piggy bank and go buy candy."

"That's not true!"

"Face it, Kat. It's who you are, a spender. But that's okay. I can't save, either, and that's not our fault—we were born to shop. We're from *South River* and what else was there to do in South River but . . ."

"Shop." Toni tossed down her glasses. "I get it. That explains your husband's line in this email, by the way, the one about fearing you'd drain the account." She underlined that line on the printout I'd brought. "I thought that was very telling."

Unbelievable. My sister and lawyer were actually blaming *me* for my husband having a secret slush fund. "Are you saying it's my fault Griff's leaving?"

Toni said, "Frankly, that's not my business. That's for a therapist to help you discern down the road. Which reminds me, I should include psychologist's fees in the settlement." She jotted another note. "All I care about is finding the basis for a fault to pin on Griff, starting with adultery."

Adultery? The awful word hung in the air like a noxious cloud.

Under her breath, Viv said, "It's not your fault."

"What I'm more interested in at this juncture is how you're going to get the money to pay not only me, but those other expenses we talked about—shelter, food, insurance, car payments. . . . That's our prime objective—seeing you become fiscally independent."

"Our mother!" Viv snapped her fingers. "She has savings and she won't tell Dad if we ask her."

That was abhorrent. I was not about to approach my elderly mother who'd managed to gather a nest egg from Dad's allowance by sewing our clothes instead of buying them and making Monday's meat loaf last for a week's worth of lunches.

"No." The image of my mother slowly writing me a check was so pathetic that it imbued me with a burst of unfamiliar resolve. "My mother will *not* pay for me to survive a divorce. Neither will my father, or, for that matter, my husband."

Toni looked aghast as I jumped from my seat and, caught up in some strange swirl of energy, pounded her desk so hard I toppled her mini Chinese brass gong. "I'll do it on my own. I don't know how . . . maybe my new client will lead to bigger and better things. Maybe Chloe will give me a raise. . . ."

"In this economy?" Viv whistled. "Not likely."

"Okay, then I'll simply cut back on everything. I will be the best saver you've ever met."

While Viv had the decency not to snort or roll her eyes again, I could tell she was holding back, trying not to laugh at my dramatics.

"I know you don't believe me, Viv. . . ."

"Who, me?" She put her hand to her chest. "Who am I to say you can't pull off saving $15,000? I didn't think a black man from Hawaii had a chance of winning the presidency, either, and look how wrong I was about that."

So she *did* doubt me.

"It's what you said about Mom that got me thinking. If our mother could put aside a so-called nest egg by spending less than the allowance Dad gave her, then why can't I?"

"Because Mom had forty years. You've got, what? Eight months?"

"That's okay." Toni nodded wisely. "An intensive savings program is the ideal exercise for your sister during these tough months ahead. It'll build her confidence and independence."

Viv said, "I know that, but I'd hate to see her try and fail."

"I won't fail." Geesh. I wasn't a child.

"Failure's not the enemy. Not trying is." Toni got up and came around, perching herself on the desk, perhaps to keep me from pounding it again. "And you never know, Kat. You might save more than money."

CHAPTER NINE

*O*kay, so there it was. I had publicly declared my intention to save at least $15,000 despite my abysmal financial history and Viv's skepticism.

Aha! What my sister didn't realize was that her doubts only further buoyed my determination. I'd show her, I would. And I'd show Toni, too. And my mother and, most of all, Griff, that I could be smart with money.

But how?

It wasn't as though one could flip a switch from consumer to saver and be done with it. There wasn't a patch or a gum that could curb a spending addiction. Nor did I have the ironic luxury of alcoholics and drug addicts in going cold turkey. I had to feed and clothe my family and that required expending money almost daily.

Knowing when to say when for me was a mystery.

On the ride home from Toni's office, for instance, I passed a dozen places where I easily could have stopped and shopped—Wegmans for groceries, the camera shop to pick up black-and-white film for Laura's photography class, the dry cleaner to fetch Griff's shirts, the pet store to buy the special—and pricey—food for my toothless dog, Jasper. Those errands alone would have sucked over $200 from my checking account in a snap.

And then I saw the Rocky River Public Library and it hit me. If I couldn't get support from my family, then maybe I could get it from strangers. Libby had been after me to go to one of her Penny Pinchers meetings for years. Perhaps now was the time. Of course, that would require me to eat a bit of crow since I'd never exactly warmed to her invitations, but . . .

"You are not going to regret this," she said the day we met to go to my first meeting. "The Penny Pinchers are going to change your life, I swear. You are never going to be a victimized consumer again."

We were outside the Rocky River Public Library a month after my session with Toni on a crisp fall morning invigorated by the snap of autumn. Kids were back in school full swing, the leaves were beginning to turn red and gold, and a sense of organization had replaced the lazy ennui of summer. I wanted to rake leaves, roast a chicken, clean out the closets and fill them with brand-new clothes for winter, perhaps some tweed slacks, a few cashmere twinsets, and cute leather boots.

But I was proud to say I resisted the temptation. Every day when yet another catalog came in the mail promising vigorous hikes through snowy woods (L.L. Bean) or cozy evenings snuggled in black watch flannel around a roaring fire (Plow & Hearth), I'd toss it immediately in the outside trash, forbidding myself from taking so much as a peek at L.L. Bean's latest offering of periwinkle turtlenecks and sage green sweaters.

"I've never gone into fall without buying at least a few new pieces," I told Libby as we headed up the library steps. "I think it goes back to when I was a kid and my mother would take Viv and me to Two Guys for saddle shoes and plaid jumpers and white blouses with Peter Pan collars to start the new school year."

And new pencils, I thought, remembering the glorious smell of sharpened Dixon Ticonderogas neatly stowed away in my brand-new zipper pencil case along with a fresh pink eraser, blunt scissors, a six-inch wooden ruler, and a protractor I never learned how to use.

"It feels as if something's missing from the fall season, not stocking up on new stuff. Don't you think?"

"Not anymore." She yanked open the heavy oak doors. "And, someday, you'll get over it, too."

Though I wondered, since it seemed Libby had a new fall wardrobe. Or maybe it was that I was so used to her in jeans and T-shirts, her hair in a ponytail, that her black boots, a black skirt, and russet sweater with a rather tasteful scarf was new only to me.

"You have to think of new ways to mark the seasons besides going on a shopping spree, Kat. Ways that don't cost money. For instance, leave work an hour early and go for a nice long walk in the park with Griff."

"Not a nice long walk in the mall?"

"Can you smell fallen leaves in the mall? Can you fill your lungs with fresh air and hear the sounds of children playing?"

No. But I could get 20 percent off at Ann Taylor, I thought, hit by a sudden case of nerves as we headed to the basement where the Penny Pinchers met. "Maybe this isn't such a good idea."

Libby hesitated with her hand on the door-knob. "Don't tell me you're getting cold feet."

A burst of laughter erupted from within, along with the distinct sound of clinking coffee cups. "When they find out I've never saved a thing, they're going to kick me out."

"It's a public library. They can't kick you out." She grabbed me by the sleeve of my leather coat. "Come on!"

All conversation stopped as we entered to find a small group sitting in a semicircle of metal folding chairs, a giant mural of Winnie the Pooh, Eeyore, Piglet, and Tigger dancing on blue walls in the background, along with stacked cushions on the floor. Clearly we were in the library story room.

Libby smiled at a man in his thirties in jeans and a half-unbuttoned button-down shirt over a tee, his hand in one pocket as he leaned back on a folding chair. I knew the pose and the clothes all too well. Abercrombie & Fitch 2007. He returned with a wink that turned Libby pink.

So *that* explained her new sweater and boots.

"Guys," she said, dragging her gaze away from the Adonis. "This is my friend Kat."

A young black woman in pearls and a gray twinset said, "You mean the same Kat you work for."

Awkward!

Libby was unruffled. "That's right. You know how long I've been trying to get her to come to one of our meetings. Well . . ."

She found out her husband's leaving her, I thought.

". . . she finally saw the light. So I hope you'll give her a warm welcome."

"Hi, Kat," they singsonged.

"That's Sherise." Libby pointed to the woman in the cashmere twinset. "She kind of keeps the group organized."

"Organized? That's rich." A guy about my age with the physique of a body builder—thick neck, big chest popping out of a white T-shirt—leaned his arm on one knee. "What she means is boss us around."

"Don't mind Steve," Sherise said. "He's a security guard and bouncer, so he thinks he has to act tough, but he's really a pussycat inside. Sit next to him and he'll keep the riffraff away."

I took a seat next to Steve. Libby had already insinuated herself between the Abercrombie guy and an old woman knitting merrily. Abercrombie planted a kiss on Libby's cheek, prompting an overweight woman in a purple kerchief and black knit skirt pawing through a huge pile of coupons on the floor to exhale in disgust.

"Okay." Sherise clapped her hands. "I don't know if Libby told you how we like to start our meetings, Kat, but usually we go around the room and brag about our successes last month and lament about our slips off the wagon."

Question: Was it possible to slip off if one had technically never been on the wagon?

"I'll start." The heavyset woman lifted herself from the coupons.

Steve put his mouth to my ear. "Keep your eye on Opal. She's a bigger tightwad than everyone else."

"I heard that, Steve," Opal said. "And thank you. You know how much that means to me, especially coming from you."

I wasn't quite sure I'd heard "tightwad" taken as a compliment before.

"This month," Opal began matter of factly, "I got forty bottles of Pantene for eighty-eight cents each at Rite Aid and with a buy-one-get-one-free deal and manufacturer's coupons plus a rebate, I actually ended up making $4 on the transaction." She pumped her fist as everyone responded with applause.

Steve said, "See what I mean?"

But I was trying to get my mind around what she'd just said. *Forty bottles of Pantene for free? What does one do with so much shampoo?*

"Any slips you regret?" Sherise asked.

"Yeah, one. I finally broke down and bought Jeremy a box of Reese's Puffs." She sighed. "Call it a weak moment."

"Bad mom," someone teased. It might have been the cute guy with Libby.

"Well, I did have a coupon for thirty cents off, but you know how I feel about sugared cereals. Next, he'll be looking for harder stuff. Like Coke."

The cute guy said, "Can heroin be far behind?"

Libby poked him with her elbow.

"You laugh, Wade, but come see my kids in twenty years when they're strong and healthy and lean and mean. And why? Because I kept them away from overprocessed foods and spared their pancreases, that's why."

Buying Reese's Puffs did not seem all that bad. I

mean, Laura used to live on Cap'n Crunch, string cheese, and fruit leather. Whatever fruit leather was.

Opal finished and we went around the room listing our successes and failures. Wade, the cute guy, claimed not to have had any failures, though he did find an awesome transistor radio in a Dumpster. But as I heard everyone else's answers, I began to worry. I hadn't really saved much since my meeting in Toni's office, aside from not hitting up Saks and quitting the gym—more of a pleasure than a hardship, really.

I did call the cable company and cancel HBO, though I wasn't quite sure these were the types to be impressed by my sacrifice of next season's *Big Love*.

Velma, the knitter, held up two balls of yarn she'd made from unraveling a moth-eaten sweater she'd picked up for free from the discards box at a church rummage sale. "They'd make a nice pair of socks," she said, "for the homeless."

Oh, my word. Not only were these people thrifty—they were *saints*. I slunk down in my chair praying Sherise would be kind and give me a pass. Alas, no. After Libby bragged that she called in the power company for a free energy audit and found she could reduce her electric bill simply by vacuuming the back of her refrigerator, Sherise skipped Steve, who claimed some sort of excuse, and came to me.

I drew a blank.

"We're all friends here," Sherise said, crossing her legs. "No need to be embarrassed. We've all been through it."

"Yeah. You gotta get used to being open about your spending. That's the only way to get control over it," said Steve, though one might point out *he* hadn't been so open.

"I suppose," I began, "my biggest success recently has been . . . finding a gas station a couple miles away where it's ten cents less than my regular one." I was actually very proud of that; I'd never shopped for gas before because saving pennies per gallon seemed too trivial.

With an edge of smugness, Opal said, "I'm part of a gas-buying co-op. Last week we were paying ninety cents a gallon. What did you pay?"

"A little more." Like fifty cents more. "Also, I quit going to The Sushi Bar in Princeton for lunch and started doing take-out to save myself from paying tips. Not only that but, are you ready for this? I completely cut out Starbucks. Totally. As of today, I am three weeks and two days venti latte free and, let me tell you, it has not been easy starting my day without that triple shot of espresso."

The group went silent. At first, I thought they might have been in awe, considering how tough it is to quit Starbs. But then I realized otherwise—they were in shock.

Wade leaned forward and grinned as if he could see right through me. "Was I correct in remembering that you pay Libby a hundred bucks a week to clean your house?"

The room got very hot. Sherise fiddled with her pearls, and Opal went back to sorting the coupons.

"That's right. I have for fifteen years."

"And was that your SUV parked outside, the Lexus?"

Steve let out a whistle. "Those things go for what, forty, fifty grand?"

"It's a 2002," I said defensively. "And I got a good deal. Why, is there something wrong with me driving a Lexus?"

"Not at all." Wade threw up his hands. "Just raises the question of why a woman with a housekeeper and a luxury vehicle would see the need to join this group. I mean, we're hardly in your income bracket. Look at me. I don't even *have* an income."

Ah, so that explained why Wade was such a jerk. He must have lost his job. Men take unemployment so hard.

"I'm sure you'll find work soon." Then, remembering a phrase I'd heard Chloe use often, I said, "Besides, the economy will turn around any day now."

"Thank you, Pollyanna." He massaged his forehead. "You're not getting it. I *quit* my job. I used to make over a million dollars on Wall Street and drive a Porsche."

Steve said, "Now he lives in his mother's back-yard. In a tent."

"Yurt." Wade sat back and crossed his arms. "It's a *yurt*, man."

Libby whispered, "No one's calling it a tent, babe. Steve just misspoke."

"Hmph." Steve flexed his bicep that sported a tattoo—Bunny—surrounded by a heart. "I'll call it a tent if it's a tent."

Tensions were rising, and I couldn't help feeling that, somehow, I'd been the one at fault. Sherise, eager to keep order, inched forward on her chair. "You know, Kat. You might want to examine if a group setting is the best situation for you right now. Have you thought of going online? There are hundreds of sites on frugal living to get you started."

"For those of you who have computers," Opal added. "Personally, I wouldn't allow one in the house. All that free porn?" She tapped her temple. "Screws with teenagers' minds."

Sherise shot her a warning glance. "What I mean is, you might get more information that way and not waste time listening to us bicker."

No one dared make eye contact. Even Libby, who'd been begging me for years to come, pretended to be fascinated by the heel of her new boots. The exact same thing happened in a step aerobics class once when, after repeatedly falling behind and tripping and being out of sync, the aerobics instructor came over and said I might feel more comfortable in a beginner class because everyone else was used to a faster pace and she didn't want to have to slow them down to help me. They wanted to get *rid* of me.

No. No. No. They could not kick me out. This was my only chance to get on the right track. If I couldn't work with a group, I'd be completely without support. I didn't want to find help on Griff's computer alone, with those emails of his only a keystroke away.

"The thing is," I began, tamping down feelings of growing desperation, "I need this group because, I know this sounds weird, but . . . my husband's leaving me."

It just came out. Even I was stunned. I don't think I'd ever before said those words—*my husband's leaving me*—out loud.

Libby hissed, "*Kat?*"

Too late now. Better to plow on. "Last month, the day of our twentieth wedding anniversary, I found a couple of emails to his assistant. He's set up a private bank account, put $10,000 of *our* money into it, and has even taken out a new credit card in his name only so he can buy her dinners and hotel rooms and whatever."

The backs of my eyes began to throb. Since my cry in the master bath, I'd been holding in all these emotions and now they threatened to burst—in front of these strangers! People who for all intents and purposes didn't like me very much. People who'd written me off as a pampered suburban housewife with a luxury car and Tod's drivers.

"But I have no money of my own. None. So if I don't start saving now, I won't have anything when my husband walks out the door after our daughter graduates from high school this June."

Opal walked over to me on her knees. "He's going to leave you in June?"

"That's what the email said." I could barely blubber out the next line. "That is . . . if he can *put up with me that long.*"

"Oh, oh." She got up and, pushing Steve off his own seat, brought me to her, placing my head on her nice warm chest that smelled vaguely of lavender and yeast. "You should have told us right off."

"I'm so sorry," Sherise said. "Is there anything we can do?"

"Yeah," Libby said. "We can stop being a bunch of reverse snobs and help this woman. She's a friend of mine and she's in pain."

It was so true! I choked back a sob and Opal handed me a dingy handkerchief. No bleach.

Velma put down her knitting. "I'm not very familiar with how much it costs to get a divorce nowadays, having been left by my own husband thirty years ago when he walked out to get a quart of milk and never came back."

Wade said, "Here we go. The weekly male smackdown. Is it possible for us to go a month without one?"

"So," she went on, "how much, exactly, do you need to save?"

I didn't want to say, not with people like Wade who intentionally didn't earn a living. But Steve said, "Remember. You gotta be up front with us, Kat. It's part of the program."

Opal pushed back my hair, her voice warm and motherly. "The beauty is, once you tell us, then it becomes *our* problem, too, not just yours. That's what we're all about at the Penny Pinchers: overcoming financial anxiety with communal support and savings strategies."

What a lovely idea! Why, if I had other people to share this with, then I wouldn't have to lie awake at night thinking about it. I could pretend they were lying awake with me.

I hiccupped. "Fifteen thousand."

Velma said, "Oh, my. That's more than I live on in a year."

"Chump change." Wade flipped his wrist. "I used to spend $15,000 on a weekend in the Hamptons and never miss it."

"Well, la-di-da, Mr. Rothschild," Opal scolded. "We're not talking about you and your former life as a Wall Street playboy, are we? We're talking about Kat." She went back to stroking my hair. "Now, be honest, hon. How much do you have saved already and don't exaggerate. That won't help a bit."

I pinched my thumb and forefinger together to make a zero, a symbol that should be etched on my tombstone.

"Zero?" Opal pulled away. "As in nothing?"

"Zip, zilch, nada."

We sat there, flummoxed, until Libby said, "Truth is, she doesn't know how much she has."

"Of course she knows how much money she has," Sherise said. "Unless she was like me, with a trust fund and Daddy's accountants handling everything."

"No accountants," Libby said. "She's just clueless. I was at her house when her sister and her friend were going over her finances and looking for evidence that her husband was cheating and I could overhear them. With all due respect, Kat"—she gave me a dutiful nod—"you're a financial idiot."

It was a shocking statement, albeit an honest one.

"Is that true?" Sherise asked.

"Pretty much."

"That I don't get," Steve said. "I'm raising two kids on my own and if I didn't know how much money I had in my wallet, those suckers would rob me blind."

I tried explaining it this way: "You know how some people have a fear of heights or spiders? I have a fear of bills. They should come up with a name for it, Visaphobia or something."

No one laughed.

"Then it's obvious," Opal said, turning to the group. "This calls for an immediate Penny Pinchers audit." Setting me right in my seat, she went to the coupon pile and fetched her clear plastic accordion file. "We'll follow you, Kat. I take it from Libby you don't live far."

Steve checked his watch. "I gotta be at work in a couple of hours, so we have to make it snappy."

"Count me out," Wade said. "The suburbs make me nervous."

Libby let out a little moan in disappointment.

Hold on. Hold on. Were they about to do what I thought they were about to do? Was this the end of the meeting or . . . were they really going to come to my house and go through my records?

Velma said, "Do you have coffee, Kat? Because I made a delightful lemon coffee cake for the meeting that I'll just take to your place."

Oh, my God. They *were* going to go to my house!

"Excuse me!" I raised my hand tentatively. "This is really wonderful of you and all, but . . ."

Sherise, buttoning up a smart fire engine red coat that I could have sworn was Valentino, said, "But what?"

"But I can't let you go through my personal stuff."

"Why not?" Steve asked. "We did the same thing for Sherise when she showed up a few years ago like you."

Sherise agreed. "That's right. And now I run the group."

"What's the matter?" Steve folded his arms. "Don't you trust us?"

"I do . . . it's just that, I'm not sure—no, wait—I *know* my husband would have a fit if he found out I let total strangers comb through our files."

They stared as if I'd had the audacity to object.

"Your husband?" Velma flipped him the bird with one of her knitting needles. "His vote stopped counting when he decided to cheat on you."

"And I, for one, am slightly offended you consider me a stranger after fifteen years of scrubbing your toilets," Libby said. "That Adele on the other hand? Now *she* was strange."

"Besides, you gotta bite the bullet and find out what your situation is," Sherise said. "Otherwise, how do you know where to go if you don't know where you are?"

CHAPTER TEN

*W*hen the Penny Pinchers do an audit, they don't stop at adding up your income and debt. Oh, no. They check out *everything* until there's nothing about you they don't know."

This was Sherise's warning as we drove from the Rocky River Public Library to my house. Of course, the Penny Pinchers carpooled, which was why she was in my passenger seat explaining not only how the group operated but how she came to seek their help years before.

It was the idea of her father, a wealthy investment banker who'd spoiled her rotten, after he read an item in the Rocky River Public Library newsletter about a group of frugal-minded people who wanted to start up a club devoted to trading coupons and tips on savings.

Back then, he and Sherise were barely on speaking terms, so disgusted was he by her careless disregard for his hard-earned money, putting clothes, shoes, trips, and even nights on the town for her friends on his credit cards. The Penny Pinchers was a last resort.

"I was, like, what did I do wrong? *You* were the one who sent me to boarding school and college without so much as mentioning tuition. *You* were the one who gave me the charge cards and never made me look at a bill. How was I supposed to know that stuff costs money?"

It was a sort of childish question and, yet, I understood it fully. If her father hadn't wanted her to rack up huge bills, then he shouldn't have made it so easy. Kind of strange how parents can talk about drugs and sex with their kids, but when it comes to money, they clam up. Griff and I were no exception. Laura had no concept how much—or how little—we made, and that was just the way we liked it.

I waited at the front of our development for Opal,

who was hauling the rest of the group—Steve, Velma, and Libby, Wade having thumbed a ride back into Princeton—in her minivan. He was, Libby said with much reluctance, "adorably antisocial."

Sherise went on. "Then one day I came home from college and was ambushed by my parents. All the bills were laid out on the kitchen table and my father said, 'Sherise. You have to get control.' I thought he was talking about something else to buy. I said, 'What's control?' "

Opal pulled up behind me, flashed her headlights, and I took a left, snaking our way through the roads of Waldorf Farms until we got to our modest blue colonial with its basketball hoop and lone elm in the tiny front yard.

"And here I am, years later, a financial adviser with a five-year investment plan and an IRA." She unsnapped her seat belt. "Ask me how much I have already saved for retirement."

"How much?"

"Twenty-five thousand, six hundred dollars and I'm only twenty-six. Now *that's* what you call control."

Steve helped Velma out of the minivan while Libby, acting as though this were *her* house, took the liberty of leading Opal inside, lifting up the front mat and helping herself to my spare key. "This way, people. Wipe your feet."

Velma said, "What about the killer dog you were telling us about in the car?"

There was a halfhearted bark from Jasper in the garage. "He won't bother you. He's ancient, anyway." Libby unlocked the door.

What happened to her threat to pepper spray? Suddenly my vicious dog was *ancient*?

Velma passed in front of me carrying her foil-covered coffee cake like I was invisible.

"Libby tells me you got three TVs." Steve scratched his head. "Oh, man. I don't even know where to begin. You gotta jettison two, at least, though it's better not to have even one. Those shows like *Gossip Girl* send kids the wrong messages. Makes them think they're entitled to be driven to school in limousines and drink and do drugs and such."

I studied his crew cut and the chain hooked through his faded jeans and thought it somewhat astounding that a muscled rent-a-cop like him had even heard of *Gossip Girl*.

"See? I told you they just take over." Sherise pulled tight her lovely red coat against a breeze through the elm. "My advice is to relax and let them do it. They live for this. It's their raison d'être."

I tried to relax, but it wasn't easy with Libby acting as tour guide, pointing out my most egregious possessions. The PS3 we used to play Blu-ray movies, for example, was not only a pricey toy, but also a huge energy sucker. Steve found a button in the back and snapped it off. "Saved you a dollar a day right there."

Meanwhile, in the kitchen, Opal was taking an inventory of my food, noting with dismay the tubs of prepared pesto in my refrigerator, wrapped cold cuts, and, yes, collection of boxed cereals. "Don't you know anything that comes in a box is a rip-off and probably loaded with carcinogenic preservatives?" She tossed a box over her shoulder. "Get yourself some glass jars at the Dollar Store and fill them with pasta, rice, and homemade granola from the bins at the co-op. Maybe some oatmeal and raisins, too. Organic, of course."

I said, "Of course," knowing full well that in a million years I would never trot down to the Dollar Store for glass containers, that I would never take the time to fill them up with staples from the Whole Foods store in Princeton.

"Do you have a downstairs freezer?" She held open the cabinet doors with both hands.

I shook my head no.

"That's your next purchase. It'll pay for itself in the long run." She quit the cabinet to assess what I had under the kitchen sink. According to her, I didn't need most of the chemicals there except for dishwasher detergent and ammonia. "Most everything can be cleaned easily and, more important, safely, with vinegar and baking soda." She pinched a bottle of mildew remover as though it were nuclear waste. "Overpriced and causes asthma. Throw it away."

Velma was at the top of the stairs to the basement, a slice of coffee cake on a napkin, a cup of coffee in her hand. *Did someone make coffee?* "Is this where she keeps her records, Libby?"

Libby, pouring herself a cup, said, "Yup. Griff's got a Quicken program. That should be a start."

"Libby!" Not even I, his wife, knew Griff had a Quicken program. How did she? "That's going too far."

"What? It's Velma and Sherise. Not like they're gonna hack into your bank account." She sipped her coffee. "Not like there'd be any money in there if they did."

With everyone preoccupied, now was my chance to grill her about the man she'd been hiding. "So what's up with you and Wade?" I asked, getting my own cup of coffee.

Libby shrugged, like it was no big deal. "He's a friend. That's all."

"Yeah? Well, I have lots of friends and none of them nuzzles my neck like he was doing."

"Okay, so we're kinda hot and heavy." She dipped her finger in the coffee coquettishly, giving it a slight twirl. "I haven't exactly been singing it from the rooftops because we're taking it slowly, on Wade's advice. He's been kind of burned in the past and, you know, he wants to make sure we're on solid footing before we go public."

That old line, I thought as Steve came down the stairs two at a time to announce he'd found the TV in *our bedroom* for a total of eight phantom appliances.

"You were in our bedroom?" I couldn't get over his audacity. I mean, I had clothes lying about. My bra!

"Yes, ma'am. And let me tell you that you put that bedroom TV and the DVD player on a power strip along with most of your other appliances like your microwave, you'll cut your energy bill sixty percent if you flick off those strips for twelve hours every night." He did not think it the least bit rude that he'd tromped into my personal space without my permission. "Now, about that water heater. . . ."

I led him down to the basement and showed him the heater room. He went over to our ancient white model, patted it, and said, "Handyman's special, this is. Your bills must be huge."

"Kat?" Sherise called. "Could you come over here for a minute?"

Sherise and Velma were at Griff's desk, envelopes divided into little white stacks. Velma was at the computer, squinting.

"As a former bookkeeper, Velma doesn't have a problem with opening your bills, but I do. I'd feel more comfortable if you did it and called off the amounts."

Thankfully, one of these Penny Pinchers could see reason.

"Anyway," she said, "it's better if we bring you

into the loop considering it was being out of the loop that got you into this mess, right?"

"Looks like about $25,000 of the $30,000 is gone." Velma stroked her chin and clicked downward. "The question is, where did it go?"

What $25,000 and what $30,000? And what did she mean by *gone*?

Sherise handed me a New Jersey Power and Light envelope. "Would you do the honors?"

I slid my finger under the flap and out fell an electric bill for $135. Not bad considering we'd had the air conditioner going into September. I called out the amount and Sherise wrote it down on a white tablet.

Next was the phone bill—$63! Pretty good, though the bill for our cell service—a whopping $212—was a stunner. Cable also was not so great. Internet plus HBO at $125 a month was hardly the deal the cable company claimed on TV and what was with all these other charges, the list of taxes and fees?

"I just got rid of HBO," I told them.

Sherise did not seem that impressed. All she said was, "Hmmm. How about that mortgage?"

I found the most recent bill—$1,548—and plotzed. Didn't it used to be much lower? And what was this other one from the bank? A $30,000 line of credit. But . . . this didn't make sense. We'd spent about $6,000 to redo the basement. So how come we were in hock for $25,000?

And why was our monthly payment for that $250?

"Ahh," Velma said, taking the credit card statement out of my hand. "That's what I was looking for."

"I'm confused." All these bills. It was overwhelming. "The line of credit was to pay to redo our basement for about six grand. So . . ."

"He's been using it to pay off credit card debt." Velma compared it to what was on her computer screen. "Smart idea since you can write off the interest on your home equity. Problem is, he's running out of funds."

"I can't find a pay stub for him," Sherise said. "Do you happen to know what your take-home is and your husband's, too?"

I told her I took home an average of $2,000 a month but I had no idea about Griff. It was horribly embarrassing to realize that I hadn't a clue about how much money my own husband earned, but there you had it. I was oblivious.

"That's okay," Velma said without the slightest tone of disparagement. "I can figure it out from his deposits. Ballpark, I'd say he's taking home about a thousand a week."

"Okay, so we're talking about $6,000 to play with per month." Sherise tapped her pencil on the tablet thoughtfully. "Subtract from that your monthly bills, including my guesstimate on property taxes and insurance, and we're down to about $625 a week for food and entertainment."

"Hey," I said, brightening. "That's not too bad at all."

Velma held up a finger. "Except, you've got a line of credit to pay off."

"The least of her problems," Sherise added. "I didn't include your credit card debt." Sherise handed me the latest Visa bill. "You might want to sit down."

The Visa envelope lay in my hand, a white sliver of doom. Again, I felt the familiar sickness, the dread of bad news and the onslaught of worry and self-loathing. It was like a bad report card for adults. "I can't."

"You gotta," Velma said. "Be strong."

"We've all been through it, Kat." Sherise smiled. "We're here with you."

"Even Velma?" The woman knit sweaters for the homeless out of recycled yarn, for heaven's sake. Hardly the portrait of a profligate spender.

Velma exchanged questioning glances with Sherise. "For your information, one time my bills at home piled up so high, I figured the town would never miss it if I borrowed four thousand to cover them."

What?

"Velma used to be treasurer for Breyers Falls in the northern part of the state," Sherise explained. "She didn't think of it as embezzlement. . . ."

"I was going to pay it back," she interjected.

"*Velma?*" Sherise glared. "Remember what the judge said about denial."

162

"All right, all right. I know now it was a crime, though back then, from my perspective, it was more like borrowing."

Sherise said, "This is why the judge suggested Velma try our group, so she'd learn money-management skills after her release from the hoosegow."

"One year, six months suspended for four measly thousand dollars. The judge way overreacted." Velma waved to the envelope in my hand. "Now, let's see what Visa sent you."

Putting aside my rational concern that a convicted felon was prying into our private finances, I ripped open the envelope, unfolded the bill, took a peek, and immediately suffered what doctors would refer to as a minor cardiological incident.

Not only had we almost reached the limit of our $10,000 credit line, if my calculations were correct, thanks to the anniversary party last month, we'd exceeded it.

So, that explained the call Griff got from the Visa people the day of the party. It wasn't a randomly generated computer thing, after all. Griff hid the truth to protect me that night because of the party. Oh, god. We were in so much trouble.

I must have let out some sort of yelp because Libby rushed down the stairs and asked, "What happened?" while Sherise came around the desk and took me by the shoulders, moving me over to the old couch covered with dog hair. "Good girl. You did it. You faced your demon."

"Yes, but . . ." Numbers began to swirl before my eyes. "We have so many bills. So much debt. Nearly $40,000. How will we ever get it paid off? How will we ever send Laura to college or save for our retirement or . . . a divorce?"

Libby plunked herself on a step and said, "Credit card bill?"

Velma said, "Yup. It put her over the edge."

"I knew it'd be bad." Libby clasped her hands around her knees. "She's not used to dealing with bad news about money. Griff's spared her."

Libby was right. This was exactly the kind of bad news that made me ill and it was hitting me head-on, as if I'd swerved into the path of a Mack truck carrying a load of debt. Moreover, if I understood Toni correctly (please, may I have misheard), were Griff and I to divorce, then not only would our assets be divided, such as they were, but also our *debt*. Which meant that I, on my own little lonesome, would be responsible for paying off . . . $18,500!

I seriously questioned whether I was in the initial stages of a heart attack. How could Griff—responsible, prudent Griff—have allowed us to get so far in the hole? This couldn't have been *all* my fault, right? Not *all*.

My cheek stung and, belatedly, I realized I'd been gently slapped.

"Snap out of it." Sherise gave me a tiny shake. "This is not nearly as bad as you're making it out to be, Kat. You've got to separate your emotions from your figures."

Velma said, "It's totally doable. You can save some money and pay down this debt in no time if you work at it."

"Look. You two are lucky," Sherise said. "You both have jobs and health insurance. That's better than a ton of people these days."

The downstairs printer warmed up and spit out a sheet of numbers. "I'm printing you a rough budget." Velma carried over the paper. "The way I see it, cut out $200 a week from your expenses and you'll save $6,400 by June. That would take hardly any effort. If you really want to go the distance, though, try to save $500 a week and you'll reach your goal: $16,000 by the time your daughter graduates."

She held the paper for me to read. It was all there in orderly columns. Income on one side, expenses on the other. Short column for the income, long column for the expenses. "As you can see, there's a lot of fat there to cut in heating, electricity, cable, and car payments. It's simply a matter of being mindful. And, um, perhaps doing away with . . ."

She turned to Libby, who said, "Don't tell me. I know what's coming."

"Let Libby go and you'll save $400 a month.

That's almost your home equity payment right there."

"We domestic workers are always the first to get cut in an economy like this. So unfair."

I began to feel better. Not about having to fire Libby; that was dreadful since Libby was more than a housekeeper. She was a friend. "Sorry." I held up Velma's budget and shrugged.

She shrugged back. "It is what it is. You'll get tired of scrubbing toilets soon enough."

No, I felt better because those numbers that had so frightened me before weren't so bad once you had them all on paper. Yes, it was daunting. Frightening, even, to see our bills were so high. But they were just these little black and white symbols. That was all.

They don't control me; I control them.

"Steve will help you get your energy costs down," Sherise went on. "He's good at that stuff. And take a couple of shopping trips with Opal and she'll show you how to live on dollars a day. That woman feeds and clothes a family of four on what you, alone, take home, Kat. Like I said, count yourself lucky."

"Thank you," I whispered, clutching the sheet as if it were the answer to all my prayers. "Thank you, thank you."

Velma took a bite out of her coffee cake and, wiping her lips, said, "I think our work here is done."

Heavy footsteps tromped down the stairs. Steve

stopped at the step above Libby and said, "By any chance, Kat, does your husband drive an old gold Honda Civic?"

Libby said, "Uh-oh."

Holy crap! Griff was home . . . and the house was jam-packed with Penny Pinchers.

"You want to tell him now?" Sherise asked. "I mean, about your budget."

I didn't know. Running around the room, collecting the bills and rearranging them into the disorderly mess they'd been before, shutting down the computer, my one concern was that line in his email—that he already worried I was suspicious. If he saw me down here going through his stuff, he might admit to having an affair.

I couldn't take him leaving now. I had to follow Toni's advice and use this period of limbo to prepare. "Let's wait," I said.

Sherise nodded. "Okay. Then what *do* we tell him?"

"I have a few choice words," Velma said.

"We don't have to tell him anything." I crumpled up the napkin and tossed it in the trash. "My mother always did say a hint of mystery sparks up a marriage."

Though, when I stopped to think of my parents and their regular six P.M. dinners followed by the nightly ritual of the news, *Jeopardy!*, and *Dancing with the Stars*, my mother's lofty advice seemed downright ludicrous.

Unless Opal said something to him first. . . .
Eeep!

Rushing up, I found Griff in the kitchen picking at what was left of Velma's coffee cake. Steve and Opal were nowhere to be found.

"There you are," he said jovially, coming over to kiss me on the cheek like he always did. "I had a free afternoon, so I thought I'd come home for lunch." He kissed me again, this time on the lips . . . and with meaning. It wasn't lunch he'd come home for, that was for sure.

Over his shoulder, I caught sight of Velma shaking her head.

"You have friends over?" he asked, nodding at Libby.

"Uh-huh. Griff, this is Sherise and this is Velma."

Sherise and Velma nodded as politely as they could manage.

"Nice to meet you," Griff said, squinting, as if trying to place them. "I'm sorry, but I don't think I've ever heard Kat mention you before."

"That's because we just met," Velma said. "Well, we better get going. I assume Opal's waiting in the van."

"I think she might be," he said, his usual helpful self. "Tall woman. Purple kerchief . . ."

"Behind the wheel of the van?" Velma shot him a finger. "You should be a detective, Mister. Bye, Kat."

I waved good-bye to them and thanked them for coming over and . . . for everything. I wanted to tell them they were angels, that they had single-handedly endowed me with the courage to face my fears, but Griff was there, so I couldn't. Somehow, though, they knew. I could read it in their smile and warm handshakes.

When they were gone, Griff shoved his hands in his pockets and said, "They seem nice." It was killing him, absolutely killing him that I refused to provide any context. "A kind of diverse bunch. Friends of Libby's, are they?"

"You got it."

Then I turned and went upstairs to the bathroom where, for the first time since I'd found the emails, I sat on the edge of the tub and had a good laugh.

CHAPTER ELEVEN

After the Penny Pincher audit, I was CHARGED!

I was as motivated as a wayward stripper who'd seen the light at her first tent revival and was ready to put on her Sunday go-to-meeting dress to proclaim the Good News! I could not wait to begin my new journey down the path of frugality.

Right off the top, I conceived of a dozen easy changes that would bring me closer to saving $500 a week. Canceling the cable completely—not just HBO—was a no-brainer. Laura might balk about missing *South Park* and Griff would be bummed that he couldn't watch basketball this winter, but I was confident that he, being an intellectual academician and nature lover, would applaud the move. Honestly, did we really need to pay to watch British Chihuahuas with bed-wetting disorders on Animal Planet or sub-IQ humans crash motorbikes on truTV?

As for the Internet, Velma—who turned out to be a bit of a cyber geek—suggested approaching the neighbors and sharing a wireless connection. BRILLIANT IDEA! Why hadn't I thought of that? Or Griff? It was so stupid for each of us to be paying these exorbitant bills when wireless technology made communal Internet a snap.

Then there was my Lexus. It would have to go since those $250-a-month car payments were killing us. Better to buy an Elantra or a used diesel car I could have retrofitted to burn vegetable oil from McDonald's. (Libby suggested I hit up Wade, who apparently had ties to the underground "Mazola cartel.")

Netflix was gone, to be substituted with movies rented from the library. Ditto for my cell phone. Yes, one might argue cell phones were necessities now that all the old pay phones had been ripped out and, therefore, if I got a flat in the backwoods of New Jersey or an inner-city neighborhood harboring . . .

Okay. I'd keep the cell phone, I decided, but the

170

landline was outta there. An instant savings of at least $600 a year.

That said, there were a few big-ticket items I unfortunately had to buy. There were the glass containers Opal recommended, along with a pressure cooker so it wouldn't take days to cook the hard dried beans I'd keep in them. Since I had a job that required me to be out of the house, she also suggested a bread maker in which I would mix the ingredients, set the timer, and come home to freshly baked bread. Just like food that came in boxes, Opal did not trust food that came in chemically manufactured plastic bags. And that included bread.

Then, of course, there was the deep freeze. Steve said he could get a sixteen-cubic-foot freezer off Craigslist for under $100. I had no clue what I'd do with a freezer that large until Opal explained I could use it to store tomato sauce and vegetables freshly picked from my garden. Which might have made sense if I'd *had* a garden. Since my patch of a few withered tomato plants could hardly qualify, Opal said she'd help me with that, too.

Unfortunately, I'd forgotten to take into account how Griff would react to all this.

Two weeks after my Penny Pinchers audit, he strolled into the kitchen earlier than I expected and nearly tripped over the bread maker box. "What is all this stuff? And why is there a 'For Sale' sign on the Lexus?"

Uh-oh. I hadn't planned on telling him about my budget so soon, not until I got my first check from the work I did for Madeleine Granville. Then I planned on sitting him down and laying out my plans to start my own interior design business, gradually building up enough clients so I could finally tell Chloe to kiss off. I'd also use Madeleine's check as an excuse to explain why I felt it necessary to open my own bank account that, unbeknownst to him, would be used to not only finance my business, but also my life after he asked for a divorce.

"Because . . . ," I began, stalling, remembering there is no more effective lie than the truth, "I'm going on a penny-pinching program."

"Are you now?" His lips twitched. "And how, pray tell, does a penny-pinching program necessitate you cleaning out half of Bed, Bath and Beyond?" He eyed the brand-new Cuisinart pressure cooker.

"You gotta spend money to make money."

"Oh, I think you got that down—the spending part, that is. The question is . . . how does that make money?"

He wasn't taking me seriously. Just like Viv, who'd burst out laughing when I proudly announced that we would live on $200 a week, he thought this was just another one of my phases. Like the time I wanted to raise llamas and sell the wool.

"I know you don't believe me, Griff. But I mean it." I plunked a bunch of dried spaghetti into a glass jar, getting so aggravated by his persistent smile that I started talking off the top of my head. "I've got a plan for us to start saving $500 a week so that by the time Laura graduates, I'll have $16,000 of my own."

Griff quit smiling. "Why would you need $16,000? And why by Laura's graduation?"

Shoot. I'd practically let it out of the bag. He cocked his head and was about to ask me something else when I jumped in and said, "For Laura's college, of course. You know we have absolutely nothing set aside for her."

"You don't!"

Laura was at the kitchen door holding a venti iced mocha, her lips wearing a whipped cream mustache of shock. "You guys don't have a college savings plan for me?"

This was our gravest shame, that we'd never socked away money like other parents had—our own included. Not that we didn't try. We did. Just that whenever an unexpected expense arose—car repairs, new flashing for the roof, a new furnace—we dipped into that fund. Then, as we got closer to college and saw tuition rise to $40,000 and above, we figured, screw it. What middle-class family already absorbing the costs of raising kids was able to save $320,000 along with plowing money into an IRA for retirement?

"There's no point in saving money for college," Griff said, far more somber than he'd been minutes before when he was laughing at my penny-pinching plan. "It's a joke. The schools only count it against you when they're putting together their financial aid, anyway."

"But all my friends have college savings plans. Sylvie's parents started it when they found out they were *pregnant* with her. That's how much they cared."

We didn't know what to say. When I was pregnant with Laura, we were having enough struggles trying to pay the rent while Griff finished up his PhD.

"Don't worry about it, sweetie," he said, giving her a fatherly pat on the back. "This is your mother's and my problem, not yours."

I loved Griff at that moment. I loved him because he was calm and in control—and he was my ally in the strange war that occasionally erupts between parents and their teenage children. It was too bad he wanted out when our best years were ahead, just the two of us. At last.

"Besides, you shouldn't have everything handed to you, kiddo." I told her about Sherise, who'd awakened to a cruel reality when she discovered in her twenties that she needed to support herself instead of forever relying on her parents.

"I have a job, Mom."

The guilt I felt when she said that made me want to crawl under a rock.

"Good. 'Cause you'll need every dime."

Turning to me, Griff said, "Kat, don't you think we should talk about this in private?"

Griff had been raised in one of those starched families where money was never discussed, like sex and religion. But having had my eyes opened by Sherise's life story, I disagreed.

"Actually, I think Laura needs to understand money and she needs to hear this." I picked the venti iced mocha out of her hands. "You spent at least five bucks on this drink. That's a waste."

"It's my own money," she protested.

"Exactly. Which is why you need to hear what I have to say. You, too, Griff."

I could tell by the way the lines were creasing between his brows that my abrupt bossiness had him concerned. Money was our marital bogeyman and he had been conditioned, as had I, to avoid addressing it whenever possible.

"Geesh, Kat. I've had one hell of a shitty day. That's why I came home early, to relax. Can't this wait?"

"No, it can't, because there's something I've needed to say for a long, long time." I took a deep breath. Laura sat on the couch, hands clasped in her lap, her mouth open. "I'm . . . sorry."

"Sorry?" Griff shrugged. "What are you sorry for? Our decision not to save for Laura's college was mutual."

Laura turned to him. "You made a *decision* not

to save for college? I mean . . . that was something you did *intentionally* so, what . . . so you could redo the basement? I thought you lost money in the market crash like everyone else."

"That, too." Griff winced. This conversation was killing him.

I wanted to tell her now was not the time, that there were moments when children were better not seen *and* heard, but I figured I'd already earned enough strikes as a bad parent that afternoon. "It has nothing to do with your college saving, at least not directly. My apology is directed at Griff." I pointed to him. "Your father."

He said, "Really?"

"I'm sorry I've been such a careless spender. But mostly, I'm sorry to have burdened you with handling all the finances and for behaving like a baby when you grilled me about the Visa bill."

"Wow." Laura reached for her mocha and took a slurp. "Never thought I'd live in this house long enough to see this."

"I know I've spent a lot while you've scrimped to offset my costs. I know that, coming home today and seeing the pressure cooker and new bread maker . . ."

"You bought a bread maker? Bread costs a buck fifty a loaf! Why would you need a machine?" He got up and went to the bread maker, turned it around, and frowned. "It's huge and hideous and it'll clutter up our kitchen until we finally throw it away, like that damned chiminea. How much did it cost?"

I was hurt. I so wanted him to be grateful for my apology and proud that I was at last taking control.

"Two hundred, but . . ."

"Two hundred bucks? *That's* your idea of a penny-pinching program?"

"For your information, a loaf of good bread costs more like three dollars, and, yes, that's my idea of saving. You'll see."

I had to remember not to let my emotions get the better of me, to heed Sherise's words that I need to separate feelings from the facts.

"I know I've given you every reason to doubt my intentions, Griff, but what I've been trying to tell you is I've joined a group, Libby's group, the Rocky River Penny Pinchers. You know, the ones who meet in the basement of the library. And for the first time I think I have a shot at becoming frugal."

He remained impassive.

"By the group's calculations, if I cancel cable, sell my car, and slash our grocery bills plus some other adjustments, we really could save $500 a week. It'll take some hard work on our part"—I poked my head into the living room where Laura was eavesdropping—"on *all* our parts. No more takeout. No more shopping for entertainment. We can do something else, like . . . go on bike rides.

Or a walk in the woods. A whole-day hike, even. That doesn't cost much."

He leaned over and brushed the back of his hand to my forehead. "Are you well?"

"A walk in the woods is a thousand times more romantic than cruising Bridgewater Commons, wouldn't you say?"

"You're a woman after my own heart." There was a glint of love in his eyes, a twinkle I hadn't seen in a while.

Could this work?

"That's all very fine and good," Laura said, joining us in the kitchen. "But it doesn't explain how you guys are going to pay for my college."

Ignoring her, Griff said, "Hold on. *What* group?"

"Pardon?"

"You said by *the group's* calculations we could save such and such." He shifted feet. "You're not referring to that collection of oddballs in the house the other day."

"That's what she just said, that she joined Libby's group, the Penny Pinchers." Laura tapped her temple.

He said, "I thought you refused to go to those meetings. I thought you said clipping coupons and saving ten cents on gas was a waste of time better put to use earning money."

"Yeah, well. Things change." I bit my lip, praying he wouldn't ask *why* things change. But what he said next was much worse.

"Please tell me those women weren't in the basement going over our bills." His expression was growing dark. "Because when I went down there later that day, everything was organized. I knew *you* hadn't done it—since you won't read a bill to save your life. But . . ."

"Now I do."

"What?"

"I go through the bills . . ." I paused, anticipating the blow. "Now that I have the Penny Pinchers for support."

"Which is your way of saying they did." He paced to the other end of the kitchen. "They *did* go through our stuff. Oh, shit." He clenched his jaw. "Tell me, at least, that you did not let them go into my computer and . . ."

"Yes." I squeezed my eyes shut. "But don't worry. These are good, upstanding people. They never would have . . ."

"Libby told me one of them was a convicted embezzler." Laura sucked on her straw.

Griff smacked his head. "A convicted embezzler? You allowed a convicted embezzler access to my bank account? My social security number? Your social security number? Even Laura's? In this age of identity theft, do you know what kind of risk you've exposed us to?"

This was bad. This was really, really bad. I was even mad at myself and I was on my side. Griff was right, what had I been thinking?

"Look. It was a mistake. I just got caught up in the moment."

He clutched the kitchen counter, fuming.

"Well, I'm gone." Laura spun on her heel and headed up the stairs. "Call me when the shouting's over."

After she was out of earshot I said in a low, calm voice. "We're in $37,000 of debt, Griff. Pardon me if I'm a bit freaked out."

He closed his eyes.

"I know that's my fault. I know that had you never married me"—I was skating close to the edge here—"you never would have found yourself immersed in such expenses. That's why I joined the Penny Pinchers and . . ."

His hand reached out for mine and, still unable to meet my eyes, he said gruffly, "No, Kat. It's my fault. I've studied every aspect of economics, I pass myself off as an authority on monetary policy when the reality is I can't even balance my family finances."

My heart went out to him, in such pain and shame. I wanted to hug him and come clean about it all—the emails, Toni, the divorce plans. But something held me back.

"Plenty of doctors drink and smoke and ride bikes without their helmets," I said, trying to make light of this. "Just because you have a higher degree in a certain subject doesn't mean you're not a human being." I gave his hand a reassuring tug. "You did everything you could, Griff, to keep this family fiscally afloat."

"Not everything." He dropped my hand and studied the calendar by the refrigerator. "I haven't made enough money, for starters."

Talk about bringing the elephant into the room. This was almost a full-blown circus. I wanted to tell him how impressed I was that he could admit this out loud and how it didn't matter how much money he made because we're more than the numbers on our paychecks. However, both statements would have been exactly the opposite of what he wanted to hear.

"So what?" I shrugged. "The alternative—working for some D.C. think tank or a corporation—would have made you miserable. Probably, we would have gotten divorced long ago. Besides, where in the marital rule book does it say the husband should have to make all the money? It's not like I'm an incompetent bimbo."

He didn't even smile at bimbo, one of his favorite words. "You know how it is, Kat." He flicked through the calendar pages, scrutinizing December with its snowcapped fir trees. "It's a male thing."

"Yeah. Like athlete's foot. Though you might be happy to know I read *National Geographic* last week and I learned that the Stone Age is over. Anyway, we'll get through it because we love each other . . . remember? For richer, for poorer?"

He lifted his gaze. In his eyes, I recognized a tempest of worry and disappointment. "Your mother is right. You would have been better off marrying Ian what's his name."

A lump came to my throat. *He didn't say he loved me back.* "First of all," I replied, sticking with my resolve to keep it light, "his name was *Liam*— Liam Novak." Griff never could get it right. "And, you're wrong. I shouldn't have married him."

"You'd have been better off. You wouldn't be fighting with your husband in an outdated kitchen trying to figure out if you can bake enough bread to pay off $37,000 in debt."

I chose to pass on that. "Secondly, the correct response when your wife says you'll get through this together because you love each other is, 'You're right, honey. I do love you and where there's love, there's hope.'"

Again, no smile. I was beginning to get nervous, even more so when he said, "You know, this might not be the most propitious moment for me to bring this up. . . ."

Oh, god, here it comes if he's using words like propitious, I thought. *Just say you love me. I'll forget everything I read in your emails. I don't need the details, only the happy ending.*

"But since we're experiencing an episode of brutal honesty . . ."

Brutal? He used the word brutal?

"I have to admit to having doubts. . . ."

My nails dug into the underside of the kitchen counter. The pain was excruciating.

"Mom?" Laura opened the swinging door and held up a phone. "It's for you. Chloe. She called when I was on the other line."

I practically jumped to get it, so glad to be spared Griff's confession that I treated Chloe like I was on death row and she was the governor who'd just arrived with a reprieve. "I didn't even hear it ring," I chirped giddily, taking the phone and seeking the shelter of my living room, my heart still beating rapidly from the close call with Griff. "Chloe?"

She sounded breathless. "You'll never guess who just bought Macalester House from the university. You know the mansion I'm talking about, right? That fabulous old place with the eight fireplaces and plaster walls and hand-crafted molding from England."

Geesh. Could this woman have any worse timing? Here I was getting down to the nitty-gritty of my finances and marriage with my husband, who was a hair's breadth away from admitting he had doubts about our marriage, and she called to gossip.

"Liam Novak."

Liam? It was like the universe had been eavesdropping on my life. What were the odds that within minutes of Griff mentioning my ex for the first time in years, I would receive a call from Chloe about the exact same man?

"You remember him, don't you?" she asked stupidly.

"Yes, Chloe. Of course. Liam and I were almost married." I looked up to find Griff leaning against the doorjamb, listening. "But," I added hastily for his sake, "I haven't spoken to him in, gosh, forever."

"Well, he's gotten a divorce and he's moved back to Princeton." She was babbling a mile a minute, not hearing one word I was saying. "That house he bought is a grand old place, listed on the Historical Register, et cetera, et cetera. But the university's been using it as an inn for visiting alumni and, well, let's just say their interior decorating concerns ran more to durability than to authenticity."

Oh, no. I knew where she was going with this.

"We have got to be the ones to get that contract." Suddenly, she was being inclusive.

"You mean *I've* got to be the one to get that contract."

"You? Me? What does it matter. We're a team. Though it does make sense for you to make the first move. I mean, he did once love you madly."

I was stuck. To say no immediately would have only incurred more breathy pleading from Chloe. "I'll see what I can do."

"Is that all? I'd have expected you to be more enthusiastic than that, Kat."

Here came the manipulation. . . .

"Do you know how many interior designers have gone under in this economy? Every day Scotty Boy says, 'Chloe, it's not practical to keep Kat. The business can't afford it.' But do you know what I say to him?"

Kat is my girl Friday. I couldn't live without her.

"I tell him, 'Kat is my girl Friday. I couldn't live without her.' And do you know why?"

"Because I do everything around the office and then some?"

"Very funny. No. Because you're *loyal*, Kat. You've been with me longer than your husband and I know as sure as my name is Chloe Sykes . . ."

Which it wasn't.

". . . that you would never, ever in a million years go behind my back or try to find a job with someone else."

I thought of my first client, Madeleine Granville, and Elaine's encouragement to break out on my own and I felt the slightest pinch of guilt.

"Ipso facto," she added, "I know you would do everything in your power to keep this little boutique of ours afloat. Am I right?"

"Of course you are, Chloe. You're always right."

"Good. Then I'll assume you'll call Liam this week."

Again, I told her I'd see what I could do. I hung up and faced Griff.

After a second he said, "Liam Novak, huh?"

"Yup."

185

"To think we were just talking about him. Isn't that a coincidence?"

"Kind of. He bought a new house and Chloe wants his business. That's all. Oh, and"—I played with the tassel on one of our couch pillows—"he just got a divorce."

"I see." The muscle in the back of his jaw twitched. "So what are you going to do? I mean, about getting him as a client."

I said, "We've got $37,000 in debt and a daughter to send through college, Griff. I'm going to do whatever the hell it takes."

CHAPTER TWELVE

I should have figured Chloe would be too determined to abandon Liam when I kept "forgetting" to call him. But I never would have expected her to pull the crafty stunt she did three weeks later while I was on a penny-pinching expedition for discount toiletries.

Shopping with the Penny Pinchers was unlike any of my many, many previous retail experiences. They did everything backward. Instead of drawing up weekly menus and then buying ingredients accordingly, they culled through store fliers to find what was on sale and built menus around those. *Monthly* menus often involving chicken legs or beans that they'd purchased in huge quantities at a warehouse store.

Buying in bulk—what heretofore had seemed to me to be a massive waste—was the key, Opal claimed, to serious grocery store savings. The only problem was the bulk. After throwing out freezer-burned ground beef she'd bought on sale at Costco one day, she searched for a group with whom to share her bulk purchases and found the Penny Pinchers. They've been a team ever since.

On our most recent trip to Costco, for example, we purchased two fifty-pound boxes of chicken parts at an irresistible sixty cents a pound. Individually, one hundred pounds of thighs and wings would have been a disaster even with the sixteen-cubic-foot freezer Steve snagged for me off Craigslist. However, as a group, each of us was able to take home around sixteen pounds of chicken. (As a "nonconsumer," Wade never bought—he foraged.) Perfect for about five dinners at about $1.80 each.

The only difficult adjustment was learning to view shopping not as entertainment—as it had been during my formative years in South River—but as a military expedition mapped out by store circulars and executed through coupons. Sometimes, when the stars aligned, the Penny Pinchers were able to combine frequent-shopper discounts, manufacturer's coupons, and rebates for the mother of all discounts, what Steve liked to call "the perfect storm."

The Saturday before Thanksgiving at DrugSave

promised to be that perfect storm. Unfortunately, it was raining only tissues, toothpaste, and tampons.

If I'd known the sale was so lame, I might have passed since I'd promised my mother I'd take her to go Christmas shopping in the antique stores in Lambertville while I stopped off to see Madeleine Granville's redecorated kitchen. Also, fingers crossed, to pick up an overdue check. This was a new twist I hadn't counted on as an independent business owner—likeable clients who didn't pay their bills.

"Don't scoff," Opal said as we huddled in her minivan and divvied up coupons she'd downloaded and printed out by the dozens. "Normally tampons run about five bucks a box. With the frequent shopper card, that would bring them to $4.50. Add the buy one, get one deal and now we're at $2.25. Throw in the $1-off coupon and we're at $1.25. Combine that with buy ten and get a $5 rebate and, ladies and gentlemen, you have your $5 box of tampons for seventy-five cents."

Libby checked the van. "I think that's only ladies, Opal."

"Right. Well, those guys don't know what they're missing. If Wade and Steve were true Penny Pinchers, they would be in the trenches with us buying Kotex." She let out a snort. "As if men were capable of putting anyone else first besides themselves."

"Speaking of men," Velma said when we zipped

up our raincoats and grabbed our reusable bags to head into the cold drizzle of November. "How are you and your hubby getting along these days?"

Quieter, I thought, struck by how strange, yet appropriate, that word was. With the televisions permanently off, our house was quieter. So was our free time. We'd given up going to the movies with their blasting Dolby stereo sound effects. Nor did we eat out, ever. Meals were filled with quiet conversation instead of shouting in noisy restaurants. After dinner we usually read in near silence or we went for long walks through our peaceful neighborhood, the fall leaves swirling at our feet, the tinge of woodsmoke in the air. Even the way we treated each other was more gentle, with "pleases" inserted liberally along with "thank-yous" and mild kisses.

"You know," I said, having not given the issue thought before she asked. "I think we're . . . better. Quieter. I guess that's because we got rid of the TVs."

"Ah, I know what you mean. It's healthier, isn't it? When I feel a cold coming on, I sometimes I turn off everything electronic—the TV, the computer, even the lights—and let myself heal."

Was that what we were doing? I wondered. *Healing?*

Velma stuffed her hands into pink knitted mittens. "So what is it you do for a living exactly, Kat?"

I told her I was an assistant interior decorator.

"Does that mean you paint and put up curtains?"

"Mostly it means I put up with my boss's abuse." I guided her fragile elbow as we negotiated a puddle and had a sudden thought. "You know, I come across lots of cast-offs in my job, Velma. Decorator miss-tints that can be bought for nothing. Discarded old curtains." Gently, because I didn't want to offend her, I said, "So if you need your walls repainted or new curtains, I could do that for you—gratis."

She looked up at me and smiled, her thin lips erratically painted with coral lipstick. "Well, that's very nice of you, Kat. But I like my apartment just the way it is. However, I've joined a bartering co-op which has been great except I've had nothing to exchange for a tune-up of my old Monte Carlo. Now I'll have you."

It wasn't exactly what I'd had in mind, but that was okay.

At DrugSave, we opened the door and nearly ran into Libby, who was in one whale of a lather. "We got a problem at thirteen hundred," she whispered, cocking her chin to a balding manager standing with his arms folded by Shampoo/Feminine Hygiene. "Opal should have picked a day when he wasn't on duty. I know the guy and he's a jerk. He's got a bug up his butt about in-store rebates."

Opal boldly pushed past him, arrived at the tampon shelf, and with one motion swept half the boxes into her cart. The manager plucked a walkie-talkie off his belt and spoke into it.

"He treats her like a shoplifter because she wears kerchiefs and hippie batik skirts and reeks of patchouli." Libby clucked her tongue. "Profiling, pure and simple."

Still, Libby didn't move.

"Aren't you going to get some?"

"And risk being blacklisted by DrugSave? Heck no. This place is the cheapest in town."

Then it was up to me since Velma seemed to have gotten lost in the toothbrush section, her mittens to her lips as she debated soft versus medium bristles.

"Hi," I said to the manager.

He scowled.

"What a bargain." Doing as Opal had, I swept the rest into my cart."Okay, see you around."

At the end of the aisle, Opal gave me a wave. "Could you snag me a few rebate slips? I forgot mine."

"No problem." I yanked one off the shelf display. But when I went for another, a hand stopped me.

"One per customer," the manager said.

"Oh!" My neck went hot. Congenitally easily embarrassed, I felt it worse when there was an implication of greed. "I didn't know."

"He's lying." Opal marched up the aisle, removed his hand, and took one. "Read the fine print. It's one *per ten boxes*. It doesn't say anything about one *per customer*."

"One *per customer*," he reiterated, not bothering to read the rebate. "My store. My rules. If you don't like them, all of you can go."

I gasped. I'd never been kicked out of anything. Well, that wasn't true. The now defunct Woolworth's in South River never forgave me for shoplifting a packet of Bubble Yum when I was thirteen.

Velma turned the corner. "What's the problem?"

"It's the old one-per-customer rebate hassle." Opal made a rude gesture that obviously shocked the manager, whose eyes just about popped out of his head.

Velma slipped on her bifocals and took a rebate slip, reading it out loud for all of us to hear. Sure enough, it said nothing about one per customer.

"I'm the manager," he said. "I should know."

"You *should*," Velma said. "But you don't."

So intriguing was this showdown that I barely heard the chimes coming from my purse until Opal said, "Is that your phone?"

It was Viv with her trademark bad timing, forcing me to take refuge by the shampoo. "Call back later . . . ," I hissed.

"Where are you?"

"DrugSave on Market Street."

"So Mom was right. Curse her." She paused. "Is there a back door or something you can sneak out?"

192

A back door! "Why? And . . . no I can't leave. I'm with Opal and Velma and we've run into a bit of a snafu." Both women had their arms crossed and were facing the manager, also in crossed arms. "They need me for support."

"You never should have told Mom to meet you there. That was a big mistake." She sounded close to hysterics.

"What? Slow down, Viv. You're not making sense."

"Shoot. Here she comes now. I'm telling you . . . run! It's your last chance." Then the phone went dead.

Honestly, my sister was getting stranger by the day. Maybe she suffered from some form of post-traumatic distress after all those years of being stuck in cinder block rooms with high school students.

"We can stand here all day," Opal was saying when I got back. "Or you can let me go to the cash register and check out. I mean, that is the purpose of a store, right? To purchase items within its walls?"

"Purchase, yes. Rip me off, no."

It was then that I saw them approach in slow motion, my present and past stepping into my future.

First there was my mother in her purple raincoat and new Chooka rain boots with the cherries that gave her the appearance of a seventy-five-year-old with sixteen-year-old feet. She was strolling down the aisle, hand in pockets, wearing a mischievous grin that, in light of Viv's urgent call, made me wonder until I saw . . .

. . . A tall man in a Barbour behind her, slightly older than I recalled, his hair more fashionably cut, though not quite as bright blond, his blue eyes creased at the edges.

Liam?

It was as if a figure in my dreams had been formed and come to life. Liam. *Liam!* How many nights had I lain awake, trying to recall his smile, the way he bent to kiss me once upon a time. And now he was here, not a fantasy, but a real person whose face had been aged by what had happened to us in the interim—marriage, deaths, glorious vacations, and horrific moments of despair in the hours of 9/11. At last, we met again—by shampoos and feminine hygiene in DrugSave.

I'd stopped breathing.

"Look who's here!" Mom singsonged, though I couldn't tell if that was directed toward me or him.

Between us stood the Penny Pinchers, Opal and Velma, and the manager, oblivious.

Mom, equally unaware of the confrontation, took Liam's hand and wiggled past them. He looked as humiliated as I felt by the circumstances. If his helpless expression was any indication, meeting me in DrugSave had not been his idea.

"It's Liam!" Mom exclaimed, declaring the

obvious. "Can you believe it? I was on my way to meet you when I bumped into him on the street corner."

I said, "Outside his house?"

Liam laughed, the old familiar laugh, low in the back of his throat. "Pretty close." He extended his hand and said warmly, "Hi, Kat. Nice to see you again."

A surge of excitement rippled through every nerve, catching me completely off guard. "You, too. You look . . . fantastic."

I couldn't help smiling. I wanted to hug him, to apologize for leaving him on that beach. And yet, every pulse of my joy was tempered by the beat of guilt. I'd made my choice long, long ago, so I had no right to wish differently out of mere curiosity. He must be treated as nothing more than a fond acquaintance, a potential new client for Chloe.

"You haven't aged a bit," I added with slightly more reserve.

"I was just about to say the same about you." He was polite but distant. A proper response as always.

Mom, however, was like a precocious child from a Disney movie who'd successfully reunited her previously estranged parents. "So . . . are you almost done? I'm in no rush to go down to Lambertville if you two want to get a cup of coffee and catch up. Or . . . why don't you go to

Lambertville with us, Liam? Kat just finished designing a kitchen . . ."

It was then that a third puzzle piece appeared, bringing the larger picture into sharp focus.

Chloe—who to my knowledge had never stepped in a discount drug store since her Manville days—approached us carrying a basket that held a lone pack of Trident. "Did I just hear your mother say something about a kitchen you designed? Which one was that?"

Man, oh man. It was like I had one of those monitoring bracelets around my ankles the way she was aware of my every move.

Her gray eyes fixated on Liam. "And who's this, Kat? And, more important, does Griff know?"

Mom giggled, but I was tempted to slap my boss. Chloe knew too much about my personal life. How? That was a mystery. But somewhere along the line she'd discerned that Griff and I were riding through a bumpy patch and she'd started using this as subtle ammunition in her campaign to remain in charge.

"Liam, this is Kat's . . . ," Mom began.

"Partner," Chloe interjected, slipping him her slim white paw. "At Designs by Chloe. *Interior* designs, that is."

"Oooh," Mom gushed, right on cue. "I should have thought of this sooner, Liam. You need a professional to redo that big old house of yours." Turning to Chloe, she said, "Liam just bought the

Macalester House. You know, the old stone one with the eight fireplaces that the university sold this fall."

Chloe said, "Is that so?"

Wait. She already knew that. She was the one who told me. And how come she was in DrugSave just when I was there with Liam and my mother? And why was my mother so eager to offer Chloe's redecorating services?

Because . . . this was *a setup*! And I had been the bait. Those two battleaxes must have been in cahoots, too, since it was too much of a coincidence for all of us to be in DrugSave on a miserable Saturday afternoon.

From the other end of the aisle a shout went out. Opal.

"This is outrageous." She waved her arms madly as doors opened and two uniformed rent-a-cops burst in. For a brief second, I thought one of them was Steve—wouldn't that show the manager!—but, alas, no.

"All I'm trying to do is exercise my constitutional right to buy some tampons," Opal shouted. "Also, Kat!"

Liam's eyes dropped to my cart, filled halfway with Kotex. Mom, of that generation, went crimson, while I wished for a hole in the floor beneath my feet.

Chloe said, "What's going on?"

"You, too." The manager waved me off. "You

can buy those with one rebate or you can leave the store."

Behind his back, Velma snuck a handful more of rebate forms.

"I'll buy them," I told the manager. "Thanks."

"Then follow me."

I followed him to the cash register, piled the boxes on the counter, and prayed to be anywhere else. Since I didn't have a DrugSave frequent-shopper card—that was supposed to have been Opal's bailiwick—and since I only had about ten dollar-off coupons, the total was nothing close to the seventy-five cents per box that had been promised.

Meanwhile, Chloe used my encounter with the manager as a distraction to get her clutches on Liam, leading him away to the rainy outdoors. I never even got a chance to say good-bye.

"I cannot believe you just spent over $140 on tampons," Mom said as we got in the car to head toward Lambertville.

Frankly, it was hard for me to be civil, so furious was I at my mother's unconscionable scheming. "I cannot believe you and Chloe set me up," I retorted, gripping the wheel.

Out of the corner of my eye, I could see my mother beginning to form a denial. "Don't even try it, Mom. For you to have 'bumped' into Liam on the street corner and then for Chloe to conveniently show up after weeks of hounding me to call him so she could get the contract on that house is no mere happenstance and you know it."

But there was another hurt under the surface, one I hadn't realized was there until I'd said Chloe's name out loud. "And how could you have thrown Chloe his business when you knew perfectly well that I was trying to strike out on my own? Do you know what having a client like Liam would have done for me? It would have been my ticket to freedom!"

Mom sat back, silent and chastised, making me feel twice as bad for my outburst. How was it she could flip my emotions like that without saying so much as one word?

We didn't speak until I parked on Main Street near her favorite antique shops and I killed the engine. "I'll pick you up in an hour. I won't be long."

She toyed with a button on her raincoat. "You're right, Kat. Not about me reuniting you with Liam. I still believe you two were meant to be together. But you're right about letting Chloe get first dibs on renovating his house. I don't know why I didn't tell him about you right off. I guess I'm not that used to you having your own business."

I softened as I always did on the rare occasions when my mother admitted her fallibility. "That's okay, Mom. I know your heart was in the right place."

"I just want you to be happy, Kat, and it frustrates me to see you struggling in your forties, shopping with those Penny Pinchers, when you could have been the lady in the house in pearls and heels."

My mother's concept of the good life often seemed to be taken from 1950s sitcoms. "I like my life, Mom. Do I have enough money? No. Who does?"

"I do." She kissed me on the cheek and opened the door. "One hour, right?"

"Right."

I waited until she stepped inside Time and Again and then drove off to visit Madeleine.

But my thoughts for once were not on saving or on managing my mother. I was too preoccupied with mentally replaying my reunion with Liam and wondering why I so desperately wanted to see him again.

CHAPTER THIRTEEN

*W*hat's with all the tampons underneath the bathroom sink?" Griff asked three weeks later when I returned from saying good-bye to my beloved Lexus, having traded it for a very practical, very unsexy, very used, economical Toyota Corolla. "You cornering the market or what?"

I threw my new keys on the counter and collapsed on the couch. Our dirt cheap Charlie Brown Christmas tree, usually surrounded with presents by this time, was bare aside from six small boxes scattered over the red felt tree skirt. Griff, Laura, and I had pledged to exchange no more than one present each, an idea that seemed wise at the time—especially to Griff, who so dreaded holiday shopping, he held off until Christmas Eve—but now seemed downright depressing.

I couldn't help feeling as if the Grinch had visited overnight, what with losing my Lexus and going stingy on the presents and forgoing the tradition of a big Christmas dinner with roast beef and champagne. I'm sorry, but it just wasn't Christmas without throwing a huge holiday party.

Worse, I hadn't yet been paid by Madeleine Granville for the $3,450 worth of work I did on her house. Nor was my saving plan flowing seamlessly. We'd been hit by a few surprise expenses—the brakes on Griff's car and new snow tires for mine—that had derailed me, if not them. I was, in short, dead broke.

"That's excellent!" Sherise had said during our last Penny Pinchers meeting when I revealed that after many weeks of effort, I had little more than $2,500 to show for my sacrifice of Starbucks and DVDs, new boots, HBO, and Christmas gifts. "That averages out to $250 a week."

"Yes, but . . ." I looked over to Velma who, content as usual, knitted along, listening. "According to the budget Velma worked out, I should be saving $500. I'll never get to $16,000 by this summer."

"It's DrugSave's fault," Opal said. "You'd be at least one hundred dollars richer if it hadn't been for me and that fight I had with the manager."

During darker moments, it crossed my mind that Opal had intentionally used me to provoke the manager. After all, why didn't she get her own in-store rebate slips instead of making a big fuss by yelling to me? Whenever I had these thoughts, though, I'd chastise myself. Out of all the Penny Pinchers, Opal had helped me the most and to attribute ulterior motives to her was ungrateful and wrong.

Wade put down the *New Yorker* he'd borrowed from upstairs. "I'm telling you, Kat, forget all this coupon stuff. Unless you're minding it every minute like Opal does, it's a trap. My approach is much more logical. If you don't want to spend money, *don't spend money.* This spring you're coming with me to Dumpster-dive."

"You mean steal," Steve said.

"No. I don't mean steal. If I'd meant steal, I would have said steal."

But Steve would not give in. "Just like entering private property without permission isn't tres-passing, right?"

"So what that I take other people's trash? It's only going to be thrown out, anyway. And let me ask you this . . ." Wade held up his finger, a sure sign he was turning the heat up a notch. "Which is worse? Killing a cow, a sentient being, only to throw away the meat simply because some arbitrary expiration date has passed? Or making sure that a loving animal's life wasn't wasted."

"Okay, you two." Sherise stood and spread her arms like she was physically splitting them apart. "That's enough. How about we take a breather for ten minutes and get some fresh air."

Wade and Steve grinned sheepishly. Ever since Steve announced that this was his last meeting because he'd been hired as a cop in the Rocky River Police Department and couldn't fit us into his morning schedule, Wade and Steve had been at loggerheads, with Steve telling him in no uncertain terms that if he caught Wade rifling through garbage on private property, he would arrest him.

"Steve's a jerk," Libby said under her breath as we slipped out the back door into the gray December day. "He is on Wade's case for no reason."

"He's not a jerk. He's just under a lot of pressure these days as a single father during the holidays." I handed her a Christmas cookie, a reindeer with a broken leg, as a substitute for the cigarettes she was trying to quit. "Give him a break. It can't be easy with two boys begging for snowboards and Xbox 360s."

She took the cookie and frowned at the gimpy reindeer. "I dunno. If I keep eating like this, I'm going to be the size of a house and then Wade's never going to ask me to marry him."

"First of all, if he loves you, he loves you. It has nothing to do with size." I, who had no compunction these days about ruining my waistline, took a bite of a frosted angel. "Second, since when did you want to get married?"

"Since I walked into the meeting last summer and saw him and just . . . knew." Her shoulders slumped as she nibbled on the cookie. "He is the most gorgeous guy in the world, Kat. And smart. And sexy. And so well read. I can't believe he likes me. Me! Libby Wilson. Housecleaner."

This was where I was tempted to remind her he lived in a tent, but my better side held off. "You are not just a housecleaner, Libby. You are one kick-ass chick, a survivor, a"—I tried to think of what she was—"woman roaring."

But Libby was lost in thought over Wade. "The problem is," she added, "I see you and Griff and even though you *seem* like you're happy on the outside, the perfect married couple and all that, I run into him with Bree now and then and I think maybe marriage is not all it's cracked up to be."

My cookie had somehow ended up on the sidewalk, broken into pieces. "What do you mean," I began, unsure which part of her statement was more offensive, "that you ran into him with Bree?"

"Oh, I don't run into him all the time, just on Thursdays, when I clean up by Emerly. Sometimes

I see him and Bree together, walking, or sitting and talking at that café. You know, the one with the blue awning . . ."

"Belladonna's?" It was a bit more than a café. In fact, it was one of the nicer restaurants near campus, the place where parents took their kids out to dinner when they came for visits. "You see them at *Belladonna's*?" And here I hadn't even been to a freaking McDonald's.

"Only for lunch. And it's not like they're kissing or anything," she added quickly, finally comprehending that I might not be taking the news so well that my husband regularly was out with another woman. "They're just talking. Really close talking, though. *Realllly* close."

Sherise opened the door. "The meeting's started up again. We've been looking for you two. Come on."

I brushed my crumbs off my coat and shoved my chilled hands under my armpits as we went inside. Curse Griff. Curse him and his stupid girlfriend and their trendy vertical food lunches, the famous Belladonna's tower of asparagus, hollandaise, risotto, and grilled shrimp. Meanwhile, across town, I'd been subsisting on sixty-nine-cent tuna on thinly sliced dry rye toast and water. So much for our united front in saving money.

Plunking myself down next to Opal, I let out a grunt and eyed Libby, who nestled into Wade's arms. *Good luck,* I thought. *Marriage bites.*

Opal said, "What's eating you?"

"Nothing." I tried to rally, sitting up and pasting on a big smile, but I couldn't even summon the energy to unbutton my coat.

"I made the mistake of mentioning that I've been seeing Griff with his assistant at Belladonna's," Libby said.

"Belladonna's?" Sherise widened her eyes. "*Pri-ceee.*"

"I'll say. That's where I used to take my wife on our anniversary," Steve said. "Before she got sick."

Velma reached over and rubbed his shoulder, exactly what I wanted to do. It was hard ragging on marriage when there was Steve, his heart not quite mended over his dead wife, forever giving the impression of being slightly damaged.

"I'm just saying that it's expensive," he said. "Didn't mean to kill the conversation."

"Have you spoken to Griff about this?" Sherise said in her patient financial-planner voice. "Or are you still on the stealth savings plan?"

This produced a few welcomed laughs. "I thought we were saving together," I said. "You know: more quality time, cutting back on Christmas, and all that."

"Oh, yes," everyone agreed. No one splurged this year. Velma had knit everyone socks, and Libby was giving lamps she constructed from odd parts Wade had found in the trash.

"You'll be grateful come January when those credit card bills come in the mail," Opal said. "Not that I use credit cards. I don't. I only keep them on hand for rental cars. It's what I've heard, though, that those first-of-the-year wake-up calls can be brutal."

"So, not to bring up a delicate subject, but how much have you saved?" Sherise asked. "I mean for . . . the divorce."

It was embarrassing how little I'd put together. In three months I'd managed to save only $3,400. "I've had a setback," I said. "For the divorce fund, I've only got about $3,400. But my new client promises a check any day." Never mind that the "any day" was two months overdue.

"How can you say that's a setback? You have to celebrate every dollar." Sherise motioned for everyone to give me a round of applause.

"I just haven't been motivated. Griff and I've been getting along so well and I thought our saving was bringing us closer together." I didn't say this out loud, but it was as if Libby had reopened an old wound and I was angry at her for ruining the progress we'd been making, though reporting bad news was hardly her fault. Logically, I realized that. It was my illogical heart that was struggling.

"The thing is, now that I find he's been cheating on our budget as well as on me . . ."

"You have a whole new reason to sock it to him," Velma said. "Don't you?"

I was confused. "You mean away. Sock it *away*."

"That, too." She took a stitch. "Though, personally, I'd prefer to sock it to him. Much more satisfying in the short run."

"Not so satisfying in the long," Opal said. "Stick with saving money, honey. Having a pile of it in the bank is a woman's best revenge."

"What's got you lost in thought?" Griff sat next to me on the couch and put his arm around my shoulders. "Bummed about losing the Lexus?"

"Yeah." After much thought, I'd decided not to bring up Belladonna's or Bree since mentioning her always sent him into a weird seclusion. Better to pretend everything was hunky-dory and to do as Sherise advised: keep my eye on the goal. "Also . . . look." I gestured to our tree, which was practically raining needles already. "It's pathetic, and a fire hazard."

He considered this. "Fire hazard, yes. Pathetic, no. It cost five bucks, Kat. Plus, we gave it a home. Think of this poor little tree still on a gas station parking lot alone in the cold."

There was a time when Griff, Laura, and I would make a big deal of getting the annual Christmas tree, driving to a tree farm in Cranbury Township that offered free hayrides and hot chocolate. Back then we'd spend a fortune on a huge, lush fir that we loaded with lights. If we loaded this thing with lights, it would explode.

I leaned my head against his chest in a test of he power of positive thinking. Part of me didn't care what Libby saw. My gut instinct was that Griff and I *had* grown closer since we'd cut back on our expenses. It was a basic matter of logistics. By not spending money, we stayed at home more and in our separate cars less, watching movies from the library or simply reading on the couch, my feet in his lap, Jasper snoring on the rug nearby. As for Bree . . . perhaps they'd been out on Emerly College's tab.

"Buck up." He gave my shoulder a squeeze. "Just think what it was like for us last year this time before Christmas. You were running around, exhausted and cursing the crowds and the traffic, worried you didn't get Laura or your nieces and nephews enough gifts. Not worried about me, of course, since I don't count." He sniffed.

I gently punched him.

"Then, after the shopping orgy was done, you'd be in the wrapping orgy and then the mailing orgy. This would be followed by another orgy of baking cookies and then the ultimate orgy—the over-the-top Christmas dinner that nearly always sent you running for the Prozac."

"I never took a Prozac in my life."

"Spoken like a true addict." He kissed my forehead. "Now isn't this better? The two of us side-by-side on a gray December day simply enjoying each other."

"I miss the orgies."

"Mrs. Griffiths! What are you suggesting?"

Snuggling into his shoulder, I inhaled the smell of his wool sweater that always reminded me of Barb Gladstone's library, the books and fireplace even if Griff had stunk like a farmhand. "I keep feeling as though I ought to be doing more since it's Laura's last Christmas."

"As a high school senior. She'll be back for years. I'm afraid she's going to be one of those slackers we're going to have to kick out of the house, if we're ever going to embark on the next adventure of our lives."

Hmm, I thought. *What does that mean?* It sounded inclusive. And yet . . .

I kissed his neck, slightly salty and warm, wishing our problems could be resolved. I was so tired of being conflicted, of spending every waking minute wondering if he was or if he wasn't having an affair. I regularly wavered between moments when I dismissed my fears of divorce as wifely hysteria and other moments of pure green jealousy when Bree called or he went downstairs to his computer for hours at a stretch.

Which might explain why, instead of kissing more than his neck, I said, "Hey. You haven't seen my new car."

"Would that be the luxury Corolla? What are we waiting for?"

He bounded off the couch and I led him to the

garage. "Notice," I said, "the fine detailing in the molded-plastic dashboard and the sensuous velour seats."

"Yes. I understand 1999 was an exceptional year for the economy car." He opened the door and feigned amazement. "Are those armrests I see?"

"Two!" Like Vanna White I spread myself against the hood. "That's 120 horsepower under me, baby."

"And five speeds?" He raised his brows. "Grrr." He circled the car and wrapped his arms around me. "Why is it that there's nothing more alluring than a beautiful woman on the hood of a car?" He kissed me gently on the lips. "Especially on a hot rod like this."

"Speaking of hot rod." Seemingly on its own volition, my hand slid down the front of his jeans to find he was already getting hard. "You weren't joking about the woman on the hood of the car phenomenon."

He swallowed. "No, ma'am."

"If I'd only known sooner I'd have totally redesigned our bedroom."

"You might get a bit more purchase if I do this." He unbuckled his belt and unzipped his jeans. "Not that I'm issuing requests."

It felt so good to be like this with him, so easy, as if there'd never been worries about money or Bree or Belladonna's or disconcerting emails. Griff slid his hand under my sweater and cupped my breasts, nudging my turtleneck down until, in mock frustration, he said, "Does this thing come off? Or do I have to rip it off with my teeth?"

It came off. And it was freezing.

"Ohmigod, this garage is cold."

"Yeah?" He grasped me by the waist and hoisted me up. "Let's see what we can do about that."

His hands ran up my thighs, under my skirt, and, for the first time, I felt the thrill of bare skin on chrome. So that's what all the fuss was about with those *Car and Driver* centerfolds.

Griff covered me with his body, sending rays of warmth as his bare thighs pressed against mine.

"I love you, Kat," he murmured, breathing heavily, excitedly, as he entered gently and then, after a few purposeful thrusts, more forcefully. "God, do I love you."

It was what I wanted to hear, what I *needed* to hear as I wrapped my legs around him and met him stroke for stroke, finally reaching the kind of explosion that can never be predicted or planned.

Griff buried his head in my neck and kissed me under the ear. "You are one hot babe on a hot rod."

"Ditto."

He frowned.

"I mean reverse ditto."

"Better." He kissed my cleavage and said, "Tell me honestly. Do you think we really can move this car upstairs?"

I reached for my bra and hooked it on. "Like I said, this afternoon's given me a whole new perspective on boudoir design."

"Now aren't you glad you weren't out Christmas shopping?" He languidly stepped into his jeans.

"Or that we own a Toyota? 'Cause I'm pretty sure the front end of the Lexus is too high for . . ."

"Mom?" Laura's voice echoed through the kitchen. "Dad? Where are you?"

More panicked than busted teenagers, Griff and I hurriedly scrambled into the rest of our clothes. I ducked into the car and tried to smooth my hair in the rearview mirror while Griff ingeniously grabbed a tire gauge and bent down to the rear left tire, as if all he'd been up to was looking after my safety.

"There you are! Didn't you hear me calling you?" She was at the door from the kitchen, holding a small box wrapped in brown paper with a red envelope attached. "What's this?"

I thought she was referring to the box, which I'd never seen before. Then I saw she was referring to the Toyota. "It's my new car." I checked the hood to make sure we hadn't left any dents or other incriminating evidence.

"It's not too bad. Connor Richardson has one just like it. Maybe a few years newer."

Connor Richardson was seventeen. Seventeen-year-olds now owned fancier cars than I did.

She held up the package. "This was sticking out

of the mailbox when I came home. What's PharMax?"

Griff lifted his head from the tire. "That's the place where your mother used to work before we met."

Somehow I knew it was from Liam, though why he would have sent me a present was more than slightly intriguing.

"It must be from my old roommate, Suzanne," I lied, practically snatching it from her. "She said she was putting something in the mail for me. How nice."

The name NOVAK was handwritten above the PharMax stamp in cryptic block handwriting—distinctive to me, unintelligible to most. Including, thankfully, my daughter.

"Open it!"

"I can't! It's a Christmas present."

"Then at least take off the brown wrapper so we can put it under the tree. That would give us a grand total of seven whopping presents."

Tapping her on the nose, I said, "Now who's acting like a seven-year-old instead of a seventeen-year-old? Wanna go test-drive my new wheels? Dad will give you another lesson on driving stick, and I promise he won't yell or grip the dash." I slid the package under a box of garbage bags by the door while Laura got the keys on the counter and Griff finished with his duty of checking the tire pressure.

He lay the gauge on his workbench, thought for a bit, and said, "I didn't know Suzanne still worked at PharMax."

"Oh, sure. She's got so much seniority there, she'll never leave." I was dying for those two to skedaddle so I could see what was in the box. The curiosity was killing me.

Laura came back and jangled the keys. "Ready?"

Griff made a point of taking the long way around the car to the passenger seat, stopping to brush his lips against my cheek. "That was really great what we just did. Try to keep that in mind when Laura and I pull out of the driveway and you rip into that box."

CHAPTER FOURTEEN

*I*n the safety of my office the next day, I reopened the red envelope for the umpteenth time to reveal a snowy scene of a white country church on a starry night, your standard Christmas card. Inside, in Liam's cramped block script, it said:

Dear Kat,

I meant what I said about you looking fantastic. Clearly, life with Griff has done you good and I couldn't be more pleased to see you settled and happy.

But I've been a mess ever since. Shortly after our meeting, your mother called me at home to set the record straight: that I should hire you since you, apparently, are opening your own interior design business. Now I feel awful since I've promised the job to Chloe.

That said, being a soulless CEO type, I have absolutely no problem crushing Chloe's hopes (I crush hopes every day!) and would love you to take on this humongous project if you can stomach putting up with my horrendously bad taste.

It's been twenty years under the bridge, enough time for us to hammer out a perfectly professional relationship, I'm sure. And, frankly, the impetus is not you, it's your scary mother. There's no telling what kind of wrath Anna Popalaski could rain down on someone who fails to support her daughter. ☺

Naturally, I'll understand if you would rather not. But please let me know sometime soon after the holidays. Between your mother and Chloe, I'm afraid my phone won't stop ringing until this matter is resolved.

Merry Christmas,

Liam

P.S. You left these on my bedside table long, long ago and for all sorts of reasons that need not be explained, I was never able to return them. If I remember correctly, they were your grandmother's— right?

Two pearl earrings with tiny diamonds lay on blue satin in the tiny jewel box, a sixteenth birthday present from my mother's mother and one I could have sworn was stolen by several questionable movers when I was leaving the apartment I shared with Suzanne.

He'd saved them all these years.

The front door opened and I quickly shut the box, stuffing it into my desk drawer, the one place I was confident his note and my earrings would not be discovered by Griff.

Much to my relief, it was only Elaine arriving with lattes for both of us, her treat. Of all the sacrifices I was making in the name of saving, for some reason Elaine was most saddened by my refusal to spend $5 on a cup of coffee and foam. Once a week she brought me a triple venti, which she produced with the kind of earnestness most do-gooders display when handing out winter coats to the poor.

"You gave me a heart attack," I said after thanking her profusely.

She pulled up a seat and took a sip. "What does

that say about your relationship with your boss that whenever she opens the door, you have to reach for the defibrillator?"

"This time I have good reason." I opened the drawer and showed her the card. "Read this."

Elaine flipped it open. "Who's Liam?"

"Liam Novak. He's the new CEO of PharMax. We were dating when I met Griff in the dark ages."

"You mean the guy you almost married, the one who bought the Macalester House?"

I nodded. The latte was delicious, so much better once a week rather than (I'm embarrassed to admit) twice a day.

"Art handled the Macalester House deal." Art was Arthur B. Winchester, owner of Arthur B. Winchester Properties, where Elaine was a Realtor. He was the guy who insisted she wear the ugly navy pantsuit. "I was there when he told Chloe that Liam had bought it, and you should have seen her reaction as she put two and two together. She bragged right off that with your connection, she'd be sure to get the interior design contract."

"Except . . ." I pointed to the paragraph about him having no worries about crushing Chloe's hopes.

"Oooh. She's not going to like that." Elaine added evilly, "Do it!"

"You mean call and tell him I want the job? Chloe will fire me on the spot."

"So? If you get him as a client, you can quit first.

Hell, you can type up your resignation letter on gold leaf. Look at this."

Nudging me aside, she went on my computer and found a newspaper article that had appeared two months before in the *Trentonian*. "This is why Art decided to hunt down your old boyfriend and insist he look at the Macalester House. Also, why Chloe went berserk when she realized you and he had a connection."

It was a boring business story about the changing of the guard at PharMax. There was a picture of the outgoing CEO who was retiring and Liam looking very professional in glasses (since when?) and a nice Brooks Brothers tie.

"Not bad." Elaine framed the photo with her two hands. "And you're telling me you two were once engaged?"

"Not actually. I . . . turned him down."

She regarded me with disbelief. "Because you were temporarily mentally ill, right?"

"Because I was in love with Griff."

"Love. Hah! You know what I love? This."

She scrolled to a breakout box summarizing Liam's new compensation package at PharMax.

ANNUAL SALARY: $1.73 MILLION

BONUS: $3.5 MILLION

OTHER: $8.9 MILLION

The figures made no sense. A salary that required a decimal point? "What's 'other' mean?"

"It means he can pay an old girlfriend so well to redo all five of his bedrooms, she never has to work another day for the Mistress of Manville."

"Good." Hastily, I clicked out of the story in case Chloe burst in, as she tended to do. "Because I already called him. We're meeting today at noon at his house."

"Why, you minx." Elaine collapsed in her chair and laughed. "When did our mere Kat grow a backbone all of a sudden? Don't tell me this comes from joining the Penny Panthers, or whatever it is you call yourselves."

"Penny *Pinchers*." I hadn't thought of it before, but maybe my new courage was an unexpected benefit of learning how to say no to the influences of a world saturated with advertising. Then again, more likely it came from being broke.

As I'd predicted, Chloe threw her door open with a violent crash. Except it wasn't the front door—it was her office. Unbeknownst to me, she'd been holed up there all morning, probably listening to our every word.

She bustled across the office, her portfolio in tow, a gorgeous Escada white ostrich shoulder bag setting off the Diane Von Furstenberg zebra wrap under her camel coat.

Man. I missed a disposable income. Not that I'd

ever been able to afford Escada. Not that not being able to afford something had ever stopped me before.

"I'm off!" she announced, checking herself in the mirror by the door. "Brand-new client. *Huugely* important. Mustn't be late."

Glancing out the window, she caught sight of my new Corolla and blanched. "Call the landlord, Kat. Someone's parked in our space who's not a client. I don't pay $150 a month so freeloaders can dump their heaps outside my business."

Had it been a Mercedes I'd purchased, I guarantee Chloe would not have had that reaction.

"Oh, by the way," she said, twirling up a tube of Dior lipstick, "I'm sure Griff will be pleased to learn your ex is completely over you, Kat. This Novak character left a message on my cell yesterday extending his deepest apologies for not signing with me. Apparently, another designer got to him first." Finished coloring in her thin lips, she dropped the Dior in her bag and said, "It's a political thing. A wife of a PharMax board of trustees member who has an interior design hobby, no doubt."

That wasn't Liam's style to lie, unless he'd changed. "Did he come right out and say that?"

"Of course not. But when you've owned a business in this town as long as I have, you know how things work. Now don't forget to call the Ishings while I'm out. And check on the black marble I ordered for the ITF project. I'll be at lunch until two."

"Bye," I said.

She took a few steps, turned, and wrinkled her nose at Elaine's latte. "There are nearly five hundred calories in one of those. Coffee straight has zero." She raised an eyebrow. "FYI."

Chloe was no sooner gone than I had to pick up Elaine from the floor where she'd ended after a fit of hysterical laughing.

"No," she mimicked, "but when you've owned a business in this town as *long* as I have, you know how things work. Oh, lord." She snatched a tissue to wipe her eyes. "Part of me hopes you never do leave this job. Not a day goes by when that woman doesn't crack me up."

Macalester House was one of the oldest homes in Princeton, a huge mansion built around 1770, which had served as headquarters for the Continental Congress, as a public inn and, eventually, as a private inn for visiting alumni at Princeton. But the downturn in the economy and the cost of maintenance had been too much for the university, which sold it to Liam, who, according to Elaine, had professed to being a sucker for Revolutionary War history.

I vaguely remembered that.

Because it was only a few blocks from Chloe's office, I risked letting my Corolla remain in one of Chloe's precious spaces and hiked through the February snow to Liam's new digs with the dim hope that a little exercise might drain off the adrenaline that had caused my palms to sweat like a nervous teenager.

No biggie, I told myself. *Treat him like any other client. Be respectful and attentive. Pretend that you have no idea what it's like to sleep with him naked in the crook of his body.*

Unfortunately, the walk didn't help. I was barely able to cobble together a cogent sentence when Liam answered the old oak door in a black turtleneck and twill pants, the Saturday morning newspaper tucked under his arm.

"Hi there." I waved. Then, realizing waving was stupid and unprofessional, I tapped my portfolio and said, "I've been doing research and I have tons of ideas. You won't be disappointed."

It was going all wrong. I sounded like a Girl Scout hocking Thin Mints instead of a smart and secure designer, or an old friend.

Liam grinned and led me into a slate foyer, graciously offering to take my coat. "You're way ahead of me, Kat. I'm still at 'nice to meet you.'" As he hung up my coat in the closet, I noticed he managed to sneak in a quick take of how the rest of me had fared over the years.

My outfit was simple: slimming black pants, tan scoop-necked sweater, and seed pearls at my throat. Pearls at my ears, too. The ones he'd returned.

"Thank you so much for not tossing these in a moment of pique. You're right. They were my grandmother's."

"Oh, do you have them on? Let me see. Lovely."

I froze in place as he slid his hand under my hair, his thumb grazing my neck. "I always did like it this way the best. Shows more of your face."

"These days," I said, trying to make it light, "it shows more of my neck, a sight that often scares small children." My mother always said it was an unwise woman who pointed out her own flaws. But since when did I follow my mother's advice?

Liam—who *was* wise—let that drop. "Come on. I'll give you a tour and you can see what we're up against."

I followed him through a narrow doorway with low headroom, taking note as I went of the details that were authentic, and those that had been added by well-intentioned but tired—and maybe cash-strapped—generations.

Since it had been an inn for so long, the house carried the air of a temporary way stop instead of a home. There was a small, built-in front desk, for instance, and the living rooms, while functional, were clearly meant to accommodate small groups of strangers instead of family gatherings. Plus, there was a lot of Princeton black and orange that would definitely have to go.

Shortcuts had been made to cut costs. The shoe molding was inferior and nicked. The plaster walls that should have been bare to display their artistic glory were papered. The wide pine floors were badly in need of refinishing and were, in the kitchen—painted! But the worst sin by far was that it was decorated in a Victorian style, not in its original mid-Georgian.

He stopped at the foot of the stairs leading to the bedrooms, cleared his throat, and said, "Might as well save the upstairs for later. I'm sure you've seen enough to give you an approximate idea of what's needed." We moved into a small sitting room with a fireplace and two lead-glass windows.

Relieved from not having to see where he slept, either alone or with some other woman, I let out a breath I hadn't realized I'd been holding. "You're right. This *is* a big job. I'm assuming that being a history buff you want to restore it to its original finishes."

"That's why I bought the place even though it screamed money pit. When I die, I can return it to the town as an authentic example of Georgian architecture." He leaned against the fireplace and looked around. "I don't know what they were thinking with this cheap bead board."

"They were thinking protection and preservation." I tapped the oak hearth. "Rip that off and there's eighteenth-century brick under there. That's what they did to the inn where we used to stay in Lumberville, remember?"

It was a bold reference to not only our past, but

to one of our more romantic evenings at the Black Stallion overlooking the Delaware, the site where we'd made love for the first time, prompting an earnest young Liam to declare his love for me afterward, kissing each one of my fingers and toes.

What had my subconscious been thinking, bringing that up?

He studied me for a second as if trying to judge my intentions and said, "Exactly. Funny, I've been thinking of that place, too. If you're free some weekend, we should drive down there and get a few ideas."

"Sure." I shrugged like it was no big deal we'd be revisiting the place where we'd fallen in love. Getting back on track, I said, "There's a lot of structural stuff I'm assuming you'll want to tackle right away."

"You said it." He gestured to a brown stain indicating a burst pipe. "New roof. New flashing. Redo the outside to expose the original brick. Electrical touchups. Plumbing issues. After that, I'll let you take over. I know it might be impossible, but I'd be over the moon if we could stick to period pieces."

"Are you kidding? Absolutely!" I gushed, immediately imagining me scouring shops in Brandywine, Pennsylvania, for the perfect hutch. "It'll require tons of research. Hours at the Historical Society researching paint tints and molding styles. And, of course, antiques."

Liam smiled at my enthusiasm. "*Of course.* As I remember, you and I were good at finding those. I still have a few at my parents' house. Paige was never a big antiques person."

For a second, I lost my mind and, like a dim bulb, said, "Paige?"

"My . . . " He hesitated. "My *ex* wife."

"Oh, right." I was such a Sagittarius, forever talking without thinking. "Sorry about that, by the way."

"You mean the divorce?" He went over to the window as if preoccupied with a broken sash. "That was years in the making. It wasn't good from the start, you know."

I didn't know, but I could have surmised it since he'd married her a few months after we broke up.

"People keep saying to me isn't it a blessing we didn't have children and I suppose on some level they're right." He lifted the broken window and checked its underside. "And I think Paige would agree that we never did because we understood this marriage wouldn't last. That said, I now find myself in my mid-forties, divorced, without kids, and I have to admit it's raised the question of whether I should remarry sooner rather than later."

I thought of his bedroom upstairs that he'd stopped short of showing me. How many young things at PharMax would love to be married to a man of his wealth and stability? Would love to give him the houseful of children he'd always craved?

"Well, that's where men are lucky," I said. "It doesn't matter how old you are, you can have kids—like Tony Randall, who fathered a child at eighty-four."

"So I have some time, is that what you're saying?"

"At least forty years, if Tony's any yardstick." I laughed at the idea of a Tony Randall yardstick. "Anyway, I expect you'll be remarried and perhaps a new father within a year, my friend. I don't know if you've heard this, Liam, but young women are crazy for successful men who have bulging bank accounts. You guys are all the rage."

He closed the window gently and, in a much brighter tone, said, "You know, I do think I read that someplace."

"It's women who get the short end of the stick when it comes to finding men at our age. I am not looking forward to that at all."

Whoops!

It just slipped out, like the line about Lumberville or the question about Paige. My subconscious, as often happens, was out to sabotage me. Probably seeking retribution for suppressing it for so long.

"*Not*," I added quickly, "that I have any plans to be single anytime soon."

"Right." He checked his watch. "Hey, it's almost

one. Wanna grab some lunch? I mean, not here. I never cook. I was talking about going down to Marc's Deli."

Okay, until that question, I'd been doing fine. Except for the reference to our first sexual encounter and the slip about becoming divorced myself. Other than that, I'd settled down and become perfectly comfortable—as long as we were discussing authentic moldings and the best way to refinish old pine floors and steering away from more touchy issues, like how I'd dumped him on that beach.

But going out to lunch on Saturday when I should have been home with Griff crossed an invisible line, even if we managed to sneak in shop talk.

"Unfortunately . . . ," I began, searching for an excuse, "I'm running late as it is, and . . ."

He held up his hand. "I'm sure. Though I would like to catch up sometime. Seems weird for us to be working like this together and me not even know if you, if you have a dog, for instance."

"Jasper," I said. "He's on death's door."

"Or whether you really will be single in the near future." His lips twitched. "Not, as you said, that you have plans to be so soon."

CHAPTER FIFTEEN

*S*o what do you think he meant by that?" Sherise asked as we waited for the fog to lift outside the Shop-N-Buy.

"I don't know." I cranked the heater, sinfully letting the car run. A few more minutes and the store would be open and we could be warm at last.

Velma, Sherise, Opal, and I huddled in my cramped Corolla near dawn on a cold March morning in preparation of our big monthly grocery shop. It had been weeks since my meeting with Liam and not a day had gone by when I hadn't analyzed his sentence down to its punctuation and use of the word *soon*.

"My worst-case scenario is that somehow my mother has found out, either from Viv or Chloe, that Griff is planning to divorce me and she passed the word to him. On the other hand, I did make that crack about not looking forward to being single in my forties. . . ."

"Yeah, but that could be taken either way." Opal, next to me, checked her clipboard holding her extensive grocery list organized by aisle and discount. "What I think is that you're projecting. You want him to know you're going to be single. You want him to care."

Yeah, she was right, and I had to admit it was somewhat pathetic that I wanted—no, *craved*—

Liam's attention. Perhaps I was as needy as any other overworked mother and wife who missed the secret thrill of flirting. Or maybe I was going through a midlife crisis of my own, one exacerbated by a husband whose commitment was uncertain at best.

All I knew was, having Liam back in my life had added a spark I hadn't felt since before Laura. I felt younger and brighter. I tinted my roots (at home, natch) and did my own nails nightly in a feminine shade of light pink, in case Liam called me over for an impromptu consultation. I even went back to working out and lifting weights—at home, not the gym—so that once sleeveless season arrived, my upper arms would be toned when I held up paint chips for his approval.

"What's Griff think about all this?" Velma asked.

From what I'd been able to tell, he was amused, at least by the nails, since I'd never been "that type." As for me working for Liam?

"He doesn't know."

The car was silent. Opal put down her clipboard and said, "You mean he doesn't know that Liam asked if you'll be single in the near future?"

"*Nooo*. He doesn't know I'm working for Liam."

Opal clucked her tongue, and Sherise threw herself between the two front seats. "Are you nuts? You know he's going to find out sooner or later."

"When?" That was rich, the idea of Griff having

the audacity to throw a fit over my professional relationship with another man.

At that very moment, he was in Washington, D.C., with Bree, supposedly spending the weekend conducting final interviews and checking facts for his book. But, since I now made a habit of going online to check our credit card accounts, I could tell he hadn't reserved the hotel rooms (or was that *room*) on our Visa or Discover. Which meant he must have used his secret MasterCard because he didn't want me to see what he and Bree were up to.

"It's only a matter of months until Laura's graduation, when he's going to leave me, anyway, for his assistant, so what do I have to lose?"

In a quiet voice, Velma said, "He's not going to leave you, Kat. Don't ask me how I know that, I just do."

Velma was sweet, but for a convicted felon she was painfully naïve. "If you'd read those emails, you'd worry like I do."

"Yes, but you're still having sex."

"Velma!" Opal whipped around. "That's none of our business."

Sherise said, "Well . . . are you, Kat?"

Truth be told, we were having more sex than ever. Hot sex. And not in our bedroom, either. In the living room. In the laundry room. Even on the kitchen table, like in the movies. That episode on the Corolla had unleashed some monster within us that made me blush when I flipped open a

Newsweek and saw an ad for Toyota. *("I love what you do for me!")*

I honestly had no idea why I wanted Griff more or why he would want me when he was having an affair with his assistant, Bree. Was it because we were spending more waking hours together? Possibly. But if I'd had any real backbone, I would not have permitted myself to sleep with a man who was cavorting behind my back with another woman, even if he now made dinner four nights out of the week. (The ultimate aphrodisiac.)

Or, was it because with Liam back in the picture I simply felt more sexual, and Griff, being my husband, conveniently reaped the rewards? And, if so, was *that* akin to cheating? Or was that normal?

But I didn't dare discuss any of this with the group. "We do it occasionally."

"See?" Velma said.

"Oh, men will have sex whenever and with whomever," Opal said, taking one last inventory of her coupons. "That doesn't mean he's *not* going to leave her."

Inside the Shop-N-Buy, a manager was unlocking the doors just as Opal's watch beeped. She flipped through the spreadsheets on her clipboard, checking off this and that to ensure it was all systems go. The invasion of Normandy required less planning than Opal's Sunday morning attack of two-for-one chicken.

"It's seven," she said. "Go time." She slid out her

side of the car as Velma, Sherise, and Opal headed toward the doors where a manager, seeing them arrive en masse, stepped back with trepidation. Not as organized, I trailed behind, shoving my coupons into my purse and folding my shopping list, already beginning to crumple in the damp morning air.

"Hey, Kat."

Wade emerged from the fog holding a cardboard box and a long metal rod with a set of pincers at the end. "Can you spare five minutes?"

"Why?" I took a wary gander at that claw. "What are you up to?"

"You don't have to do anything illegal. . . ."

Bad beginning.

"I just need you to serve as lookout while I raid the Shop-N-Buy Dumpster."

Wade's Dumpster-diving was not as shocking to me as it was to, say, Steve. There'd been many a time right after college when we were so broke, my old roommate, Suzanne, and I would rifle through discarded couches, tables, and whatnot left on sidewalks after yard sales. If it just so happened an item of interest was peeking out of a trash can, well then, all the better. That was how we got our Mr. Coffee. A couple of vinegar douches to remove the buildup and it was as good as new.

But Dumpster-diving at the Shop-N-Buy? That was plain gross. That was jumping into a metal bin filled with rotten oranges and molding meat, putrid smells of decay and mildew. And, considering it was Jersey, the occasional discarded body.

"I'm not going to do that!"

"Why not?" Wade took off the long way around the parking lot, folding the metal claw into three parts so as not to be seen. "It doesn't say there's no trespassing. And this is the best time to do it, when the rest of the group goes in and the manager's making sure Opal's not clearing them out of chicken or sponges or whatever's on her list."

I should have been in there with her since the sales really were outstanding. But he'd piqued my curiosity, so I followed him.

"She'll fill two shopping carts with six types of things, use her coupons to pay squat, and be good for a year." He assessed the Dumpster and the sky above it. "I love fog. Provides all the cover of darkness without necessitating a flashlight."

I loved fog, too—even if it did magnify the odor of rotten eggs and vomit wafting from the garbage bin. In what seemed like a faraway time and place, I'd stood on a foggy beach down at the Shore only last summer when we rented a house for $2,500 a week on a line of credit I then all but ignored. Now, I was in the fog serving as lookout while Wade foraged through trash for food.

That's what I got for blithely spending $2,500 on a weeklong summer house.

"So you'll do it?"

I nodded, but I had my doubts.

Wade instructed me where to stand watch and what to say if we were caught. If anyone approached, I should claim we were searching for boxes. That was Wade's standard excuse and, so far, no store manager had cottoned on that people looking for boxes might also be looking for food to put in them.

He pulled himself up to the edge of the Dumpster and surveyed its contents, opening and closing his Unger Nifty Nabber—the pincer device—as he decided which to pick first.

I thought: *What about rats?*

"Keep your eyes peeled. This'll just take a few minutes." Bending over, he chose his selection. Lettuce. Two cartons of orange juice. A bunch of carrots. A canister of whipped cream. A quart of milk. A bag of apples. Bagels. A broken brand-new hairbrush still in its packaging. A block of cheddar cheese. Also, one package of ground beef.

"A day past the expiration date." He shook his head and jumped off, heading toward my car. "Criminal. There's also fish in there hauled from halfway across the world that men risked their lives to catch, that planes flew and trucks carried. All for naught."

"Wait a minute!" I called after him. "I wanna see."

Inside the privacy of the Corolla, we sifted through the booty. Everything he snagged—except the lettuce and the carrots—was marked by yesterday's expiration date. It all seemed perfectly fine, smelled okay, and, according to Wade, had been dumped no more than a few hours before.

I held up a slightly bruised apple. "I've paid money for produce that's worse than this."

"I know, right? Steve used to get on my case about garbage raiding being illegal. Now you can see why NOT garbage raiding is the real crime."

What Wade said brought to mind a theory Griff had about the flaws in the current consumer marketplace. In short, Griff claimed ALL of us could be paying much, much less if we learned the art of patience. If we waited, items would eventually be marked down as weeks went by. However, there was a certain secret price point beyond which retailers *wouldn't* sell. After that, it was to their advantage to actually dispose of an item rather than mark it down further.

Partially, this was because retailers needed the shelf space for new goods that would provide a greater profit. But, also, it was because they didn't want to train consumers to wait for lower prices. After all, they'd loaded millions of dollars into advertising to teach us quite the opposite, that we *shouldn't* wait, that we should hurry now while supplies last! (At the highest price.) Which was why we ended up paying twice what was fair for the newest tech toy, the recently released DVDs, or outrageously priced Birkin bags. Because we had been trained—like monkeys.

"Pretty cool." I played with his Unger. (Not nearly as dirty as that sounds.)

"Really?" He puffed up proudly, like a little boy displaying his found toad. "Bakeries first thing in the morning are better: yesterday's *pain au chocolat*, croissants, bear claws, bagels—you name it. Though you know what's the best?"

He took a deep breath. "The last Sunday night of the month. People tend to move over the weekend and they get so tired and fed up with packing and sorting that they end up throwing away great stuff that won't get picked up until Monday. You wouldn't believe what I've found after moves."

"Try me."

"Plants. I don't know what it is, but people hate moving plants. I've found ivy, spider plants, even a bonsai that was dying. Also, cheap bookshelves *and* books. VCRs. Even computers. But best of all," he added, "I've found collectibles."

Now he was talking my language. Unless he was talking about Hummel figurines or Beanie Babies. "As in . . ."

"Rare books. Artwork. *Lots* of antiques."

The magic word. I moved closer. "Go on."

He looked off, trying to remember. "Well, there was a broken bronze mantel clock I found last fall that I repaired and sold on eBay for about $150. Also a fireplace mirror that was shattered, though it had a beautiful oak frame. Had that assessed at about $1,000 before the glass was replaced."

"I had no idea you could find stuff that nice. And for free!"

"You have to know where to look. Most people don't, so they end up with crap."

Naturally, I thought of Liam and his search for period furniture. "You think there might be any eighteenth-century stuff?"

"Hmm. That's a stretch since most people assume something that old is valuable and they tend to keep it or sell it. However, it doesn't hurt to look. I can take you to where I found a pair of scissors that an auctioneer told me were at least two hundred years old."

"Could you?" Goody, goody. "I would really, really like that."

"I *could* . . ." He debated with himself. "But you have to keep in mind that, like Steve said, it *is* technically illegal to take from other people's trash. And it's not at night, when I prefer to raid, so there's a better chance of us getting caught."

"I don't care." I didn't. I was positive that with Wade's guidance I'd find an old hand-carved wooden rocker or trundle bed. I just knew it. I could feel success at the tips of my fingers just as I could feel how wonderful it would be to surprise Liam with an authentic Revolutionary War pitcher.

"You're willing to take the risk?" he asked.

"I'm willing to take the risk. But I want to get there before the fog lifts."

"Hey, you're all right," he said, rewarding me

with a genuinely bright smile. "You know, when you walked into the group that first day, I figured you'd never show again, that you were one of those dilettantes who didn't have the stamina for bucking consumerism. But you're catching on pretty fast, aren't you?"

I told him I was. And that, by the way, I had never had more fun.

"How did you get into this Dumpster-diving stuff to begin with?" It was an innocent question to kill time as we drove to Wade's mystery location.

"I'm a freegan," he said. "Stems from the word *vegan*. Freegans are anti-consumers who believe there's so much waste in the world, it's possible to live for free. Out west, they call it living by the Compact."

I'd heard of the Compact from Griff who, being a native Oregonian and being in academics, associated with that ilk. "So you don't buy anything new for a year."

"I don't buy anything new. Ever."

I followed his directions to turn onto Route 206, headed north. If my hunch was right, he was taking me to the Millerville section of Rocky River, an area of old farms that had gradually succumbed to the encroachment of office parks. Brilliant, since I bet those aging homesteads sported attics jam-packed with treasures.

"And have you always been an anti-consumer?

Or did something happen that changed your mind?" I thought of my afternoon with Velma and Sherise when they uncovered my $37,000 of debt. "Seems no one comes to the Penny Pinchers without having survived some trial by fire, like Sherise getting sent by her father or Velma getting sent to jail."

"You know about that?"

"Of course."

"Velma. What a chick." He chuckled to himself. "Well, my path to the Penny Pinchers wasn't too far from Velma's. But for various reasons—most important, your trust in me—I'd like to bury my past as an angry young man. I'd like to think I've grown into a more serene person."

"I'm sorry. I didn't mean to . . ."

"It's okay. Really." He put his hand on my thigh and gave it a pat. "I like you, Kat. Anyone who's willing to be my lookout is A-OK in my book."

He kept his hand there, making an already unusual situation that more awkward. There was no diplomatic solution, either. If I moved his hand, he'd be insulted. If I let it stay, he'd be led on. I thought of Libby and worried. She deserved a man who was loyal and kind and attentive, not one who put his hand on the thigh of the nearest female.

With a loud clap, he lifted his hand and slapped the dashboard. "Stop. Stop here!" He was so adamant, I nearly swerved into the oncoming traffic.

We were at one of those office parks, hardly the place to find antiques. But Wade insisted he knew what he was doing as he gestured madly to the right. "Now, before you miss it. The gate's open."

A nicely landscaped driveway led to the steel-gray building of E. W. Drummond, a concrete fortress packed wall-to-wall with accountants. I couldn't imagine what kind of treasure troves he'd find in those Dumpsters.

"Yes!" He pumped his fist as we passed through the gates and along the twisting road. "I love Sunday mornings. Low security and no employees. I've been waiting to get in here for-ever."

Inner warning bells went off as the wheels of my Corolla moved over the smooth blacktop, past the imposing gold and black E. W. Drummond logo and numerous NO TRESPASSING signs. *We shouldn't be here. This is not why you came with him. Back out now before he gets you in trouble.*

"Uh, Wade . . ."

"Do you know what these people do? They are single-handedly responsible for causing last year's stock market crash that pushed my best friend over the edge, literally. Everyone thinks I did what I did out of greed, but they're wrong. I did it for Eric."

I slammed on the brakes. "Hold on. Who's Eric?"

"Eric and I worked as brokers for seven years. He was a great guy. Funny. Pretty good golfer.

Ugly as sin, but managed to get women anyway 'cause he'd bring them roses and make them laugh."

He rolled down the window, ostensibly to stick out his head and check for security cameras, though I suspected Wade the rugged iconoclast didn't want me to see him being emotional.

"Last summer, Eric lost everything. And I mean everything. His job. His fiancée. His car and his house. We tried to tell him it would be okay, that the market would turn around. But then he admitted he was way overleveraged with the kind of debt no honest man could pay, to quote Springsteen. Credit card debt that not even bankruptcy court will erase. Thirty percent interest."

"Ohmigod." I gasped, knowing where this was going. "He didn't."

Wade made a diving motion with his hand. "Right into the Arthur Kill. Took two weeks to find his body."

"I'm so . . ." To lose someone to suicide over something as stupid as . . . debt! That was the worst. Debt was nothing more than figures on a balance sheet—meaningless and intangible. Life was *life*. And we only got one shot. Debt could be erased whenever.

No wonder Wade had blown off Wall Street and given up money.

"I quit my job and maybe committed some mayhem at the brokerage in the process." Under the shadow of his brow, there was a mischievous smile. "I'd do it again, too."

"Good for you." Though I was dying with curiosity to know what level of mayhem we were talking about. A few stolen Swinglines? Or petty arson? Whatever it was, I suspected it was responsible for him finding the Penny Pinchers.

Stabbing an accusing finger at the Drummond building, he said angrily, "But these are the jerks who made it so the fat cats at our brokerage could keep their second homes and pay for their kids to go to private school, not giving a damn if a stupid palooka from Scranton like Eric could or couldn't pay his mortgage. And now these guys are gonna pay, too."

I looked over to Wade and his clenched fists and clenched jaw and thought, *Shit.* Having plumbed farther into E. W. Drummond territory, the NO TRESPASSING signs had turned more menacing with threats of prosecution and imprisonment and pledges of twenty-four-hour surveillance. Cameras dotted the trees.

It was becoming clear that what had begun as an innocent hunt for a chipped vase was about to quickly turn into something very criminal. And as much as I sympathized with Wade and felt horrible about his friend Eric and understood his frustrations with our system's corrupt usury laws, I could not allow myself to become corrupt myself.

"Wade, what are we doing here?"

"Dumpster diving, of course." He reached in the backseat to fetch his Unger. "You can park here and I'll hoof it so security won't go ballistic. Man, I can't get over it. Usually, this place is closed down like Fort Knox."

No, no, no. My mind raced for a way to stop him since I knew simply telling him to stop would have the reverse effect.

"I don't think you're going to find any free lamps or bedsteads here," I cried, leaning out the window, calling after him as he crossed the drive. "What are you looking for?"

"Just old office furniture. I'll be back in five." With that, he tucked the Unger into the waistband of his shorts and slinked along the hedges, becoming one with the green bushes in the fog.

I did not think he was looking for office furniture.

Killing my engine, I slid down in my seat, though it was already too late. My license plate had been taped by a camera in the elm behind me, and if Wade returned with anything more than a bent paper clip, we were doomed.

Sure. "We were just looking for boxes" might con the dim-witted manager of the Shop-N-Buy, but not the FBI. Raiding a Dumpster for corporate secrets required a higher grade of lying.

Five minutes turned into ten, and then twenty. Finally, after a full half hour, after watching the automatic sprinklers click on twice in the March fog, I decided to see what was what, crossing the access road and following the hedges like Wade until I found the relatively pristine dark blue Dumpster where there was no sign of my brash accomplice, though there were plenty of signs warning of my immediate arrest should I so much as dip a toe into that trash.

"Wade?" I called in a low voice. "*Wade?*"

Nothing.

Circling, I nearly tripped over his cardboard box melting in the rain.

"Wade?" I called a bit louder. "Stop screwing around."

In the distance a rustle turned out to be a squirrel hunting for nuts in the bushes. But then, I heard another—a low, horrible sound. A moan.

"*Ughh.*"

It came from inside the Dumpster.

Wade! Hauling myself onto the side, I got to the point where I was able to deduce that the Dumpster's black rubber cover must have closed him in. By pulling with two hands, gripping the sides with my knees, and trying very hard not to think about what that cover had touched during its tenure shielding New Jersey waste from rain, I managed to yank it back.

Sure enough, there was Wade lying facedown in a pile of shredded office paper fast turning red with blood.

"Ohmigod!" I screamed. "Wade! Are you okay?"

His cheeks were as ghostly gray as the HP printer nearby that must have hit him on the head. "Keep it down," he mumbled.

"I will NOT keep it down. You've got a head injury. We've got to get you to the hospital." And, by the way, how did he expect me to rescue his 170-pound carcass?

"No hospital. No health insurance." He winced. "Give me a minute. I'll get myself out. Right now, I just need a little shut-eye."

Eeep! The first sign of a concussion. No time to waste! With more effort than a woman in her forties should have to expend, I climbed to the Dumpster's edge and threw over a leg. Throwing all caution to the wind, I jumped in and landed with a soft thud on the shredded paper. There were worse dumps, I told myself, than ones filled with paperwork and accountants' empty bags of Doritos.

"Let me take a look." Gingerly, I pushed back his hair to reveal a deep red gash. My stomach did a double flop. "Not too bad. A Band-Aid and you'll be fine."

He cocked open one eye. "It's not a Band-Aid and you know it. This totally screws up my plans."

Elevating his head onto my lap so the blood ran down instead of out, I weighed my options and decided I had none besides somehow forcing him to climb with me out of this hellhole.

Luckily—or, unluckily, depending—voices

gradually emerged outside, growing louder and louder. In the gray sky above us, I could just barely discern the reflection of revolving blue lights. We were in trouble, true, but, with much relief, I realized Wade would get help.

"Oh, great," Wade grumbled. "That's all I need. The fuzz."

"Count yourself fortunate." Gently letting his head down, I pulled myself up to find not only E. W. Drummond security but, also, the Rocky River police, including our former Penny Pincher, Steve, in full uniform. Thank god!

His jaw dropped. "Kat?"

"It's Wade," I said. "He's been hurt."

"How bad?"

"Bad. Head injury."

The cop next to him said, "You know her?"

Steve lifted his radio and said, "I'll call for an ambulance."

He wasn't helping us. I couldn't believe it. How could he be so cruel and unkind?

"You're on private property, ma'am," the other cop said, extending a hand to help me out. "You're in a high-security waste repository that may or may not contain classified information pertaining to certain corporations protected under federal statute."

As he rattled off my violations, it dawned on me that he wasn't just being helpfully informative, he was leading up to reading me my rights. I looked to Steve hoping he would set the record straight and tell this man that I was not some sort of thief, that I was Kat Griffiths, mother, upstanding citizen, *Penny Pincher*, but Steve remained as still as a statue. It was so confusing and . . . heartbreaking. So not like him.

"You got it all wrong, Officer." Wade had managed to drag his bloodied self out of the Dumpster. "There's no drama," he said, staggering toward us. "No raiding of corporate secrets, gentlemen."

Steve shook his head. "Damn it, Wade. I knew this would happen eventually."

"Just that age-old story of a man and a woman who gotta get it on."

What!

And before I could stop him, Wade planted a deep kiss that was so long and so passionate, by the time he finished, I was so woozy it barely registered that I'd just been slapped with handcuffs.

CHAPTER SIXTEEN

And that's it." I clapped my hands on the metal table and faced Rocky River Police Officer Ramone and FBI Agent Wasko, who, after listening to my hours of blow-by-blow recitation of how I ended up in the E. W. Drummond Dumpster, were bleary-eyed and somewhat dazed themselves. "Not stealing corporate secrets. Not out for sabotage. Simply looking for an eighteenth-century rocker."

Wasko rubbed his temples. Ramone took a sip from his Styrofoam coffee cup and, finding it empty, hooked it into a wastepaper basket.

It had all been true, every bit of my story except, perhaps, that teensy-weensy part about Wade searching for office furniture. Though he did say that's what he was doing. Technically.

"I guess what I'm not clear on," Wasko said, flicking a pen at me, "is whether or not you two are an item."

"Please"—I held up my left hand to show the gold band and Griff's diamond—"I'm a married woman."

"Yeah, right. As if that stopped anyone before."

There was a knock at the door and Steve entered, so sheepish he couldn't look me in the eyes. "If you're done here, I wonder if I could have a moment alone with you two before you bring in Wade."

I was worried about Wade. He'd refused medical care, so the paramedics had released him with a bandaged head and a list of warning signs. Libby would no doubt sit by his bedside throughout the night, holding mirrors to his nose to check if he was breathing, but even her smothering attention was no substitute for an MRI.

"Okay, Mrs. Griffiths," Wasko said, "you can go. But my advice is that you call a lawyer."

That lawyer comment was unnerving and so was Steve, who kept his focus squarely on the metal table as I left the room and found Libby practically sitting in Wade's lap, stroking his forehead and clucking in sympathy. Two seats over in a white trench and Italian silk scarf, the vision of calm, sat Viv, trying very, very hard to keep a straight face.

Honestly, I have never been so glad to see my sister.

"Dumpster diving?" She arched an eyebrow. "That's taking this penny-pinching thing too far, don't you think?"

"I am so glad to see you," I cried, opening my arms to give her a great big hug.

She flinched. "Ewww. You'll get blood all over my new coat. It's Juicy Couture."

It was then that I noticed the ratty sweatshirt and jeans I'd worn for schlepping in a grocery store were spattered with Wade's blood. With my pony-tail and Keds, I could have stepped out of a teenage slasher film.

"I can't believe you came," I whispered, taking the seat next to her, being careful to keep my distance. "How'd you find out?"

She nodded to Libby, who was fetching Wade another paper cup of water. "Wade used his one phone call to contact her, and Libby used her unlimited phone calls to contact me. Are you okay?"

"Fine." A random frightening thought. "Did anyone call Griff?"

"Not me. Isn't he in D.C.?"

"Yes, thank God." At least that was one less worry.

"Why? *Do you not want* him to know?"

"No!"

"Kat, what the hell is going on?" Viv bent her head so close I could make out where she'd messed up on her aqua eyeliner. "I thought this Penny Pincher's group of yours was just a bunch of coupon clippers, and now Libby tells me that one of them has a record." She didn't use his name, but she didn't have to. "And he lives in a *hut*."

"A yurt. And he's not the only one with a record." A slow headache was beginning to throb behind my forehead as I began to register my depth of troubles. "It has nothing to do with Wade. It's all my fault. I never should have gone with him to hunt for antiques."

"Antiques? You were caught in the trash bin of E. W. Drummond. What kind of antiques could you find there aside from a mimeograph machine?"

There was no way to get around this without telling her the truth. "I've made a mess of things, Viv. I haven't told Griff and I haven't told you because I don't want Mom finding out, but . . . I've been working for Liam, restoring the house he bought to its original mid-Georgian decor."

"You mean the big one the university used to own?"

I nodded. The headache was getting so bad I wondered if concussions could be contagious.

"For *free*?"

"Of course not. He pays me and he pays me pretty well." Already a thousand for consultation.

"How long has this been going on?"

"Since February. Don't tell Chloe, either. She wanted the job and I got it. I had to, for Laura's sake."

"Oh, Kat." Viv adopted her disappointed older-sister voice. "It all comes back to money. If you and Griff weren't so strapped, you wouldn't have gotten yourself in a situation where you were being paid by your ex."

Sometimes Viv had a particular way of phrasing things that was nothing short of jarring, I thought, as she excused herself to make a phone call.

The door to the conference room opened and Steve emerged, somberly followed by Officer Ramone. "Mr. Rothschild?"

Wade carefully unhooked Libby's arms from where they'd been around his neck as, shuffling in his shackles, he passed Steve without saying a word, like icebergs drifting in the frigid Northern Atlantic.

"I'll wait for you," Libby wailed as the door behind him slammed. Her eyes watered and she blew her nose loudly on a damp ball of tissue. "It's so unfair. Just when we were inches away from getting married."

"It'll be fine, Libby," I said, though I had absolutely no way of being able to promise such a thing. "Wasko and Ramone are actually really nice."

"Maybe to you. But you're not Wade. He's on a different . . . level." She caught sight of Steve, who was off to the side, hovering, and said coolly, "Some help you were."

"Hi, Libby, Kat." He did a slight bow and took off his hat. "I'd like you both to know that I went in there and explained about the Penny Pinchers and how Wade was an odd fish, but he wasn't a criminal, even if he did overreact now and then and dive in Dumpsters for food."

"He is so not an odd fish," Libby said, forgetting to thank Steve for putting his reputation on the line by defending Wade. "He's wonderful."

"Thank you, Steve," I said. "It really helps." This reconfirmed my belief that most people want to do the right thing; sometimes it just takes them a while to come around.

"It won't help. Nothing can be done." Libby began to cry again. "Not with his background."

What *was* his background, anyway?

Viv returned from her phone call, hands in her pockets, and gazed at Steve. "I don't believe we've been introduced."

My word. My sister's blue eyes were actually sparkling and she had that glow she gets whenever she meets a new man of interest. Ah, yes, the uniform. Sailors, cops, and any man in the military made her weak in the knees.

"This is Steve Adams, who used to be in my Penny Pinchers group. Steve, this is my"—I passed on the "older" part—"sister, Viv. Viv Popalaski."

He shook her hand and murmured "Popalaski" like it was exotic.

"Adams! Wait! I know you." Viv wagged her finger. "I bet you're Kyle and Jason's dad."

Steve's face fell. "Uh-oh. What did they do now?"

Viv threw her head back and laughed, revealing a long length of relatively wrinkle-free throat. "They didn't do anything. Oh, maybe they forgot to turn in a couple of papers, but . . ."

Steve kept staring, waiting for the other shoe to drop.

"My sister's an English teacher at Rocky River High," I explained.

"Whew." He drew a hand across his forehead in exaggerated relief. "With those two kids of mine, you never know."

"No, they're good boys." Viv examined her nails, which meant she was lying through her teeth. "I had Kyle last year, and now I have Jason for American Writers. You know, his paper on *The Grapes of Wrath* was not bad. In fact, as I recall, he wrote an excellent analysis of the selfishness motif."

Steve helped himself to the chair between us, pulling it out between his legs. "*The Grapes of Wrath*. That's Steinway, right?"

"Stein*beck*." Viv, who loved nothing more than to show off her knowledge of high school English, added, "You know, *Of Mice and Men. East of Eden*."

"I saw that movie. James Dean. I love James Dean."

Viv twirled a strand of hair, entranced. "Me too. *Rebel Without a Cause* . . . I must have seen that ten times."

"Fifteen." Steve crossed himself. "No kidding. Swear to God. You know, there's a James Dean film festival every spring in Princeton."

"Is there?"

"We should go."

"We *should*."

I got arrested, and my sister got a man. How did that work?

For the first time since I'd fired her, Libby playfully rolled her eyes like she used to when Viv did or said something outrageous. It was her moment of forgiveness, and I could have kissed her for it.

"Mrs. Griffiths?" Wasko appeared at the door. "Mind stepping in for a minute? We have a couple more questions."

It was the office furniture fib, I just knew it, I thought, rubbing my sweaty palms up and down my thighs.

Steve said to me, "You don't have to say boo, you know. By law, you can ask for a lawyer anytime."

Viv squeezed his arm and said, "Thank you for saying that. That was *so* sweet."

"It's part of my job as an enforcer of the law." He grinned in a way that would have made his beloved James Dean proud.

Oh, brother. Get a room already, I thought, glad to give them their space. As I passed by her, Libby flashed me a thumbs-up and whispered, "Tell Wade I love him."

It was quite a different scene from what I'd expected to find in the questioning room. Wade's hands and feet were unbound and up on the table, and he was laughing with Wasko like they were old friends. I took a seat and tried to appear upstanding.

"All right. Listen up, folks, here's the deal." Ramone hitched up his belt. "The good news is, I'm not charging Mrs. Griffiths with attempted theft, and Agent Wasko's not going to pursue the federal counts."

It was as if a hundred pounds had been lifted off my chest. *Thank you*, I mouthed to Wasko, who wrinkled his nose, like it was nothing.

"Mr. Rothschild makes a convincing case that Mrs. Griffiths was only in the E. W. Drummond Dumpster because she'd heard him cry for help, and after her own extremely lengthy description of the events leading up to this incident, we believe her."

It was weird the way they referred to me in the third person.

"However"—Ramone pulled out his ticket book—"the bad news is that I *am* charging her and you, Mr. Rothschild, with defiant trespassing, New Jersey statute 2C: 18-3b, since her car was on private property after hours despite numerous 'no trespassing signs' and since you were in the Dumpster."

"Come on, Ramone." Wade swung his feet off the table. "Defiant trespassing's a bullshit law and you know it."

Wasko fixed him with a glare. "Now, listen, Wade. . . ."

The door opened and a plump woman with frizzy strawberry-blond hair poked her head around the dispatcher. "Sorry to bother you, but there's a Liam Novak here. He claims he's got urgent information about a Mrs. Griffiths. You want me to tell him to wait?"

Liam? What was he doing here?

Ramone jutted his chin at me. "Who's this Novak?"

"My client." My heart was thumping in my chest. My mouth was dry. I couldn't tell if I was excited that he'd come to my rescue or mortified that he'd find me under arrest. "That's why I was searching for antiques—because he's redoing his house. It's a mid-Georgian."

"Whatever mid-Georgian means." Ramone scratched his head and said, "I'll talk to him," and walked out, leaving Wasko, Wade, and me in awkward silence.

"Defiant trespassing," Wade snorted. "That's a joke."

"That's thirty days in jail and not more than a $500 fine," Wasko said. "Doesn't seem so funny to me."

Two minutes later Ramone returned, motioned for Wasko to join him, and they both left. As soon as they were gone, Wade covered his mouth—I supposed so no one on the other side of the two-way mirror could read his lips. "Who's Novak?"

"A friend . . ."

He placed my hand over my mouth and motioned for me to continue.

"A friend and client of my design business. He's the one on the hunt for antiques."

Wade said, "Is that it? What's he do for a living?"

"He's the CEO of PharMax."

Wade scrunched up his face, trying to connect the dots. "That's bizarre."

It *was* bizarre. In fact, the whole morning had been bizarre, starting with raiding grocery store refuse in the fog, to being questioned for hours by the feds, to Liam advocating for my release. For one, I was glad Griff was out of town, even if he was with Bree. He'd never have understood why my ex had come to my rescue.

After what seemed like hours, though it was in all likelihood only minutes, the door opened and Ramone said casually, "Yeah, you two can go."

Wade hopped up, no questions asked, and split. I, on the other hand, was frozen to the table in shock. "What happened?"

"Your charges were reduced to simple trespassing and they'll probably be dropped after the prosecutor gets hold of the case." Ramone waved me out like a traffic cop. "Come on. Don't you want to go home?"

No, actually, I didn't because I knew as soon as I walked out that door Liam would be waiting for me and I was a mess. "How do I look?" I asked, smoothing a strand of hair behind my ear.

Ramone was put off by the question. "I don't know. . . . You look like you got caught raiding trash. That's how you look."

Bravely, I pasted on a confident smile and exited. Yup. There were Viv and Steve, standing impatiently as if itching to be somewhere else, and there was Liam in his Barbour, a white scarf casually and way too debonairly thrown around his neck.

"Thank you for whatever you did," I said. "But how did you know to come?"

Liam cocked his chin to Viv. "Viv called me. Something about you getting in trouble with the police because you were on the hunt for antiques and a group called the Penny Pinchers. I came as fast as I could." His gaze dropped from my greasy hair to my bloodstained shirt and jeans and returned to meet my eyes with a look of pity. "Poor kid."

Poor kid. A favorite phrase of Liam's I hadn't heard in years.

"Excuse me." Viv gave Liam a look of gratitude before turning to me. "I just want to know if you're free to go. Because, if you don't mind, Steve and I want to step out for a cup of coffee. His break ends in ten minutes."

"I'm going to show your sister this new coffee shop," he added, as if he needed to justify their impromptu date.

"Go ahead, go ahead. I just want to go home and take a bath, anyway."

Viv sighed and came over to give me a kiss on a cheek, a not-so-subtle attempt to hide her whispered words of advice. "Be careful, Kat. You're kind of vulnerable these days."

Spinning around, she hooked her arm in Steve's, an inch or so shorter than he. At five foot nine inches, Viv's greatest obstacle to finding love had been finding a man who didn't need to wear elevator shoes. Steve had passed the first test.

When they were out the door, Liam said, "You're not going home."

"Why not?"

"Because you don't have a car, for one thing."

"Yes, I do." I gestured out the window to my trusty Corolla.

Liam, an inveterate snob when it came to such things, turned a pale shade of green. "*That's* your car? That does not seem Kat Popalaski's style at all."

He used my maiden name! "I used to drive a Lexus, but then I traded it in for this right before Christmas."

"Because . . ."

"Because," I began, remembering the Penny Pinchers mantra that there was no shame in being frugal, "because I didn't want to spend $250 in monthly car payments."

Liam remained stock-still. "No husband, no quality wheels," he said. "We need to talk. Alone."

CHAPTER SEVENTEEN

*L*iam boldly took my hand and led me out the police department double-glass doors into the misting rain. That was just like him to step in and take control. Next, he'd be ordering my entrees and making my dental appointments like he used to.

"Here." His BMW was parked illegally in a space reserved for cop cars. In a million years, Griff never would have done such a thing.

I got in and slammed the door with the impressive thud of German engineering. *Ah, luxury*, I thought, running my hand over the buttery seats, drinking in the smell of fine leather. *Oh, how I've missed you.*

Liam started up the car, reversing and stepping

on the gas like we were hightailing it out of Dodge. "Unbelievable." He brushed his bangs to one side and checked the rearview. "For them to interrogate you like that for two hours for trespassing. It's harassment."

"Well, it was a Dumpster for a high-security firm."

"That's no excuse. They only treated you that way because you didn't have a lawyer." He hooked a right with one finger on the wheel. "Though, I gotta say, Kat, what the hell were you doing in some company's trash to begin with? Yeah, yeah. I know about the search for antiques. Viv said you did it for me, which was why I rushed down here with enough cash to bail you out for murder. But I don't want someone else's trash. It's not like I'm lacking in resources to buy what I want."

He wasn't getting it. Dumpster diving was a chase, a pursuit. The brief thrill I'd had from trespassing and lusting after Wade's booty from the Shop-N-Buy must be, on a larger and cruel scale, what big-game hunters experienced on a safari. Anyone can *buy* something—meat, antiques—but finding it in the wild? Ahh, that was the ticket.

"It's hard to explain," I said, looking out the window at my town as Liam whizzed past the turnoff to our development. "Where are we going?"

"To my house so you can clean up and I can do a little interrogating myself."

I gave him a look.

"That's right—*interrogation*. My brief discussion with your sister while you were in that room was very revealing, as was that Toyota." He braked hard at a red light. "You've been lying to me, Kat."

"Don't take it personally." *I've been lying to everyone.*

"First, let's get you to my house and out of those clothes. . . ." He slapped his forehead. "I mean, into some *new* clothes while those wash. Also, after going through garbage, you kind of . . ."

"Stink?"

He shrugged.

Great. How positively, ultimately humiliating. So much for the dyed hair and polished nails and trying to impress the ex. Liam had seen right through me. Or, rather, *smelled*.

The implications of visiting the house of an ex-boyfriend to shower and talk while my husband was out of town were not lost on my tired brain. It had been dangerous enough agreeing to work for him and letting him set up a line of credit while telling Griff none of this. But visiting his home on a nonprofessional basis was one step over a very important line.

There were no showers on the first floor, so I followed Liam up the narrow stairs to a guest bathroom. He handed me a couple of towels and stood outside the door so I could toss him my sweatshirt and jeans; I hoped he wouldn't be nosy enough to check the size on the waistband.

Warm water and soap were exactly what the doctor ordered. I shampooed and toweled off, feeling like a new woman. When I got out, I found a maroon terry cloth robe slung over the counter, along with a pair of socks. He'd come into the bathroom while I was in the shower and put them there.

This was wrong. Really wrong.

But if Liam shared my concerns, he didn't show it. I found him in the kitchen wearing a plaid flannel shirt and jeans at the stove mixing scrambled eggs as casual as could be. Coffee was being brewed, a cantaloupe was sliced on a cutting board, and the sports section of the *Trentonian* was folded and propped up against the toaster. We could have been any other couple on a lazy Sunday, except I was married and he was not.

"A late brunch," he said, smiling at my robe. "Feel better?"

"A thousand times." I sat on a high wooden stool and took in the kitchen with its outdated cherry cabinets and oversized soapstone sink, a leftover from when this house used to work as a farm. This was going to be the biggest part of the renovation and one we planned on saving for this summer, when Liam could take off a month to spend at his family's compound in Avalon.

He poured me a cup of coffee, adding a splash of milk and about three grains of sugar. "You remembered?" I exclaimed as he slid it to me.

"Hard to forget, Kat. I never met another woman who was so persnickety about her coffee."

I had already noticed two cups in the sink from this morning. Also, a pink razor in the bathroom. Women were so crafty the way they marked their territory.

"But," I said, "you *have* met other women."

He turned off the stove. "You know me. I'm not the type to kiss and tell."

"That's a relief." I went over to the drawer and took out two forks. Liam insisted on cloth napkins, instead of paper, which I found in a tidy stack in another drawer. A woman's touch? Or had my ex, who'd been known to toss his old socks so carelessly that they could be found on light fixtures, changed his bachelor ways? Perhaps his neatness was Paige's influence.

I set the thick pine table and Liam brought over the plates. We were working in perfect synchronicity until he surprised me with a pitcher of fresh orange juice and a bottle of champagne.

"To celebrate your emancipation," he said, popping the cork, holding the bottle away from his body as the foam exploded over the rim. "Also, I thought it might be welcomed after the day you've had."

The champagne was incredibly thoughtful and incredibly Liam. When we were dating, he was forever pulling rabbits out of the hat like this— roses sent to me at work for no reason, a private masseuse at my door after a stressful week. He'd spoiled me forever, I thought as he mixed the mimosas. I needed to make sure I didn't slip into the shrewish habit of comparing him to Griff.

"To you!" He lifted the orange juice and champagne. "And what I hope will be the end of your trash obsession."

If he only knew how fun Dumpster diving could be, I thought, taking a sip. It was delicious and swiftly intoxicating. In the course of becoming a Penny Pincher, I must have lost my tolerance for bubbly—a sad side effect.

Across the table, Liam was amused. "Your nose still goes red right away."

"Pardon?" I put down my glass and, starved, took a bite of the eggs.

"Only with champagne, nothing else. One sip and you're like Rudolph."

"Oh!" I said, horrified. "That's awful."

"It's not awful. It's adorable." Liam buttered his toast.

"I didn't know."

"Hasn't Griff ever noticed that?"

"If he did, he never told me." I delicately bit into a piece of melon. "Then again, it's not like we drink a lot of champagne."

I should have been more mindful. Liam took advantage of that thoughtless aside to probe into my affairs further. "Yeah, I wanted to ask you about that."

Uh-oh. I pretended to become very fascinated with the china pattern on the saucer.

"Viv tells me that the way you ended up in Drummond's trash is that you're a . . . Penny Pincher."

"That's right. It's a club. The Rocky River Penny Pinchers Club." I figured if I made it sound as innocent as a book group, he'd let it drop. "Which reminds me. Have you considered bar iron penny nails in the wood floors? Very authentic for the time period."

"Ah, ah, ah." He wagged his finger. "You're not getting off that easily, Popalaski." Holding up his hand, he ticked off the evidence against me. "You raid a Dumpster. You're part of some coupon-clipping group that meets in the bottom of the library. You've traded your Lexus for a Toyota, and"—he frowned—"your husband doesn't meet you at the police station."

We regarded each other evenly in a match of resolve. Liam, an expert negotiator, would not be the first to declare uncle. That much I knew.

I said, "So?"

"So, you gave me the impression that you were happy."

I poked at my toast, now dry and cold. "Look, Liam, just because I don't guzzle champagne or go around burning gas in an M3 doesn't mean we're not happy. We're regular people, Griff and I, and we have a daughter to put through college.

So, yes, I'm on"—I rolled my eyes—"a budget."

"You?" His shoulders heaved. "A *budget*?"

"Why not?" I dropped the toast on the plate. "For your information, I'm doing quite well. I've got my spending under control, I've got several thousand—*more* than several thousand—saved and, thanks to you, I'm starting my own business."

"Congratulations. But I didn't ask how your finances were going." He paused, grinning. "I asked if you were *happy*."

"*Of course*. Of course I'm happy." Was it hot in here? It certainly felt like a furnace, I thought, loosening the heavy robe. I wanted to ask when my clothes would be out of the dryer so he could drive me to my car and I could be free of my second interrogation of the day.

Liam sat back, tenting his fingers, trying to decide whether to pursue this line of questioning further. "Then what about Griff?"

"Griff didn't come to the police department because he's in D.C. doing research for this book he's writing on the Federal Reserve. I guess it's kind of like an exposé of where they went wrong, if the Fed was responsible for the economic crisis, et cetera, et cetera." I rolled my hand, figuring if I kept babbling he'd quit pestering me about my so-called happiness. "You understand. Business school stuff."

"So, it's more of an academic treatise than nonfiction for business travelers?"

"Strictly small university press."

"You know, a small university press pays shit while a major publisher willing to promote a book that could get on the *New York Times* nonfiction bestseller list could help put Laura through NYU."

"It's not set in stone that this will be a small press book. For example, it won't be if Griff snags an interview with Hunter Christiansen, though that's a long shot. The man hasn't given an interview since he stepped down as chair of the Federal Reserve and, apparently, has decided to publish his memoir posthumously. Super secretive. I don't know if you know about this Christiansen . . ."

"Actually, I talked to him just last week."

I nearly choked on my coffee. "Get out."

"No, really. I tapped him to be on this Wharton alum board I oversee. Hunter's a great guy. He got a bum rap back when he was at the Fed."

"That's what Griff thinks, too."

"Then we agree on something. I mean, besides . . . you."

My fingers drifted to the opening in the robe that, having loosened for air, I now pinched a little tighter.

"I don't want to make this awkward," he began, fiddling with his spoon. "But, I can't help but feel somewhat protective of you, Kat. You were my first great love, the woman I was sure I'd raise a family with and sit with on the porch to watch the sun set in our golden years."

I swallowed back a torrent of emotions, thinking of how many hopes he'd invested in me—and how I'd dashed them on that beach in Avalon. Now was not the time to break down, not while we were alone and I was so vulnerable, as Viv had wisely noted.

"Liam . . ."

"Please. Let me say it and then I'll shut up. The thing is, I may be totally off base, but I sense a sort of dissatisfaction inside you, like life didn't turn out the way you expected. Maybe as someone who feels the same way, I can sense disappointment and regret in another person, especially in someone whom I once loved and of whom I remain very fond."

I was silent.

"I just want you to know that you will always have my love and respect, Kat. As a friend, if nothing else. And also that I'm here for you as a shoulder to lean on when those days—or nights— get dark. I mean that."

He dropped the spoon and reached out his hand. I took it.

We regarded each other. Old friends. Former lovers. Once almost husband and wife. I'd seen him, heard him, felt him hold me in my dreams. Maybe I *had* made a mistake. Maybe Griff had been a convenient diversion that I, in my early twenties and immature, had used to escape the adult world of marriage, kids, and responsibility that came with committing myself to Liam. If I'd been older and not so alarmed by the prospect of ending up in suburbia raising the next generation of little Novaks, Liam and I might have had a happy, productive, loving marriage.

Maybe he was my soul mate after all.

"Thank you," I said, gently removing my hand. "I may take you up on that offer someday."

"I hope you do." He exhaled and got up from the table, taking his plate and mine. "In the meantime, why don't I put in a call to Hunter, explain who Griff is, that he's coming from a friendly position, and see what he says. I happen to know that despite Hunter's reclusive nature, he's mellowed recently and has been talking more about getting his side of the story out in the open."

The buzzer for the dryer went off. "That would be awesome if you could swing that," I said, going down the short hall to get my clothes. "You really think he'd change his mind?"

Liam turned on the water and threw a dish towel over his shoulder. "You never know. He might be ready. Like everything in business—or in life—it's all about timing. Wouldn't you agree?"

But Liam already knew that I did.

CHAPTER EIGHTEEN

*L*isten up, people." Sherise clapped her hands
so we'd settle down. "We have a lot to go
over today and not much time 'cause I have to
leave early. Final job interview in NYC!"

A "whoo-hoo!" went up from Opal and we all
gave Sherise a round of applause. Sherise was one
of two contenders for a lucrative financial planner
position with a major Manhattan bank. If she got
the job—and how could she not?—it was guaran-
teed that she'd be moving out of her parents' house
in Rocky River and into an apartment of her own
by the first of June, right around the corner.

"Sex in the city, baby." She raised her fists. "I
am sooo ready."

Opal and I exchanged wordless understanding.
To be young and smart and in the city with no
children and no responsibilities aside from
pleasing a boss and getting to work on time.
Girlfriends. Shopping. Nights on the town. The
two of us sighed in envy.

Heaven.

"But before we start talking about what's on
sale this week and what coupons are hot, I need to
first welcome back a very important member of
our group." Sherise waved to Steve, who shifted in
his chair. "It's good to see you again, my friend.
We missed you."

"I'll say. There was no one to piss off." Wade slapped him on the back. "Just a bunch of girls."

Libby gave him a sharp nudge.

"Yeah, well." Steve bowed his crew-cut head shyly. "You knew I couldn't stay away for long."

Opal said, "And you brought company." She nodded to the woman nervously holding his hand. Viv.

That's right, my sister, she who once claimed to be allergic to the ink used in printing coupons, had begged Steve to take her to a meeting. Hello? What was I, chopped liver? I'd been going to these meetings for months and not once had she so much as hinted for me to let her tag along.

Steve said, "I always knew I'd be glad when Wade finally got busted for raiding other people's trash. But I had no idea why."

Steve and Viv bumped noses, Eskimo kisses, and Libby stuck her finger down her throat in a pantomime gag.

"Anyone else have other big news to report?" Sherise looked around the room, where we sat in our semicircle munching on popcorn Opal had brought from home. "Not that anything can quite compare to finding true love."

Viv giggled.

Velma put down her knitting and raised her hand. "I do. As of last Tuesday, I am officially off parole."

"What does that mean?" Opal asked.

"That I can cross state lines now and don't

have to check in with my parole officer." She bit her lip guiltily. "That I can handle other people's money and finances."

What?

Sherise said, "Let's give it up for Velma being able to touch other people's money."

I applauded tentatively. Good thing Griff wasn't here. He would have thrown a fit knowing Velma had gone through our stuff illegally.

"So aside from Opal, who's saved up enough to take her first vacation in ten years . . ."

"To Florida." Opal waved her brochure featuring sunny beaches and palm trees. She'd been showing it to anyone who would look. "Four days in Fort Myers for $340 a person. I cannot wait to get in that sun after that long winter and stick my toes in that sand."

Sherise slapped her with a high five. "All right, Opal. Okay. Anyone else?"

Libby looked to Wade. "I don't know if this counts as good news."

"Sure, it does." Wade gave her an encouraging nod. "Absolutely."

"But," she went on, almost unable to contain herself, "Wade and I are planning on moving in together, just as soon as he can find someone to buy the yurt."

Good for Libby. Weeks of ministering that head wound of his had finally paid off in his first steps toward commitment. Either that or the concussion hadn't healed and he was delusional.

Steve said, "You mean in a bona fide apartment with a roof and running water?"

"And no mom?" Opal added.

"No mom." Wade turned to Libby. "Do you want to tell them or should I?"

"Go ahead. It's such good news."

Wade said, "You don't have to worry about me being a freeloader, Steve, because I have joined the ranks of the employed."

Stunning. Way more stunning than Steve dating my sister or Velma being out from under the eyes of the law. Wade had been so opposed to any trappings of the capitalistic system that for him to get a job could only mean that he had found something larger than himself.

Or, that Libby was pregnant.

"It's not being a broker again. Forget that. In this job I'll actually be contributing to society because I'll be working at a nonprofit in Trenton offering micro loans to regular, everyday people who want to start their own businesses." He inclined his head toward me. "Like Kat, maybe. You can be my first client."

Sherise said, "Wade might be onto something there, Kat. What do you think?"

What I thought was that all our lives were changing so fast. Sherise would be moving to New York and leaving the group. Opal was off to Florida, and Wade and Libby were settling down to build their lives. Even Viv was so wrapped up in Steve, she rarely called to chat. Everyone was moving forward except for me.

I was being left behind.

Laura's graduation was weeks away and that meant Griff would soon be asking for a divorce. She'd be off to NYU and he'd be off with Bree. And I would be alone.

"I think I'd like to look into that," I said, my eyes stinging. "You know, considering I'll be on my own soon."

A big tear plopped onto a coupon for thirty cents off Palmolive clutched in my hand. Quickly, since it was so embarrassing to be caught in a moment of self-pity, I swept it away, though it was followed by another. And another, until the Palmolive coupon was soaked and wrinkled.

It was soon covered by Libby's hand. And then by Wade's. And Steve's. And Viv's. And Opal's. And Sherise's. And, lastly, Velma's tiny fist. All of them were gathered around me.

"Don't you know," Velma said, "that when you're a member of the Penny Pinchers, you're never alone."

Opal cracked, "And take it from me. That's not just a promise, that's a threat."

I was so lucky to have found them.

Chloe breezed in the front door, coffee in hand, newspaper under her arm, and headed for her office. "What's on my agenda today, Kat?"

277

"Wall coverings." I finished an email I was writing to Liam, closing out of it fast. "For the McWilliamses. They like the Maya Romanoff."

"Excellent. I adore Maya Romanoff." She held up a copy of the *Princeton Pen*, the town's monthly newspaper. "Harry the coffee guy mentioned there was a story about you in here today. Can't wait to read it."

"About me?"

At first, I couldn't imagine why the *Princeton Pen* would have written about little old me. I'd been in the *Pen* twice before: One time had been a random photo of me trick-or-treating with Laura when she was small, and the other was when I stood up at a school board meeting during a teachers' strike to defend Viv. I couldn't think of anything I'd done recently that had been photographed or . . .

The police blotter! But, wait, the cops wouldn't have filed a report about Wade and me if our charges had been dropped, right?

"You know, Chloe," I said, swinging around from my desk. "We really need to get cracking on the McWilliams project. Those people are going to be back from Italy soon and . . ."

"They're not going to be back until the end of summer. We have oodles of leeway." She spread open the paper and studied the front page. The newsprint looked very out of place on her white Louis XIV desk with the gold-leaf legs next to her hand-painted pink and cream lamp. I couldn't ever remember seeing Chloe read a newspaper or anything besides catalogs.

"Hmmm. They're raising the price of parking downtown. We should complain about that."

"Let's write a letter right now."

If Chloe found out I'd been arrested, it would be the end of my job. No question. My hands shook as I riffled through my desk drawer for a pad and pen thinking I could not, absolutely *could not*, afford to be fired. Yes, I wanted to be out from under her. But not now. Not when we needed savings for Laura's tuition.

Not when Griff was just about to leave me for Bree and I needed money to pay Toni and . . . survive.

"I don't see it in the first section. Let me try local."

Oh, god.

"To the Princeton Parking Authority," I began, drafting her letter of complaint. "As the owner of Interiors by Chloe, I was disheartened to discover that, once again, the Borough of Princeton is intent on thwarting business. . . ."

"I wouldn't say that." She placed a finger on the paragraph where she'd been reading. "Why, I happen to be very good friends with the mayor of . . ."

The front bell tinkled right as Chloe's phone rang. In my paranoia, I pictured every one of her clients bursting through the front door and burning up the telephone lines in outrage over my behavior as reported in this morning's *Princeton Pen*.

"Better go see who it is," Chloe said, picking up her phone and shooing me away.

I would have gathered my purse and marched out then and there if the person waiting on the chintz couch wasn't a small woman with short curly hair dressed head to toe in black. My first client, Madeleine Granville, holding a copy of the *Princeton Pen*.

She waved the paper. "I was waiting for the nine-twenty back to New York, reading in the Princeton Junction station, when I came across this delightful item about you!"

I hid my face in my hands. "It's not how it appears. There's a back story. . . ."

"Oh, I'm sure there is." Madeleine laughed. "Wade Rothschild III? How did you ever get hooked up with the likes of him?"

How did she know Wade? "He's just a guy from my Penny Pinchers group who happens to enjoy the occasional Dumpster dive, that's all."

I thought Madeleine would bust a gut. "*Penny Pinchers group? Dumpster diving?*" She could barely get out the words, gasping between *Dumpster* and *diving*. "*Wade?*"

"Is that surprising?"

"Uh, yeah. Don't you think?"

I blinked.

She furrowed her brow curiously. "You mean, you have no idea that the guy you went Dumpster diving with has got to be worth at least fifty million dollars?"

It was as though the wind had been knocked out of me. "I don't think we're talking about the same person."

"Oh, yes, we are. He's the son of another Wade Rothschild. You know, as in the Rothschild hotel chain."

I'd never heard of him or the Rothschild hotel chain. Sitting down next to her on the couch, I said, "The Wade I know lives in a tent in his mother's backyard and eats garbage."

"Well, he may be eating garbage now because he's dropped out of society," she said. "But once upon a time he had his own private jet and lived in a condo overlooking Central Park. I should know because I interviewed him in a documentary I did for VH1 on children of the super rich."

According to Madeleine, Wade was born in Princeton but moved to Fifth Avenue to live with his father after his parents divorced. He graduated from Princeton University and from Columbia University's School of Business and had been working as a broker, learning the ropes of finances in preparation for taking over the family empire, when a close friend (Eric) committed suicide in distress over his losses on Wall Street. That prompted him to turn his back on business and drop off the face of the earth, never to be heard from again.

"Until now," Madeleine said. "I had no idea he was right here in town all along."

This explained so much, why he'd been distrustful when I joined the group, why he didn't want to talk about his past, why the cops were so fascinated with our simple trespassing case that they interrogated us for hours and brought in the FBI. Why Libby made that reference about Wade's background.

Did she know? I wondered since, as far as I was aware, she'd been practically supporting him, buying him food, clothes, and acting as his chauffeur. The thought of that made me suddenly very mad. How could he, an alleged multimillionaire, soak off a poor cleaning woman who barely made enough money to afford McDonald's? Maybe that was why Steve was always on his case.

"He's a hurting bird," I said, thinking of how proud Wade had been when he'd announced that he had a job working for a nonprofit at a salary that, in his previous life, would have barely covered his shoe-shine bill.

Madeleine said, "He's no average hurting bird. More like he's the golden goose, Kat. That guy could buy us a thousand times over."

Chloe's door opened, her seething anger wafting to me like a plume of red-hot indignation. "Could you step into my office, Kat?"

I'd almost forgotten about the *Princeton Pen* article. But seeing Chloe teetering on a rage, I remembered very fast. "I'll be right there, Chloe. I'm with someone."

Madeleine hopped up excitedly. "Chloe Sykes. I've heard so much about you from Kat."

Chloe brushed me aside and took in this new person, her all-black Armani suit and Birkin bag, and decided she liked what she saw. "And this is . . . ?"

"Madeleine Granville."

"And you're a friend of Kat's?"

The words that formed on Madeleine's lips were like hammers driving in the final nails of my coffin. I wanted to stop them, to slap my hand over her mouth as Wade had done in the Rocky River police interrogation room, but it was too late.

"Not a friend, actually," Madeleine said sweetly, "a *client*."

That was it. I was cooked.

Chloe didn't miss a beat. She shook Madeleine's hand politely and let it drop at the exact right time. But, her displeasure was evident. Even Madeleine intuited that she'd uttered a fatal faux pas, which she unsuccessfully tried to correct by explaining that I'd only done a small job for her. And only one at that.

"You'll have to excuse me. I have a very busy schedule." Chloe weakly gestured to her office. "Kat . . . if you don't mind."

"Right." Pushing myself up from the couch, I thanked Madeleine for stopping by. "You can reach me at home from now on. Or my cell."

She mouthed, *I'm sorry*, but the damage had been done. The only thing left for me to do was to walk into my boss's office and take my punishment, or pink slip, or both.

Chloe was already at her desk, the newspaper spread wide, an item circled in thick red pen. "Have a seat, Kat."

I took a seat, praying that Chloe would be merciful, that she would remember I had worked for her for twenty years at rock-bottom pay. That I had come in Sundays and Saturdays and my days off, that I took her phone calls at five A.M. and listened to her neurotic ramblings at midnight. That I, as she liked to say, was her partner. *My girl Friday.*

"You have not been the most perfect employee," she began, her long red nails glinting in the light of her lamp. "I have not been the most perfect boss. But what's the one thing I demand?"

I closed my eyes, detesting the fact she put me in the position of having to answer like I was her naughty child. "Loyalty."

"That's right. Loyalty. We're in a competitive business in a rotten economy, Kat. I don't think it's too much to ask that you don't go out and steal clients from my boutique, do you?"

"I did not steal clients, Chloe. Madeleine was a

one-time shot. A very small job for which I was paid a pittance." Not exactly true.

Chloe blinked. "Madeleine? You mean that shrimp of a woman in the Armani ripoff?" She snorted. "Of course she paid you a pittance, because she's peanuts. That's not what I'm talking about. I'm talking about this."

She rotated the paper for me to read. As she did, I had a flash that maybe she was mad because I hadn't introduced her to Wade or, as I'd earlier feared, that I'd been arrested. But then I saw it was a feature photo of a library I knew well. It belonged in Liam's home. And, in fact, Liam was pictured reading in a wing chair.

Below it was a caption about how Liam had purchased Macalester House for preservation and how he planned to restore the place to its original decor with the help of a relatively unknown local interior designer. Me.

My peripheral vision turned black, and at the center of my focus was my name, KATARINA POPALASKI, which meant the information must have been given to the reporter by Liam, who refused to call me by my married name.

Chloe would fire me for this, of that I had no doubt. But at that moment in Chloe's office, amidst the sound of her *tap, tap, tapping* her pen, I was struck by a far more pressing fear.

Griff.

He would read this and learn I'd been working

for my ex boyfriend and hadn't told him. Intentionally.

There was only one thing to do, and that was hightail it to his office as fast as humanly possible to explain—before he read the paper.

"Excuse me, Chloe," I said, pushing back my chair and jumping up to go. "I'm sorry."

"Well, it's a little too late for apologies." She refolded the paper. "You should have thought of that before you went behind my back to undercut my deal with Liam. There's absolutely no way I can retain an employee who did such a thing. If I could do worse than fire you, I would."

"No," I said, "I have to go. Now."

"I think not," she said. "There are letters to be mailed and samples to be picked up. I can't be expected to fetch marble on my own. You owe me that much, at least."

But I was already halfway out her door. "Sorry, Chloe. But when a girl's gotta go, a girl's gotta go."

And I went, grabbing my purse and nothing else as I got in my car and drove to Emerly College, praying it wasn't too late. How long had that paper been out on the stands? I wondered, revving the engine at each red light. And why did I care when he'd be leaving me, anyway? When I'd spent months saving in preparation.

Because I loved him, I thought, getting out of my car and running to the stone building that held political science/history/sociology/economics, bypassing the elevator to take the stairs two at a time. He was my husband, father of my daughter.

He had to understand. I would make him.

I yanked open the doors to the economics department and heard her tinkling laughter flow out of his office into the reception area. Bree. She was with him in his office, alone.

Janice, the department receptionist, looked up and did a double take.

"Kat? What are you doing here in the middle of the day?"

I rarely visited Griff's office out of respect for his need to keep his worlds separate—not easy in academics, where students fired off emails at two A.M. and called at all hours begging for extensions.

"He's in?"

She picked up the phone. "Maybe I should buzz him."

"No, please. A surprise is more fun."

Janice opened her mouth to say something, perhaps to advise me against busting in on Griff and Bree in cahoots, but I was a tigress on a mission, following my rival's young, feminine voice as though it were a scent leading me to my prey.

Sure enough, I found them side-by-side on his couch, his arm around her shoulders, laughing. I must have stood there for two whole minutes before they even bothered to look up and see me at the door.

"Kat!" Griff leaped off the couch.

Bree pushed down her short skirt.

"Hey, guys." I would have loved nothing more than to give them a casual wave, but I was shaking too hard to pull it off. "What's up?"

"What brings you here?" He came over and graced me with a kiss. His trademark smell of books and library dust was replaced by the sickening sweet scent of Bree's perfume.

She gave me a sheepish finger wave. I wanted to slap her.

"You have perfect timing. We were just celebrating." He took my hand and guided me toward the couch sitting me next to *her.* "Guess what our big news is."

This could not be the moment when he would announce he was leaving me. He wouldn't be so cruel right in front of Bree. But whatever it was, she was already several steps ahead of me because she was gazing up at him with devout adoration while I, his wife, was in the dark.

"After months of negotiation and emails on my part and on Bree's"—he inclined his head toward her—"I am pleased to report that it's official."

I couldn't breathe.

"Next week, Bree and I are hopping a flight to Alaska . . ."

Oh, god. Oh, god. Please, no . . .

". . . to spend a week interviewing . . . Hunter Christiansen."

Stars danced before my eyes, and there was a sound like a dentist's drill in my ears. Fainting was a distinct possibility.

Griff slapped his thighs. "I can tell you're shocked."

"I . . ." I pressed my fingers to my temple, trying to focus my thoughts. "So you're *not* leaving me?"

"I am for a week. Unless you'd like to be holed up in a log cabin outside Ketchikan with the former chairman of the Fed talking monetary policy nonstop with a couple of wonks like us."

"I'll take a rain check." It was beginning to dawn on me that he *wasn't* leaving. At least, not for good. There was still a chance.

Except, that also meant he would be spending a whole week with Bree up in the woods of Alaska, far, far away from me. My relief that he wasn't leaving for good gradually dulled as I fathomed this excursion presented another chance for Bree to lasso my husband to herself. Griff hadn't even considered asking me, either. It was as though I didn't exist in their little universe.

Liam. He was responsible for this, for calling Hunter and making it happen and finessing it so well that Griff remained under the false impression that he and Bree had scored a coup. If he only knew that in doing so, he had further jeopardized my marriage.

Unless that had been part of his plan, too. No.

Not Liam. He wouldn't have made the call to Hunter just to get Griff out of the picture for a week. What was wrong with me? Between being fired and the shock of finding Griff laughing it up with Bree, I had become temporarily delusional.

"You know what this means, don't you?" Griff was saying. "It means this is a whole new book I'm writing now, Kat, a commercial one, not academic. It means for the first time in twenty years, I finally have the chance of breaking free."

I couldn't help but notice he didn't say "we." And that was no delusion.

Chapter Nineteen

*T*he day Griff and Bree left, I put Laura on the train to Penn Station for a weekend at New York University aimed at wooing prospective students. This reminded me of when she was nine and I sent her to pirate fantasy camp. Just as much fun, just as much of a snowball's chance in hell of becoming a reality. Not when NYU, the third most expensive college in the country, had the audacity to charge more than $50,000 a year. At that price, I'd have rather she spent fifty cents on a fake eye patch than mire herself in the kind of debt swamping her parents.

Hours before, I'd schlepped Griff and a very morose Bree to Newark for their long flight to Anchorage and then to Ketchikan, where the reclusive Hunter Christiansen lived sequestered in a huge lodge surrounded by trees and bitter memories.

Inconsolable Bree insisted on sitting in the back-seat and peering out the window longingly, as if the spewing smokestacks off the New Jersey Turnpike were the waving gold wheat fields of home and the gray skyline was not cloudy all day.

Every once in a while I'd glance in my rear-view and catch her dabbing at the thick black mascara streaks or blowing her red, raw nose. It was killing me that since she was within earshot I couldn't ask Griff what was wrong. Then again, Griff was off in his own Hunter Christiansen dreamland, rehearsing his questions, mulling over his stats and theories.

Planning his escape.

"This is so exciting, guys!" I slapped the steering wheel, determined to show Griff what he was sacrificing, a woman of self-confidence and opti-mism in contrast to his moping Bree. "You think you'll see a moose? Any grizzly bears?"

He dropped his hand and grinned. "We're not going on safari, Kat."

"I should think not. You'd be headed in entirely the wrong direction if you're looking for a safari. Africa's over there."

Only Griff laughed. "It'd be nice if we saw some wildlife, but I'm not counting on it. My biggest concern is that we're going to get there and

Christiansen's going to choke and tell us to go home. He has a history of being fickle."

"I'm sure you have a note card for that. In 1992, Hunter Christiansen addressed Congress and announced that he was fickle. The Dow plunged two hundred points. Right, Bree?"

Bree grunted. "Right."

Griff reached behind him and stroked her knee— her knee!—in consolation. "Don't worry, Bree. I bet your cell will ring as soon as we touch down in Anchorage and it'll be Dewitt calling to apologize."

"I don't think so." She sniffed loudly. "It's over."

This would have to happen, I thought. Conveniently, right before jetting off to a secluded retreat with the man she secretly loves, Bree and her fiancé had had a fight and called off the engagement. I could see right through her. She was *so* transparent!

And what was with the waterworks? She was getting what she wanted—my husband.

"Bree's gonna need some TLC, I'm afraid," Griff murmured after she got out at Newark Airport, tugging a blue pull-along listlessly.

"She's not the only one," I said, making sure to leave him with a long, sexy kiss.

He put his arms around me, defying the airport cop who clearly had no truck with long, teary good-byes. "I'll miss you, you know."

"Will you?" I cocked my head doubtfully. "Oh, I'm sure you'll manage."

"And you? What will you be doing with your-self while I'm gone?"

"Working. What else?"

He gave me a questioning look. "Are you sure you're not up to something? You've been acting sort of strange lately."

What could he mean by that, I wondered, since, as far as I was aware, I'd been acting perfectly normal. "Don't worry about me. This is the inter-view that's going to change your career, remember?"

The cop in his fluorescent yellow vest tapped his watch. "Five minutes, folks. This is a drop-off zone. Parking's over in the garage if you want to make a scene out of it."

Griff gave me a quick peck. "See you in a week."

"Knock him dead." I thought about that. "Though not literally." Hunter had to be at least in his eighties.

I watched as Griff in his leather bomber jacket disappeared through the automatic glass doors and got back into my car, ignoring the cop's glare. That was it. I was alone for a week, maybe longer. Maybe for the rest of my life.

Usually, I didn't mind being alone because in the past I'd use it as an opportunity to shop without fear of Griff's third degree when I arrived loaded down with bags. This time, though, it was dif-ferent. No shopping, no money. I didn't even *want* to shop, which was, frankly, not normal.

The very idea of logging into my checking account and seeing it had been depleted by a whimsical purchase of, say, a $600 pair of flats from Italy was enough to keep me up nights. That was my new addiction, in fact, checking my online bank account five or six times a day to make sure all was well.

The thing was, Griff and I had been spending so much time together, just hanging out, that I was used to him. Now what was I going to do? I didn't have him. Or Laura. Or even a job.

But I did have the Penny Pinchers, two of whom—Libby and Velma—were in my driveway when I got home, sitting in Libby's truck because Jasper was loose. Even though loose, by her definition, meant Jasper was half comatose and curled up in a ball.

"We thought it might be tough for you," Velma said as I helped her out of the truck. "What with being alone." She produced one of her foil-covered cinnamon coffee cakes, along with her legendary fruit salad with the marshmallows.

"Yeah, after your"—Libby searched for the right word—"*breakdown* at the last meeting, we got our marching orders from Opal to not let you have a minute's peace."

That was probably true, I thought, unlocking the door, tickled by Opal's motherly ways.

"Sherise got the job." Libby took the coffee cake from Velma and plunked it on the counter.

"You won't believe how much money she's gonna make, too."

Velma said, "She won't need to pinch those pennies anymore. Speaking of which, how did Griff react to you getting fired?"

"I didn't tell him because I didn't want to ruin his trip. Guess you could call it my lovely parting gift." I got out a knife and plates for the cake while Velma helped herself to my coffeemaker, filling it with her own decaf.

"You know," Libby said, pulling herself onto the counter, "Wade was serious about the micro loans. It's a really simple process, and he'll walk you through it so you can at least get enough money to buy some material and advertising or whatever it is interior designers need."

Slicing the cake into tiny wedges, I tried not to think about my life after Griff, even if it did involve starting my own business. All that planning, all that saving, and yet, having him gone for a week had brought it crashing home. This was what it was going to be like when he left me for Bree. Lonely. Cold.

Sensing my reluctance, Velma artfully turned the conversation back to Wade and Libby. "How does he like his job, anyway?"

"He loves it," Libby said. "I just wish the money were better, though. I'm struggling to make ends meet more now than before he moved in."

Okay, I thought, *that's it*. Putting down the knife, I said, "You do know, don't you, that Wade is worth about fifty million dollars?"

Velma screeched. "What?"

"Oh, sure." Libby swung her legs. "But that's family money. That's not his."

"Who cares?" Velma rounded on her. "*Mi familia es su familia,* as the saying goes. That is, if it's true he's that rich."

"It's true. His father owns a bunch of hotels."

To drive it home, I added, "Wade grew up on Fifth Avenue."

"The one in New York? Or the one in Princeton?"

Velma could be such a hick. "New York. As in overlooking Central Park. And he had a private plane and went to Princeton."

"I don't care," Libby said, lifting her chin. "Sure, it'd be nice not to be so strapped for cash all the time, to be a little less anxious when the bills come in. But we have everything we need in my cozy apartment. We have each other."

Velma made a face. "Which would you rather have? Fifty million smackeroos or a man?"

"Not any man." Libby bowed her head. "Wade. He's all I need."

Libby's gushing love reminded me of when I was young and felt the same way about a piss-poor grad student. If it meant not being with Griff, I, too, would have spurned millions—heck, I did by turning down Liam. I remember the warm feeling of anticipation at the end of the day, driving home from work, knowing we'd be together in our own tiny apartment, just the two of us. I'd felt so lucky in those days, so blessed to have Griff as my own. What was money compared to that kind of bliss?

"Well." Velma threw up her hands. "Not my business."

"Not mine, either," I had to agree. But still!

After Libby and Velma left, I called in Jasper and headed for our basement, which served as refuge and reminder of the home improvement loan we were still paying off. Whenever I flipped on the lights and saw that expensive shag carpeting, the entertainment center, the idle Barca-loungers, and *huuuge* television, I cringed. It was like the "fat picture" dieters tape on the fridge to remind them to stay out. *Never again*, I thought, sitting at Griff's desk. *Never again.*

Turning on the computer, I ignored the bouncing postage stamp indicating Griff had new email and logged into our checking account. $4,634. Enough to cover the mortgage, the home loan, the electric bill, and make a few more payments on Discover and Visa. (I often paid them two or three times a month in tiny amounts just to drive them nuts.)

The postcard kept bouncing.

No! I was not going there again. Too painful.

Ripping open the mortgage, I grabbed a checkbook and carefully wrote out the amount, adding $50 more to the principal. Then I recorded it in Quicken.

What to do about Wade and Libby?, I wondered, turning my thoughts to gossip while I paid the bills, a trick I'd learned to lessen the pain of draining my checking account.

Should I call him? Take him out for coffee and explain how Libby, who'd been born and raised with nothing, would surely appreciate a taste of luxury? Or should I do as Velma suggested and stay out of it because it was none of my business?

Bounce. Bounce. The postage stamp would not give it up. I'd made a firm resolution after the incident last summer to never, ever check Griff's email again. I was so proud of myself. And yet . . .

Bounce. Bounce. Bounce.

. . . We *had* been getting along so much better lately.

Bounce.

So maybe, just maybe, one of these emails might be positive, I thought. What if he'd written b.robeson@emerly.edu to say plans had changed and he did love me after all and had absolutely no intention of leaving me and that was the real reason Bree was crying in the car? Sure, that was a fantasy. But if it were true, wouldn't I feel better about him being in the woods of Alaska with her?

Of course, I would. The future of our marriage hinged on whether or not I read those emails. Not just our future, but Laura's, too.

I was seconds away from clicking on the postage

stamp when the phone on Griff's desk rang and I snatched it up, hoping it was him.

"Griff?"

There was an awkward pause. "Actually, it's me. Liam."

Liam. I hadn't spoken to him since the article ran in the *Princeton Pen*.

"I tried reaching you at work, but some new girl answered the phone," he said. "Is it true you're not working there anymore?"

How to break it to him in a way that didn't make him feel guilty? Certainly, it hadn't been his intention to get me fired. "Afraid so."

"Please tell me it had nothing to do with the photo that ran in the paper."

I didn't answer.

"Shit. I was worried that was the case. I thought your name in print would be some free publicity since . . ."

"It's all right, Liam. Don't worry about it. Chloe was . . ."

"A piece of work." He chuckled. "Still, I feel bad. I know it's not like you can afford to . . ." He stopped short of calling me broke. "Look, I might just have a solution."

"Solutions are good. I'm listening."

"The family getaway in Avalon. You've always loved that place."

The very place where I broke his heart. "Are you kidding? Your house is a gem. I mean, there can't be that many rambling nineteenth-century frame structures still on the beach, right?"

"Whatever ones there were have been torn down to build bigger, sturdier showplaces. That's what my brothers and sisters want to do, but I want to preserve its decor of shabby chic. I told them I'd foot the bill for a spit-and-polish if they'd give me a chance."

I held my breath. To do two jobs for him, not just one, smacked of extreme charity. Or more than that. Yet, the potential income would be hard to resist. I was in no position to turn down job offers, not with Griff and Bree executing the final stages of their escape.

"And before you conclude I'm doing this out of guilt over the *Princeton Pen* article or some other reason"—he cleared his throat—"rest assured that my primary motivation is purely logistical. You've been a great help on my house in Princeton, Kat. You understand me and you listen and you're easy to work with. I know you'd be the same with this project."

"I'm speechless."

"Obviously not," he joked, "because you just spoke."

"My only hesitation is Griff."

"Ah, yes. You still haven't told him about the Macalester House, have you?"

"I was getting around to it. Haven't quite found the right moment to bring it up."

"Though it has been almost five months."

I winced. "It's complicated. It'll be bad enough when he finds out it was your one phone call to Hunter and not his months of emails that got him that interview."

"So he *did* get the interview?"

"He's in Alaska as we speak. Somewhere over Canada, I presume."

There was a pause on Liam's end. "Look, I'm afraid you might take this the wrong way, but . . . I'm headed to Avalon this afternoon to open the house for the summer. How about you join me tonight, before the rest of the family descends tomorrow? We can talk and generally brain-storm."

My chest went hot. It was bad enough that I hadn't told Griff about working for Liam or about my run-in with the cops and showering at Liam's house. For me to spend a night with him down at the Shore would be inexcusable. It would deal a serious blow to our marriage.

"That's very nice, Liam, but . . ."

"But what? It's perfectly on the up-and-up, Kat. It'll give you a chance to look the place over without being under the microscope of my family."

"So it would definitely be just the two of us."

There was a beat before he said, "Is that a problem?"

Another flush of heat.

"Look, Kat, there are five bedrooms, as you may recall. All have locks on the doors and I promise not to use my secret master key, though you can't blame a guy for trying."

I couldn't help but giggle. Flirtation, as my mother used to say, made the world a nicer place, and Liam was proof of that.

"Ah, at last I made her laugh. So, what say you?"

Before I gave in to my lesser half, I said, "Think I'll have to pass on it tonight, but thank you. It sounds divine."

"I assumed as much. Hey, if you change your mind, call me. You know my cell."

I told him thanks again and hung up, feeling totally conflicted. Liam was looking after me, I knew that. Despite his claims to the contrary, he was throwing me work to keep me afloat. That was just his style because he, like I, worried about being financially secure.

I had to admit there was something very alluring about a man who went out of his way to protect me with such respect and dignity. Even if that man was not my husband.

Sighing, I turned my attention to the bills and caught sight of that dancing postcard. What the hell, I thought, clicking on it. After the sacrifice I'd just made by not taking Liam up on his offer, reading a few emails didn't seem like the biggest sin in the world.

I scrolled past a new email from the department

secretary to find an old one from Bree to Griff. Oddly enough, it began with her thoughts on the calculating economist, Ayn Rand.

You mustn't feel that way, Griff. I know you're no fan of Ayn Rand, but as a devoted disciple and confirmed Objectivist, let me reiterate the value of "rational selfishness." Why should you have to put your life on hold for your wife when you're meant for greater things?

Kat can look no farther than her own backyard of Jersey. Her world is the superficial one of shopping malls and consumption, while you were meant for loftier goals and purer surroundings—mountains, woods, books, reflection, and deep intellectual thought.

Now, thanks to me ☺ you have the opportunity to chuck this job and this trap of suburban life and follow your bliss, as they say. My advice is to tell her everything when we get back from Alaska.

After that . . . let the chips fall where they may.

B.

The pain under my sternum was so sharp, it was as if the wind had been knocked out of me. This Bree, this awful, selfish *Ayn Rand lover*, was urging him to leave me. For her. For the woods, mountains, and deep intellectual thought.

Oh, please.

Crazed with heartbreak, furious with resentment, I scrolled through his inbox searching for more. But Griff must have kept faith with his promise last fall to be more careful, because there were no other messages from her.

And only one from him to Bree in his outbox.

```
Your advice is well taken. Let's
discuss in Alaska.

Griff.
```

Curse him.

Without thought, without reproach from my inner voice, my hand reached for the phone and dialed the number I'd come to memorize.

"What time do you want me there?" was all I said.

"I'll be there around six." Liam's voice was low and gruff. "You don't know how happy I am that you changed your mind."

CHAPTER TWENTY

*T*he Novak estate was a rambling white house of many stories on an unkempt oceanfront lot. Its overgrown grass and crazy split-rail fence lent a wildness to it that made the neighboring pristine homes with their tidy, white sidewalks and pebbled yards seem foolishly prim. It remained a beautiful destination with splendid white beaches that never suffered from the overcrowding just a few miles to the north. Since Liam and I had dated, though, the real estate values here had inflated to ridiculous proportions. Elaine told me the other day that a simple two-bedroom bungalow, two blocks from the beach, went for two million dollars.

I couldn't begin to calculate the worth of Liam's 4,200-square-foot estate.

The churning ocean was steely gray since the sun had almost set when I arrived around seven thirty on the unseasonably chilly May evening. A spring breeze was tinged with salt, and a fine mist cut through the black turtleneck that had been enough to keep me warm back in Rocky River but here was as worthless as Kleenex. But that didn't stop me from lingering outside to inhale the invigorating air and listen to the steady thunder of waves crashing in the descending darkness.

"It's awesome, isn't it?" Liam came down the wide front steps.

He took my bag and kissed me lightly on the cheek, adding absently, "I'm always on my secretary Lilly about her cavalier use of *awesome*. It'll be a shock to that generation when something awesome really happens and they've run out of words to describe it."

I said, "You're beginning to sound like an old man."

"Old men aren't so bad. We have our talents. And experience." He put an arm around me and rubbed my shoulders. "You're freezing. I've got just the ticket to warm you up."

"A fire?"

"I was thinking more along the lines of a fiery cabernet, but I've heard this fire thing works well, too."

Possibly afraid I'd turn and flee, he hooked my bag over his shoulder and led me by the hand up the stairs, my mind racing. *What am I doing here? What possible positive outcome can result from this?* Fire was right. I was playing with it and I had a very good chance of getting burned.

Liam had been spot-on about the shabby chic since every item, though ratty, was of high quality. The beautiful hammered-tin ceilings showed signs of slight rust corrosion in the corners from exposure to salty air, and the Southern yellow pine floors were scuffed and darkened with age and sand. Faded antique throw rugs, small enough to shake outside, set off a thick farmer's table and a Franklin rocker mended at the joints. An old cast-iron woodstove provided some heat, but not enough to combat the drafts blowing through the chinks.

"See what I mean?" He flicked on a light in the kitchen, and an overhead brass candelabra flickered precariously. "Definitely due for a renovation."

"It's fantastic and you know it." I kicked my bag to the door, ready for a quick getaway. "Every other place in Avalon is white tile, yellow walls, and vinyl siding. It's like a Florida retirement community."

He opened a drawer for a corkscrew. "Remember this?" It was an old scoop with SPRINGER'S on the side, the name of the ice-cream parlor we used to hit almost every night in Stone Harbor for mint chip.

"Where did you get that?"

"Keith stole it when he was fifteen." Keith was Liam's younger brother, the token reprobate of the family.

"That's not all he stole." He riffled through the drawer for more. "Ashtrays, towels, can openers, corkscrews, glasses. Entire furniture sets. And you know what gets me? My mother just took the stuff and never questioned why the new kitchen stool said 'Windrift,' or how come all our glasses bore the names of local bars and restaurants."

The late Mrs. Novak would get along with Wade. "Did she raid Dumpsters, too?"

There was a *pop!* as he removed the cork. "Of course. She had eight kids. You don't think she was dumb enough to buy new, do you?" He poured out two glasses and handed me one. "A toast."

"To Springer's and your mother."

"To Springer's and my mother and . . . to what we were and what we'll always be to each other. How's that?"

"The rude half of me wants to say corny, but the polite half says it was touching."

"Always did prefer the rude half of you. To rudeness!"

"Hear, hear."

We clinked glasses and Liam leaned against the wall, taking in my outfit—jeans, ribbed black turtleneck, modest silver hoop earrings. "You're more gorgeous than ever, Kat."

I zeroed in on my wine, unsure of how to respond. He was making an advance, had thrown the ball into my court, and how I returned it could very well determine what happened with us that night.

"Music to the ears of any middle-aged woman," I quipped.

"You're not middle aged. That kind of attitude is dangerous, you know. You have to think young, vibrant!"

He inclined his head toward the living room.

"Come on. Let's make a fire and then head to the beach. I'll loan you one of my coats."

I sat on the old red couch with its ugly crocheted throw as Liam messed with the woodstove. Underneath his navy cashmere sweater and white cotton T-shirt, I could make out a still strong back. The Novaks had always been an athletic bunch—football in the fall, skiing in the winter, sailing in the summer—and it was paying off with the reward of a fine physique later in life.

What had happened with his marriage? He was so handsome and easy to be with, so big on family. How could a man this noble, this loving, be alone?

"Have you ever read any Ayn Rand?" I asked.

He threw in a handful of kindling. "Geesh. What makes you ask a scary question like that?"

"I was just wondering." I took a sip of wine. "I read something about her today and I've been thinking about her 'superiority of the individual' crap and it occurred to me that maybe men, when they get to a certain age, have to test if they can be out on their own. You know, one last adventure in the wilderness before they surrender to hearth and home."

He got the fire going and closed the door halfway. "Are these the kinds of intellectual conversations you have with Griff?" He joined me on the couch, close. "Analyzing Ayn Rand."

"Unfortunately, no. That's the problem."

He arched his eyebrows. "So, my hunch was

right. All is not paradise between my former love and her current one."

"Do you honestly think I'd be here if it was?"

"I suppose not." He put his wine down on an old steamer chest that served as a coffee table. "I kind of had an inkling when you didn't call Griff after your arrest. If I'd been your husband, I would have dropped what I'd been doing and come to your rescue in a heartbeat, even if I was in D.C.—or, hell, China."

I know.

Leaning his elbow on the back of the couch, preparing for a tearjerker, he said, "What, exactly, is this dire problem?"

"Ayn Rand, like I said. I think he's spent so many years teaching Milton Friedman and Alan Greenspan and their Objectivist tripe that he might be starting to believe it." I paused, debating how much to confide. "After this book is researched and Laura's out of high school, he's leaving me."

Liam didn't move a muscle. "He told you that?"

"No. I've found emails."

"Shit." The room warmed and he pushed up his sleeves before going to the fire and adding another log. "Sorry to hear that, Kat. All I can say is, marriage is tough. Having been through a nasty divorce, I'm here to tell you, avoid it if you can."

"At least you and Paige never fought over money, I bet."

"That was one issue we were spared, yes."

"Did you know money is the leading cause of divorce in America? Not infidelity, like most people think. It's okay if your spouse screws around on you, just watch out if they run up the credit cards."

"Trust me, there are worse things than money that can ruin a marriage." He gave the fire a couple of stiff pokes. "There's coldness and cruelty and manipulation."

"I assume we're talking about Paige."

He hung up the poker and thrust his hands in his pockets, his face red from the stove. "She was my wife and I feel guilty trashing her behind her back, but it was a nightmare, Kat. Her hair-trigger temper. Her need to control. It was as though every move I made was a mistake and she was there to record it and hold it to my face." Turning to the fire, he added, "I hated coming home."

Her need to control, I thought. *Well, there's a switch.* Seemed Liam had finally met his match.

"All I ever wanted when I signed up for marriage," he continued, "was love, companionship, family, and some regular sex. She didn't have to be the perfect hostess or a champion equestrian. She just had to be . . . nice."

We nodded, understanding. This was a vulnerable moment, a thin spot, in our lives. By either chance or the vagaries of middle age or divine intervention, we had reunited at our weakest states and I had better step carefully.

Reading my mind, Liam said, "I have to watch out that I don't take advantage of you tonight."

"As if you could."

He grinned. "That's what I've missed the most. You weren't just lovely and sexy. You were my best friend. You could take it as easily as you could dish it out."

Ditto, I thought. Already, despite our stated reservations, we were getting way too complimentary with each other, especially since we seemed to be treading on that rosy path to nostalgia.

"You know what, Liam? I think we could do with a walk on the beach."

Fresh air and a bracing breeze sounded good on paper, or maybe in a personal ad, but was nasty business in practice. Liam pulled a sweater over my head and zippered me into a windbreaker. But the wind whipped to my bones as my feet sank in the cold sand and he steered me to the breaker for shelter.

"Too bad we don't have fireworks," he yelled over the ocean's roar. "I always loved setting off Roman candles at night over the ocean."

"In this wind, they'd dive-bomb us," I yelled back.

Once hunkered down amidst the craggy rocks, however, the wind, even the rain, seemed to disappear. I brushed back my hair, already thick with salt and sand, and said, "Okay. You brought me down to the Shore for a reason and I'm guessing it doesn't have a thing to do with redoing your family beach house."

"You're right. And maybe I ought to lay it on the line."

"You'd better, and fast. It's freezing."

He took my hand and covered it with both his hands. "Here's the situation. When you started working for me, I resolved to put the past behind us."

"Me too."

"But, that's been getting more and more difficult to do. I keep thinking about you, Kat. We get along so well together. It's so easy and natural. I can't stop asking what went wrong."

I leaned into him, partly for warmth, mostly because I wanted to feel him close to me. "This is really dicey territory we're entering."

"I know. And you don't have to answer me if you don't want to."

"I do. I must, especially if we're going to be working together in the future." I stopped to think. What I was about to say had to be said carefully and with consideration not only to Liam, but to Griff and our marriage. "The truth is, Liam, that when I was twenty-three, I knew what went wrong, and now, two decades later . . . "

I tried putting myself back to when I was twenty-three and so madly in love with Griff that I couldn't help relating every simple act to him. The coffee I drank was the coffee Griff preferred. The book I read, he'd suggested. My favorite shirt was his favorite shirt, the one he casually commented made me look hot. The music I listened to was the stuff he liked. The food . . . the newspapers . . . the politics . . .

Gradually, I remembered how great it was. The electricity and anticipation of seeing him again. His intelligence and sly wit. All of them used to make me swoon. And all of them I'd come to take for granted.

"Nothing went wrong," I said. "It was simply that I met Griff and fell in love because Griff was . . . Griff."

Liam laughed. "I see," he said knowingly. "Then it really wasn't me, it was him."

"In a way, yes."

"Then that's good." He patted my hand. "It makes me feel so much better. You were in love, Kat. Really, truly in love with him because true love can't be described or quantified. You can't say I love so-and-so because she's got a mean serve or shares the same conservative values."

I noticed he used the past tense; he said I *was* in love with Griff.

"And that's what you used to say about Paige."

"When I met her, she fit all my criteria. I didn't even know I *had* criteria. But suddenly it was like I had a mental checklist. Physically fit? Check. Catholic? Check. Republican? Check. It made committing myself to someone after you so much easier. Just the facts, ma'am."

I let go of his hand. "Hold on. You're a *Republican*?"

"Used to be. In my tax bracket, it's inevitable." He took back my hand. "But you know what I used to say when people like my mother asked why I wanted to marry you?"

"You said I had the smokingest body *ev-er*."

"I said, because she's Kat. That was all I could come up with. She's Kat."

"And here I thought it was because I was the spitting image of the Madonna that hung over your grandmother's bed."

"Oh, yeah. There was that. That was creepy." He ran his hand up my arm, slowly, sensuously.

The waves crashing nearby sounded far away, like when you hold a shell to your ear. "We're stuck," I said. "You know perfectly well neither of us is going to make a pass at the other."

"Not when you're still in love with your husband, no. I'm a cad, but I'm not dumb enough to let you break my heart again. He might be planning to leave you. And for that I'm sorry since it's obvious you're mad for the guy. Still."

Liam said out loud what I'd been too frightened to admit. For all my planning and preparations, including the meeting with Toni Feinzig, despite our money woes and near bankruptcy, despite his emails to Bree, I loved my husband. I realized that the day the *Princeton Pen* story appeared, and I knew it the moment his plane took off for

Alaska and I was alone in my house without him.

I loved him and didn't want to be with Liam or anyone else.

"And if I didn't love Griff?"

He pulled me to him, pressing my head to his chest. "Then I would make mad, passionate love to you for days on end until you forgot him entirely."

"You think you could do that . . . at your age?"

"Wise guy." He kissed the top of my head. "I think I could manage."

He stroked my hair as I let myself sink into his warm chest, his heart beating steadily under my ear, the comforting smell of his cashmere sweater mixing with his aura of solid responsibility. Why is it that men who exert restraint are so much sexier than their opposites?

I sighed, safe and comfortable. Glad to know sex was off the table. Well, partly glad.

There was a strange peace, I'd learned from my months of penny pinching, that came from tying one's self to the mast while negotiating the swirling seas of desire. Whether it was lust for a luxurious leather sofa or a charming ex, virtue had its own rewards. Or was that membership? Never could quite remember.

"So where does that leave us?" I said, fingering the hem of his sweater. His style was impeccable. "Besides stuck, I mean."

"Friends? Allies? Admirers? I don't know."

"Or perhaps," I said, everything coming

together, "there's a way for us to stay in each other's lives, happily."

"I'm listening."

"It involves money."

"Yeah? Show me anything worthwhile in life that doesn't."

So I did.

At first, Liam insisted on just giving me a blank check for $10,000 which he dismissed as "a minor fee." But then, I was able to convince him he would benefit from our arrangement the most if he had creative input, too.

"You know you're better at design than I am," I said, tossing the salad in his mother's antique wooden bowl. "If you hadn't had a bunch of He-Man brothers and a father who'd order you to bench-press something if he heard you so much as comment on the drapes, you'd definitely have gone into interior decorating rather than business."

He acted doubtful as he gently flipped flounder filets at the stove. "You know, it's not like I work at Burger King, Kat. I'm responsible for thousands of employees in over one hundred countries. People depend on me to keep the company at its best. They depend on me for their livelihood."

Which was why his iPhone had gone off four-teen times this evening until we both agreed to turn off our cells.

"I'm not asking you to get out there and meet

with Mr. and Mrs. So-and-So about expanding their master bedroom. What I'm suggesting is that you be involved. Help me choose styles, set our direction. Make our online firm an outlet for your creativity."

He turned off the stove and cut up a lemon.

"And you never know," I added. "If this pharmaceutical CEO thing doesn't work out, you'll always have Interiors by Kat and Liam."

He winced.

"Lemon in your eye?"

"No. Kat and Liam. Sounds like a bad folk group. Kat and Liam sing 'If I Had a Hammer.'"

"If you had a hammer," I said, plunking the bowl on the table, "you'd use it to fix the shingles that have flown off this roof."

By the morning, Liam and I had a rough sketch of our new business: an online individualized consultation service for regular, everyday homeowners and apartment dwellers who needed advice on paint, lighting, flooring, furniture, window treatments, you name it, but who couldn't shell out the big bucks.

Most of the $10,000 would go toward developing a top-notch website and software that would accurately replicate the colors and lighting of digital photos sent by potential clients. If we were successful, it would mean the rich man's province of personal interior design would be available to the masses.

Like Madeleine Granville.

Perhaps it was because I'd had Madeleine Granville on my mind that I resorted to her as an excuse when Griff called me the next morning while I toodled up the Atlantic City Expressway, rejuvenated and inspired, itching to get started on my new adventure.

"Hey! You got in okay." The clock said eight thirty—four thirty Alaska time. "Can't sleep?"

"Haven't slept all night." His voice was strained, terse. "Where the hell were you, Kat?"

"What? Why? What's wrong?"

"Laura's in the hospital."

CHAPTER TWENTY-ONE

*W*ithout looking, I dangerously moved right and slowed down as I drifted into the breakdown lane, the fluttering in my chest so rapid I feared I was having a breakdown of a different sort. "I can be there in an hour. Is she okay?"

"She's fine. *Now*. Already back at NYU. They think it must have been food poisoning. She went with a group down to Chinatown for dinner and . . . that's not the point. I couldn't reach you last night, Kat. Laura needed her health insurance info and I didn't have it. Hell, I was in Anchorage four thousand miles away!"

I'd never heard him so angry and I couldn't say

319

I blamed him. "Calm down, Griff. It's not helping—"

"I don't care who it's helping. It was a nightmare. I left a dozen messages on the machine and tried your cell."

How could I have been so neglectful? Laura might have really needed me and I would have been unreachable. What was I saying? I *was* unreachable.

"Did she get the info?"

"Only after Viv used her spare key to get into the house and found it in my home office in the basement." There was a beat and he added, somewhat sinisterly, "Your sister certainly seems to know her way around our personal stuff."

Busted, I thought back to the afternoon of our anniversary party when she and Adele were permitted carte blanche to sift through everything. "Yes, well, she's been helping me sort out the finances." Boy, was he ever going to love *that*.

"I'm not sure that's wise, letting Viv in on our private financial mess, but I'm too beat to get into it with you right now. The bottom line is you needed to be available, Kat. You're her mother. Where were you?"

"I was . . ." Wait. Why did I have to explain to *him* where I was? I wasn't some servant who was expected to be at the beck and call of my family 24/7. "You wanna know where I was? I was working, that's where I was. I was with my very own client Madeleine Granville. But you wouldn't know about her because you're too wrapped up in that stupid book to know that I'm trying to break out on my own."

There. Take that, Mr. Self-Righteous.

He returned my snap with an icy response. "You're back to your old ways, Kat, aren't you?"

"Pardon?" I checked my side-view mirror and pulled onto the highway. Laura might have been okay, but I needed to be closer to her in case she needed me. "What old ways are those?"

"Secrecy. One of the best outcomes of this frugality phase of yours—or, at least, so I thought—was that you'd become more open and honest about everything, including your spending. You don't know how much it bugged me that you'd come home with a new skirt that you claimed you bought for $100, when really it was twice that."

"Look, if I did, it was because I was fed up with having to justify every purchase to you, like you were my father."

"Not your father. Quite the opposite. A *partner.* Have you forgotten that we're a team, that we're married?"

A huge yellow Hummer was beginning to tailgate me, annoyed that I was on the phone AND maintaining the speed limit. As the days of flipping the bird were over for safety's sake, I gently applied the brakes to really drive him mad.

"You know, you're right. I might have forgotten we're married. Not exactly hard to do when you spend more time with your beloved Bree than your wife."

The Hummer passed and leaned on the horn while Griff contemplated that zinger.

When he spoke again, he used the calm, rational tone that bugged me to no end. "I don't know what it is with your obsession over Bree, but I'll tell you one thing. She takes an interest in my work. She doesn't roll her eyes or hint about being bored when I bring up the book, which I rarely do."

"That goes both ways, pal. You don't care about my work, either. You couldn't tell a stripe from a paisley and you don't want to."

"Yeah, well," he said, turning nasty, "there's a difference between a job and a hobby."

The car began to shake as my foot pressed down on the gas going way, way too fast. "It's not a hobby, Griff. That's my living."

"Really? That's news. Say . . . how's business these days? Been to the office lately?" The sarcasm dripped.

He knew I'd been fired. But . . . how?

"Oh, that's right. *Another* secret you kept from me. Too bad Chloe called right before I left to say she'd mailed you a box of your belongings. Also, FYI, your ex-lover's been calling the office, looking for you."

I stomped on the brakes, hard, as I crested a hill

and spied a spidery state trooper hiding in a U-turn. Too late, I realized. For my driving record . . . and my marriage.

That's why Griff had been so silent on the ride up to Newark, why he'd asked what I'd be doing with my week, why he'd graced me with nothing more than a brush of the lips before flying to Alaska. He hadn't been daydreaming about interview questions or statistics, he'd been steaming about my lies.

Guilt poured over me like hot oil.

As did outrage. I was tired of keeping mum about *his* infidelities. There he was presenting himself as so high and mighty and he was anything but. To hell with Toni and her advice. To hell with waiting and saving for the moment when he decided to ask me for an official divorce. The truth was, I was sick of waiting, and didn't what I want matter? For once.

"For your information, I didn't mention losing my job because I wanted to spare you some worry," I began, the words flowing out fast and furious. "As for Liam, I'm helping him restore the house he bought, that's it. I didn't tell you to protect you and your precious ego."

"Oh, please. Liam Novak doesn't even begin to impress. Corporate CEOs are a dime a dozen."

"Perhaps. But my hiding the fact I lost my job doesn't even begin to compare with the fact you opened a secret bank account with $10,000, money that you didn't want me to know about because you're going to use it to run off with Bree as soon as Laura graduates."

Griff was silent for a few seconds. "Where did you get this?"

"From your—*our*—computer in the basement. That's right. I read the emails. You can be pissed if you want, but put yourself in my position. How would you like to learn from Mac mail that I was planning on leaving you? How worthless and isolated and unloved would you feel if you were me?"

The phone went dead.

Good.

I tossed it onto the floor of the car, wishing I could grind it into a million pieces as the flashing blues of the New Jersey State Police filled my whole car, reflecting my inner pulsating craziness.

That was it. My marriage was over. It was done. *Bring it on,* I thought as the trooper took his sweet time checking my plates. *Because I am fiscally in shape and ready.*

Later that day, after checking in with Laura and discovering that, indeed, she was fine, I had a good cry in a long hot shower. The old saw is that your life flashes before you when you die. If that's so, then in my experience, the same was true for a dying marriage.

I could not stop the mental loop of snapshots, one after the other, over and over. Griff at Barb

Gladstone's library table. Him at the Alchemist & Barrister joshing with the students. Kissing me outside the gates of Princeton. At our wedding in "Our Lady of Perpetual Pain," as Viv called our childhood church in South River. Later, biking through the golden vineyards in California on our honeymoon.

Our first apartment with the loud upstairs neighbors and numerous roaches that Griff tried to extinguish by blocking every possible hole in those eight hundred square feet. Laura's birth, so fast and furious there hadn't been time for anesthesia. Her babyhood as Griff and I took turns pacing the floors so she'd stop crying. Taking her for walks in the stroller, dipping her toes in the baby pool. Our vacations down at the Shore when she chortled at the sight of soaring white seagulls.

Christmases. Fourths of July. Anniversaries. Our life speeding up as the years went on, as we fulfilled the pledge of our wedding vows to become one. Sex, glorious, passionate moments of the physical expression of our love, was the icing on the cake. It was all so wonderful, not one moment could be held out as the best.

And, now, it was over. And I was devastated as if half of me had been ripped out of my body and discarded.

I checked the phone again. No message of apology from Griff. None on my cell, either.

"Here." Viv came over the next day with a triple venti latte from Starbucks. "It's your favorite. Drink."

I couldn't. It made me sick. All I wanted was to lie on the couch in my pj's and robe. Was that too much to ask?

"Laura's going to be home in three hours," she said, thrusting out the coffee again. "You'll need this."

"So she can find her mother not only depressed but also *caffeinated*?"

"No. So you'll get some energy and get dressed. You've got to pull yourself together for her sake, Kat. And, if I may be so bold to point out, you've also got to do some explaining to this Madeleine Granville."

I lifted my hands from where they'd be doing an adequate job of keeping the sunlight out of my eyes. "Why?"

"Because you used her as an alibi for spending the night with your ex, that's why. Think what would happen if Griff were to get nosy and make a few phone calls."

She was right. So right that I got dressed in a flash and drove down to Lambertville on the off chance that, being Sunday, she'd be in.

She was—a good and a bad thing. Bad because I didn't have an excuse to wimp out and drive home to Rocky River. Good because I could ask for her discretion in a matter involving my husband.

"Come in," she said, opening the door to her painted checkerboard floor.

I took small pride in seeing that the place had been transformed from a somber, dusty church outbuilding to a cozy cottage with warm golden walls and a red-walled library. Inexpensively black-framed photographs covered the walls, making her seem not so lonely and desperate. There were books everywhere and the fireplace in the living room roared merrily, staving off the spring chill.

"Check out the kitchen." She led the way in slippers and jeans, a loose William & Mary sweatshirt falling almost to her knees. "I did as you said."

Even on a gray day, the kitchen glowed. She'd run bead board halfway up the walls and topped it with a chair rail, all painted a soft white. The rest was painted in "Tiffany Blue." The appliances had been updated with stainless-steel varieties, and the counters were made out of maple and inexpensive soapstone tiles. The room coordinated with the white, yellow, and red rugs on the refinished floors.

A refreshing change from the stained-ochre walls and brown refrigerator.

"So," Madeleine said, pulling up a whitewashed stool. "What could I possibly have to do with your husband?"

It was not easy telling a relative stranger that I'd mentioned her name as an alibi so I could spend a night with an ex-boyfriend. Fortunately,

Madeleine had very little interest in my private life, aside from the fact that Griff was in Alaska interviewing Hunter Christiansen.

She was far more interested in Wade Rothschild and the fact that he was living off Libby.

"Do you mean to tell me that this guy who could afford to buy her the nicest house in town is forcing her to pay half the rent of a crappy walk-up downtown?"

I told her I suspected it was more than half. "I've been thinking about it, and Wade's predicament is more complicated than it would seem. Having come to know the guy slightly, he acts like a man who's been hurt, who doesn't trust people easily."

"And no wonder." She slid off her stool and went to her shiny Sub-Zero refrigerator. "Do you know what it's like to have that kind of money? No one is your friend—or your girlfriend—just because they genuinely like you. Or maybe their feelings *are* sincere, but you can never be sure because you're so rich, there's no way to tell if it's you they're after or your bank account."

I watched her pour out iced teas for both of us. "So, what's the answer?"

"If you're Wade Rothschild III, I guess the answer is to run away and hide in your mother's backyard." She slid the glass to me. "Lemon?"

I nodded.

She rolled a lemon on the wooden counter thoughtfully. "Then again, that's not entirely fair.

A year or so ago, I did a follow-up documentary for VH1 on some of those rich kids, just to see how well they adapted to adulthood."

"And?" I got a spoon and went on a hunt for her sugar. Three grains, nothing more.

"I'd say about half of them had been in and out of rehab. Another quarter had followed in their parents' footsteps: homes in the Hamptons, kids in the same private schools they'd attended, et cetera. But there was one guy I met who really impressed me." She handed me a lemon slice. "He's the heir of a hotel family, just like Wade. Super rich, just like Wade."

I squeezed the lemon and listened, the germ of an idea beginning to take seed in my mind.

"Instead of living a lavish lifestyle, he became a musician, married his college sweetheart, and raised five kids. He also put ten million dollars toward a charity he and his wife founded so underprivileged minority kids could get scholarships." She tasted the iced tea and sighed. "That's what I don't get. Why doesn't Wade do what he did? Why doesn't he give his money away if he hates it so much?"

Perhaps, I thought, no one explained to him that when it came to having money, generosity was always the best option.

Maybe it was about time someone did.

CHAPTER TWENTY-TWO

*T*here were far more pressing matters in my life than Libby and Wade—like my marriage, for starters. But as each day passed without so much as an email or phone call from Griff, as each hour of silence tolled the mourning bell of our life together, I found myself increasingly preoccupied with *their* future instead of my own.

And so, the day before our June Penny Pinchers meeting, two days before Griff got home from Alaska, I decided to take action.

"Call Wade and pretend to be interested in buying his yurt." I handed the phone to Viv, who had stopped over with Steve to check on my well-being.

"You're procrastinating," Viv said, handing it back to me. "You can't face the fact that your marriage is over and so you're spending all your waking hours focusing on someone else instead of meeting with Toni and getting prepared for Griff's big announcement."

She was so blunt about it, as though we were discussing getting rid of old carpet instead of an old husband.

"It won't do any good, anyway," Steve threw in. "The guy is a confirmed vegan, or whatever. He'll never change his ways."

"Yes, he will, and he's a freegan, not a vegan." I clasped my hands together in prayer. "*Please,* Viv. If Libby answers, she'll know right away it's me and she'll be suspicious."

Viv groaned and called Wade while I listened in. Five minutes of chatting and she'd arranged to take a tour of his yurt with an eye toward purchase.

"Like I'd even stay at a Red Roof," she said, hanging up, "never mind sleeping in a tent."

It wasn't until I turned down the private road to Wade's mother's house that I finally understood why Wade got so defensive when Steve referred to his yurt as a tent. It wasn't a tent. It wasn't even close, unless the Big Top and Barnum & Bailey's Circus is one's idea of a pop-up.

Wade's yurt was about as wide as our house, twenty feet in diameter, and set on a cedar platform. With its domed roofline, it looked like someone had chopped off the top of a muffin and set it down in the backyard of the former Mrs. Rothschild, where it fit in nicely on the new green spring grass, with banks of pink roses and a fragrant English garden making for an elegant backdrop.

I parked my car and slammed the door just as Wade threw aside a lightweight door. He stood, barefoot, in his jeans and navy T-shirt, wearing a puzzled expression. "Where's your sister?"

"She couldn't come. I'm her substitute." I trudged up the grass, my heels slipping into the moist sod beneath. "Well," I said, taking a gander at the white structure. "Isn't this something."

"I told you it wasn't a tent."

"I see that."

He held open the door. "Come on. I'll show you inside."

Inside was one big room cordoned off into a kitchen area, a sleeping area, and a living area, including a small woodstove. Wooden rafters led to an opening that could be pulled tight. It was comfortable and airy and the cedar floor made it feel like a tree house.

"There's a bathhouse I built out back with a composting toilet," he said, like that would flip my switch. "Libby talked me into building a sauna for the winter. It's pretty sweet."

Thank goodness he brought up Libby. "You know," I said, looking around, "I'm surprised Libby made you move into her place."

"Oh, she didn't make me move."

I opened and closed the small woodstove. "No?"

"She likes this place."

I went over to the kitchen, where a tiny refrigerator hummed. It reminded me of one I'd had in college. "Then how come you're moving?"

"My mother. She's the one who wants it gone."

Mother, I thought. Figures.

"Now that you've seen it, are you interested?" He swung his arms. "I'm thinking maybe four, five grand. You could live in it fine after your husband leaves. Either that or . . . he could live in it. Great temporary housing for couples going through divorce."

"Graves are even better." I helped myself to a seat on Wade's futon with its Navajo blanket. "You ever been married, Wade?"

"Nope. Nor do I plan to be. Look at you and your husband. Twenty years and . . ." He drew his hand across his throat. "That's it."

This might be more difficult than I'd hoped. "Marriage is a risk, but when it works, it's great. Just because my husband and I went wrong somewhere along the line doesn't mean it's not for you."

"Trust me. It's not for us." Antsy, he stood on tiptoe and touched the beams. "This thing's extremely easy to break down and build back up. Unlike"—he smiled—"marriage."

I patted the futon. "Sit down and let me have a look at that bump."

Like a dutiful child, he sat and let me paw through his hair until I found the scar. "Healed nicely. You can barely tell."

"That was Libby's doing." He sat up and finger-brushed his hair forward. "She rubbed cocoa butter on the scar. Gave it elasticity. If it hadn't been for her, I'd probably have died or something. She stayed awake all night and held a mirror to my face to make sure I was still breathing."

"Wow." I acted impressed. "She must really love you."

"That's the truth. I've never had anyone care for me like she does."

"Not even your mother?"

He flicked a glance at his mother's white ice palace, just barely visible through one of the clear vinyl windows. "Are you kidding? My mother only cared about me as long as my father was in the picture because I was her link to him and his money." He shot me a look. "Libby told me you found out about . . . everything."

"Word gets around when you're the town's resident multi-multimillionaire."

Standing, he put his hands on his hips and said, "That's why you're here, isn't it? You don't want to buy the yurt, do you?"

"No, Wade, I really don't."

"You want me to marry Libby and make her a Rothschild, bring her into that sick world of disgusting wealth, the kind of money that separates soul from body. You don't know what you're pushing, Kat, because you haven't lived it."

"You're right," I said, standing, too. "I haven't. But neither, in a way, have you. You haven't lived the full potential of your money."

I reached into my purse and pulled out a DVD of Madeleine Granville's follow-up documentary on children of the super rich. "There are tons of stories of people just like you, Wade, with your wealth and resources, who instead of running away from the world and hiding in their mother's backyard have had the courage to do just the opposite, to meet the world head-on and make it a better place." I handed it to him. "Watch this and see. There's one guy in here who reminds me of you."

He fingered the DVD tentatively, like it was radioactive. "You're not telling me anything I don't know, Kat."

"Look, if you were with any other woman, I would never have come here and rudely suggested you get married. But this is Libby I'm talking about, a friend who's spent fifteen years scrubbing my toilets, a woman who is willing to live with you in poverty because she loves you."

I pushed him down on the futon. "She knows what it's like to live at the short end of the stick, Wade. As, after rifling through Dumpsters to survive, you do, too. Don't you see? She's your destiny. Together, the two of you can achieve amazing things."

Wade rubbed his brow. "You don't know. You can't possibly begin to understand."

"You're right. I can't. But I can help you see there's another way to live, Wade, which is what the Penny Pinchers—you included—taught me. Another way to live." I tapped the DVD in his hand. "See you at the next meeting."

Because I was pretty sure it was going to be his last.

● ● ●

Madeleine opened the heavy bathroom door of the Rocky River Public Library and headed toward Viv and me. She'd dressed down for the occasion, I thought, donning simple black pants and an understated cream sweater. She looked nice.

"Do you think he'll recognize her?" Viv whispered.

"I doubt it. It was years ago that they met. And she won't say a word. She just wants to observe."

Viv was unsure. It was Sherise's last meeting before she moved to New York and the idea of bringing in a stranger, *a non Penny Pincher,* felt wrong to her.

"Thanks for letting me sit in," Madeleine said, adjusting her bag. "A group of strangers meeting once a month to trade coupons and savings tips. Could make a great documentary down the road."

Viv brightened. She liked anything having to do with TV.

We shut up as Wade and Libby strolled down the hall, hand in hand. Wade was in battered jeans and a button-down shirt, usual fare. Libby was dressed as nicely as usual, in a skirt and light spring sweater.

Aside from the perfunctory hellos, Wade took no further notice of Madeleine.

"He is so different from when I interviewed him years ago," she gushed. "He would never have been caught dead in ripped jeans and Birkenstocks. The guy used to drive a Maserati."

Viv said, "Unbelievable."

Sherise opened the door. "We're going outside. It's such a beautiful day, I can't stand the idea of being holed up in a dark basement."

She was right. The first Wednesday of June was a far cry from the biting cold one in October when I'd stood outside the library with Libby, too chicken to face a group of savers.

The air was fresh with hope and the heady perfume of day lilies planted along the library's back wall. We settled ourselves under a spreading oak, Viv with Steve, Libby with Wade, Velma on a folding chair Steve had brought, and Sherise on a blanket. Opal sat in the middle guarding the coupons from a sudden breeze and handing out lemonade. I couldn't help remembering how odd she'd seemed months ago, how stern when she bragged about buying co-op gas. Such a contrast to what she was, a true Earth Mother.

"Okay, everybody," Sherise began. "You can bet this is a pretty bittersweet meeting for me. I start my new job next week, so this is my last one. But I am determined not to cry!" She held up a finger. "And the first person who makes me has to help me move."

That did it. Opal and I, about to hug her, snapped our arms down, fast.

"I thought so." She smiled. "Anyway, one of my duties is to pick a successor to lead this ragtag bunch. I am open to suggestions, starting immediately."

I raised my hand. "Opal. She's been here almost as long as you, Sherise, and there's no one who knows more about saving."

"No can do." Opal shifted sides and leaned on her left thigh. "This is the last year the kids will be home-schooled, much to my regret. They took a vote and they want to become corrupted by the public school system. Therefore, I have to go out and . . ." She mumbled a curse to the blue sky above us. "Get a job."

"A real job?" Velma said. "But you've been a stay-at-home mother for years. What can you do?"

"Pretty much anything, I guess, with a law degree."

"Where are you going to law school?" I asked, thinking Opal should look into managing DrugSave.

"*Went*, my dear. Temple Law, right across the river. What? You think I got this pushy naturally? It took three years and two bar exams to develop my thick hide."

I'd had no idea. There were surprising depths to these people, average folk I wouldn't have given another thought to had I bumped into them on the street. Velma the secret felon. Wade the secret millionaire, and now Opal the secret lawyer.

"Therefore," Opal began, "since I have a job and you don't, I vote for Kat."

Me? I was flattered, especially when everyone applauded. Viv gave me a thumbs-up and even Wade agreed I'd be perfect for the job.

"You've come the farthest," Wade said. "Aside from Sherise."

"Which is why you'd be good at running the group," she added. "Look at you, Kat. Look at how much you've done in eight short months, how much you've saved."

Viv said, "How much *have* you saved?"

"Yeah," said Madeleine, getting interested, "and where, exactly, did you start?"

"Tell her. Better yet, show her." Sherise handed me a notebook from her purse and a pen. "Write it down."

I took a moment, trying to get all the numbers straight. "When I came here last fall, Madeleine, I was too afraid to touch a Visa bill. No kidding. But then, I found my husband was planning to leave me and then I went to see a lawyer, who said I had to have at least $15,000 ready when he did."

"What a nightmare that was," Viv said, ripping apart a dandelion. "I've never seen my sister so pale as when Toni told her that."

I pointed the pen at her. "Nor so determined. Remember how you laughed . . ."

"I did not!" She looked around. "I really didn't.

I might have been skeptical, but I had good reason. You should have seen what my sister was like. She once closed down the Bridgewater Mall."

Velma said, "Go on, Kat. Get to where Sherise and I slapped you with a reality check."

I recounted that magical and frightening day when the Penny Pinchers descended on my house, Opal rifling through my pantry, Steve just strolling into my bedroom. "As carefree as could be," I said, much to Viv's delight, "supposedly to check out my TV."

Steve said sheepishly, "All I cared about was the TV."

Viv said, "Yeah, right. You snoop."

"And then?" Velma said. "Come on. Get to the good part."

"And then, Sherise and Velma went through my records, even though Velma was not allowed to, by law . . ."

Madeleine said, "Why?"

"Skip it." Velma dismissed her question with a flick of her knitting needle. "Immaterial."

"Which was when," I finished, "I found out that we were $37,000 in debt and that if I wanted to save up enough money for a divorce, I had better change my spending drastically."

"Whoa!" Madeleine shook her head. "In eight months? How much did you save?"

I wrote the number on the notepad. "By cutting

back on utilities, by getting rid of my car payments, lowering my insurance, ditching TV, cable,
and movies, as well as, of course, slashing our
grocery bills, I was able to save an average of
$1,650 a month. Not $15,000, but close."

Turning the notebook around, I showed them the
figure. $13,200.

"Also, we slashed our credit card debt to almost
nothing." My proudest accomplishment, though
I'd done that largely through my freelance interior
design work.

Everyone applauded except for Madeleine, who
gaped at me in shock. Viv blew me a kiss and
mouthed, *I'm so proud of you.*

"My, that certainly is progress," Velma said. "I
can't say I've saved anything, except that the
group does allow me to live on my retirement. Oh,
I also gave approximately $6,000 last year to The
Women's Prison Project, which fights recidivism."

"Velma!" Steve exclaimed. "On your fixed
income? You amaze me."

Indeed. How did this little woman with no
income to speak of manage to save $6,000 to give
to charity?

"It wasn't hard," she said. "When you give, you
get, you know."

Steve said, "I saved four grand for my kids'
education. Not bad for a widower."

Viv patted his thigh. "Not bad at all."

"Hope I don't have to use it for bail," he said,

half kidding. According to Viv, his sons were more than okay. Good, strong boys who benefited from seeing their father sacrifice himself for the community's protection.

My sister, I feared, was so in love she was a goner.

Sherise said, "How about you, Libby? Since we're sharing our success stories."

Underneath her eyelashes, Libby shyly eyed Wade, whose hand she'd been holding throughout the meeting. And for good reason, I noticed, my heart doing a little leap. Because something bright on her left ring finger had just caught the ray of the June sun. "Do you want to tell them?" she asked. "Or should I?"

Wade lifted her hand and kissed it. "Not quite sure how to put this, but I'm thinking maybe Libby and I . . . this will be our last meeting."

Everyone in the room stirred.

"It's no secret in this group that I come from, well, means. Until recently, I'd been denying that because, you know, more money means more problems. I can't tell you how freeing it's been to live simply, to find food on my own, to find the love of a good woman." He kissed her hand again. "Which is why I decided last night to ask Libby, if she could put up with me, would she mind being my wife."

Sherise burst into tears.

"Hah!" Steve clapped once, loudly. "You did it, you fool. Now you'll have to move her."

Wade put his arm around Libby. "I don't mind. Right now, I'm so over the moon, I could move heaven and Earth." He gave me a warm smile. "Right, Kat?"

"I certainly hope so," I said, overflowing with admiration for him and happiness for Libby, as well as love for this whole group of odd, but wonderful, people. "No. I'm *sure* of it. The two of you together? Anything's possible."

"Of course this means I'll have to help Sherise move, too," Steve said, pretending to be begrudging. "I can't let him be the only man here."

"Also," Viv offered, "your sons. A little physical labor never hurt any boy."

"Good point."

Sherise blew her nose and dabbed her eyes. "I just realized something. Who's going to be left after I go? Libby and Wade are going to be living high off the hog. I'm going to be in New York. Opal's going to be fighting for justice and the American way."

"I'm moving to my sister's in Florida," Velma said. "Now that I can cross state lines. No more Jersey winters for me."

Velma! In some ways I'd miss her most of all.

"Okay, so, Viv, Steve, and Kat. That's going to be—"

Steve interrupted. "Actually, they're switching me to weekdays, Monday through Friday, seven to

343

three, so I can be on my boys' schedule. Wednesday mornings are out, therefore. Sorry."

Sherise shook her head. "So that leaves Kat and Viv. The sisters."

"I'm okay," Viv said. "I just came to support Steve."

All eyes turned toward me. But, honestly, what did I need the Penny Pinchers for? I'd saved my money, or enough of it. I'd learned how to stack coupons and the value of store rain checks, the importance of sending in those rebates and plugging appliances into power strips. I didn't need the tips or the coupons.

I needed *them*.

"I guess that's it," I said, tears coming to my own eyes. "We're no longer a group."

"Never." Sherise took my hand between both of hers. "We might not be up to our ears in debt. We might not be out of control with spending. But we will always, *always* be a group."

I thought:

AMOUNT OF MONEY NEEDED TO PAY FOR A
DIVORCE: $15,000

AMOUNT OF CREDIT CARD DEBT: $10,000

HOME EQUITY LOAN: $27,000

COST TO ATTEND NYU FOR ONE YEAR: $50,000

A group of friends with whom you can openly and honestly confide about money, who will listen and not judge you, who will hold your hand when you have to open those bills, who will give you their coupons, drive you across town to the discount grocery stores, who will teach you how to forage through Dumpsters for food, and who will make you laugh all through the whole journey.

Now *that* was priceless.

"I can't believe the group disbanded." Viv sighed.

"These things have life cycles," I said as we sat in my driveway. "Someday someone will find themselves with $30,000 in debt and another person will end up with fifty pounds of chicken parts and they'll realize they can't handle it alone, that they need a group."

Viv peered through the windshield. "Why are there lights on in your kitchen?"

It wasn't like me to ever leave the lights on—all that energy wasted! Laura's car wasn't here. Jasper was asleep in the garage, so it couldn't have been a burglar. Which meant . . .

Griff!

Without saying good-bye, I opened the car door and ran to the house, dashing through raindrops.

Griff!

He'd come home to me. Here I'd been afraid that he'd stay in Alaska with Bree forever, but he came home!

"Griff?" I called, throwing my purse and keys by the phone and checking the kitchen. Nothing. He wasn't in the living room, either.

I ran upstairs, a strange sort of panic overcoming me. *Where is he?* "Griff?"

Why isn't he answering? I thought as I searched all the bedrooms, even the bathrooms.

Finally, I found him in the basement. At the computer.

He looked good, scruffier, but good. His face was tanner from the midnight sun and he'd let a slight beard grow. But it was not a friendly face and he was not glad to see me.

"I won't be staying." He went to the printer and retrieved some papers.

A shot of anxiety. "What do you mean not staying?" It was like my heart was ready to leap out of my chest. All these months of planning for this moment and still I was unprepared. "You can't go. This is your home."

Griff didn't reply. Walking around the desk, he handed me the papers. Legal documents. Contracts. Divorce papers of some sort. Separation decrees. Icky things.

I couldn't look at them. I refused.

"Kat." His voice was serious. "Read these and they'll explain about the money and the bank account and the MasterCard. I didn't tell you last year that I got a New York publisher for this book or an advance because, well, frankly because

I needed the advance to cover my research expenses and I was afraid . . ."

"I'd spend it." With one eye, I glanced at the papers. They had nothing to do with my marriage. They were copies of book contracts, the $10,000 highlighted in yellow.

"I'm sorry that you read my emails and that you thought I was leaving you after Laura's graduation. My plan was to tell you after Laura's graduation because by then the book would be mostly researched and there'd be no money left for you to take. The MasterCard was strictly for tax purposes, to make sure research expenses didn't mix with our home expenses."

And, let's face it, because you didn't trust me.

"Since then," he said, looking so sad it made my heart break, "there've been developments."

My knees began to shake. They weren't going to hold me and I had to lean against the desk simply to remain upright. "What kind of *developments?*"

"Some good ones, like the publisher is increasing the print run in light of the Hunter Christiansen interview."

"Congratulations." That was good news, though it was humbling to realize Bree had learned of it long before. "And . . ."

"And others that have had me thinking."

"About Bree?"

He closed his eyes. "I don't know how many

times I have to tell you that Bree and I don't have that kind of relationship."

"But you work together. Constantly. You email and call."

"So do you and Liam." His jaw clenched. "That's what I mean by other developments." Softening somewhat, he took my hand and led me over to the couch where Sherise had taken me before to break the news of our debt.

"Throughout our marriage, there's always been Liam."

"But—"

He placed a finger over my lips. "I'm not saying that's all your fault. Your mother, for example, won't let the guy go. She seems to think he's the second coming. It wasn't so bad when he was married and out of our lives. Now, though . . ."

Oh, no. No, don't say it!

"Now, he's back and you're with him."

He had that wrong. "I am NOT with him, Griff."

He smiled that patient smile he used with students when they were trying to bullshit about why their papers were overdue. "Don't lie, Kat. Or, rather, *stop* lying. It was bad enough that you did the renovation for his house and didn't tell me. But spending a night with him at the Shore the night Laura got sick in New York . . ."

"How did you . . ."

Griff turned grim and cold. The silence between

us was suddenly so loud it was almost deafening. "I thought as much."

He didn't know. He'd *tricked* me into admitting it.

Like a robot, he got off the couch, grabbed a bag he'd packed, and headed toward the stairs.

"Nothing happened!" I twirled around and ran after him. "We haven't even kissed or anything. We just talked."

He took another step. "The fact that you even had to say that, Kat, speaks volumes."

"No! Wait!" I ran after him, up the stairs, and out the door. "I don't love him," I shouted. "I love you!"

But I'd lost my chance. Griff backed out in his old beat-up car and headed out of the neighborhood. He was gone for good.

One week before Laura's graduation, right on schedule.

CHAPTER TWENTY-THREE

I had $13,000, little credit card debt, and no husband. If I wished, I could have called Toni Feinzig and told her I was all systems go. I had done as she'd instructed, photocopied all the documents I needed. I was prepared like I was supposed to be.

All except for my heart.

As a steady rain poured down, beating mercilessly on the roof, I sought my one and only refuge of a bathtub. But this time, I couldn't call Griff to tell him what had happened, that my best friend and love of my life had walked out the door never to return. Viv, who'd called as soon as she got back to her place, was no comfort.

Nothing anyone could say, no money I had saved, could solve the worst crisis of my life. As I lay in the cooling water, staring at our cracked ceiling, listening to the rain, sobbing softly so Laura couldn't hear, it occurred to me that the last time I'd felt so overwhelmed was not in my bath, but in the basement when Sherise and Velma made me own up to spending my family into disaster.

And yet, I had managed to pull myself out of that dark hole to vanquish what then had seemed like an unconquerable monster, one that threatened to steal our very home and send me hurtling into bankruptcy.

A calm feeling of quiet strength came over me as I reasoned that if I could overcome my financial crisis, then I could overcome a marital one, too. It would require the same sort of determination and confidence that had freed me from debt. It would require the same honesty.

And so, though it was almost midnight, I forced myself out of the bath and into clean clothes. Then I headed for Liam's to take the first step in mending the hole I'd torn in the fabric of my marriage.

Liam was awake. Perhaps that was the most amazing thing, that he was up at that hour when I banged on his door like a crazed woman. If the house had been dark, I might have run off and my marriage wouldn't have stood a chance.

It wasn't until he opened the door in his navy cotton pj bottoms and nothing else that it crossed my mind I might have interrupted him with another woman.

"Remember those dark nights you warned me about?" I began. "Well, this might be one of them."

He squinted. "Kat? You look like a drowned rat." He pulled me in and shut the door. "You're soaked."

"It's not raining that hard. I was in the bath." I slipped off my hood and watched his expression shift from curiosity to alarm.

"What happened?" He went into the living room and returned in his maroon robe and holding a blanket.

"Griff left me tonight."

"Holy . . ." He took my coat, threw it on the floor, and wrapped me in the blanket. "Come on."

I followed him into the living room, where he pushed me on the couch. "Sit," he said, though I was already sitting. Then he opened a cabinet and pulled out a bottle with something dark inside. Pouring a shot or two into a glass, he handed it to me and said, "Single malt, twenty years old. It helps."

The scotch burned and warmed. *Twenty years,* I thought, *how apropos.*

Pouring himself some, he pulled up a leather hassock and positioned himself across from me. Liam could have been a model in a Chivas ad, handsome in his opened robe that allowed a tantalizing glimpse of his bare chest. Perfect age, not too old, not too young. Wealthy. Mature. In control, as always.

"Okay, tell me everything."

I did, sparing nothing. I told him how he had always been a presence in our marriage, how when he stopped being a presence my mother would do her best to bring him back. I confessed to being in deep money woes.

"You should have told me. I could have loaned you whatever you needed."

I gave him a look. "*Loans* were what sank me, Liam. But, thanks."

Then I filled him in on the fight Griff and I had on the phone the day I left Avalon and how I'd lied about where I'd been.

"Understandable," he said. "Go on."

Finally, I delivered Griff's rational explanation for the emails. "He's had a book contract all along and he didn't want me dipping into his funds. That's why he had the MasterCard."

"Probably he was advised to keep a separate account," Liam said, taking a sip of his scotch, "for business and tax purposes."

"You got it. But that's not why he left. He left because he thinks I'm still in love with you."

Liam stared down at his drink. "I see."

I wondered if this was a victory for him, that having destroyed the marriage that had broken his heart, he, vindicated, could get on with his own life.

We sat for a while saying nothing. There was nothing to say.

"So, I suppose the obvious rejoinder to that," Liam said, getting up and helping himself to more scotch, "is . . . what are your feelings for me?"

"I don't know." And that was the truth. I didn't. "It's been a helluva night. My husband who hasn't spoken to me for a week has come to tell me he must be going and you're standing there drinking single-malt scotch looking like you could swing as a *GQ* centerfold."

Putting my drink down, I clutched my head, wishing for the gift of rational thought.

"Then, let me help you out." He sat across from me again and put both hands on my knees. "I love you."

The words hung there like a smoke *ka-boom!* in a cartoon.

"I have always loved you," he continued. "Ever since we first met at PharMax. I remember, you were coming back from a sale . . ."

"In my case, *not* a sale."

". . . and you were crossing the parking lot lugging a big bag of samples. I was new to the place. In fact, Charlie Worthy was showing me around and I took one look at you and said . . . "

That's my future wife. I'd heard the story a million times.

"But, then, you know what I said because I've told you so often." He smiled to himself. "It wasn't a joke and years later I never forgot the feeling of knowing—just *knowing*—you'd be my wife. I had no idea if you were married or single. We hadn't been introduced. I just knew."

It would be so easy for me to have taken this gift of his love and cherish it. It wasn't just the security or protection Liam offered, it was his uncanny ability to instinctively know what I needed before I knew myself.

Most of us want to believe we have found and married our soul mates, and yet, how many of us in the hard light of day can be honest with ourselves and admit we haven't. That somewhere out there is the person we're meant to be with and that each day is a day wasted with the wrong one.

I said to him, "I sense a big *but* coming on."

He rubbed my knees. "There is a big *but*, as you would say. And it doesn't mean I love you any less or that if you gave me the least little sign I wouldn't take you in my arms and take you upstairs and never let you out of my bed."

My cheeks felt hot and it wasn't only because of the scotch.

"*But* . . . as a survivor of divorce—and I use that term tentatively—I love you too much to be a party to putting you through that torture."

I looked up, studied him, tried to get a clue. "You want me to stay married to Griff."

"I know you love him, Kat. I've given you numerous opportunities to take our relationship back to what it was. I purposely created those opportunities. And you know I would have been more than discreet, would have never jeopardized your marriage. Yet, with all those open doors, you never once stepped in. . . . Kat, look at me." He lifted my chin with one finger. His blue eyes shone with sympathy. "I love you and I'm always here for you. But Griff's your soul mate, not me."

I would never know if Liam himself believed that or if he said those words because he knew I needed to hear them in order to save my marriage. What I did know was that true love is proved not by what it does for us, but what it makes us do for those we love.

"Thank you," I whispered, leaning over and kissing him for the very last time.

Elaine followed me through the house, making notes on her clipboard as she went. "You're wise to put it on the market now, before July. Last two weeks of June are my best weeks."

She was trying to make me feel better, but

nothing could make me feel better about selling our family home.

"And, with Laura moving out to go to college, you'll need the money." She opened and closed the linen closet, took one glance at my mess of poorly folded towels, and said, "It'll help if you clean the place out a bit, remove some of the clutter."

We walked down the hall, past the line of framed photos, snapshots of our family life. I didn't dare look at them in case they made me cry. Again.

"Coffee?" I suggested, heading toward the kitchen.

"Kat." Elaine slid an arm around me. "Maybe it's too soon. You two have been separated for only weeks."

"I know. But . . . it's what he wants."

"Yes, but is it what *you* want. You love this house. Sure, it's nothing special." She frowned at our old blue linoleum counter with the chipped corners. "But, you know, it's your home."

I dumped the old grounds into the trash and put in a new liner. "Griff hates Jersey. The only reason he ended up here was because he followed a girl-friend. Then he met me and I got pregnant and we were stuck." I poured in the water and flipped it on. "Stuck. Twenty years, stuck."

"And what are you going to do?"

Get a condo like Beth Williams and stock shelves at Wegmans, I thought.

"You have money saved, right?" she pressed.

"I *did*. I had $13,000," I said, opening my bare cabinets, searching for cookies or anything to put out with the coffee.

"What do you mean you *had* $13,000? Don't tell me you spent it?"

"All of it." Aha! An unopened box of Girl Scout Thin Mints. How did I miss those? "Every last penny just like that." I snapped my fingers.

Elaine slapped her cheek. "After all those months of coupon clipping and no cable and foraging through *Dumpsters*, you're telling me you blew through it."

I handed her the plate of Thin Mints and took a bite. "It was easy. I forgot how easy it was to spend money. And how much fun."

She took a cookie but didn't eat it. "What did you buy?"

"A second chance."

There was a knock at the door and Elaine and I looked at each other. "Griff," I said, going to get it. "He knocks now."

Sure enough, it was Griff, in a white shirt and jeans, too together and relaxed for my own liking. Did he have to look so fit and happy? "Hi, Kat."

"Hi, Griff." I waved him in. "It is your house, too, you know. For a while."

Elaine tensed. "Hi, Griff."

"You're looking good, Elaine." He bent over and brushed her cheek with a gentlemanly kiss. Not even I had gotten so much as that. "Are we ready?"

She patted her briefcase. "Have all the paper-work right here."

The moment I'd been dreading had arrived as we sat down around the kitchen table and Elaine distributed documents for us to sign. "You know, this is gonna sound dumb, but these are simply your agreements with me. Should you at any time choose to change your mind for whatever reason, you can. I will come over and rip that 'For Sale' sign out of the lawn myself, faster than you can—"

Griff reached over and took her hand. "It's okay, Elaine. I think Kat and I are agreed. Aren't we, Kat?"

Because Elaine was there and he wanted to be polite, he turned and smiled, the first smile he'd given me since the night he left. I wanted to freeze the moment, frame it to put with the other family photos in the hallway so I'd have it forever when he was long gone. "Yup. We're agreed."

Elaine sighed and took out her pens. I'd never met a Realtor so unhappy to sign on new clients. I pretended to listen to her go through the agreement, about the 7 percent and if we'd found a buyer and not her and blah, blah, blah. At one point during her little spiel, I looked over at Griff and he seemed dazed, too.

Finally, it was over and we were able to sign. First Griff, then me, then Elaine. And then it was over.

Elaine stood and shook our hands, as if we'd achieved something miraculous. "Ooookay," she said, snapping up her briefcase. "I guess I'll be going then."

Griff shoved his hands in his pockets. "There's a little matter I've got to discuss with Kat."

I said, "I'll walk you to the door, Elaine."

"Nope!" She backed up. "I know where the door is." She practically did the four-minute mile to get away from us.

When she was gone, Griff motioned for me to sit. "So," he said, clasping his hands, "how do you feel about selling the old homestead?"

I loved the way he called it "the old homestead," like it was some rambling ranch out west and not a crappy aluminum-sided colonial in Jersey. "I think it sucks. However"—I nodded—"I think it's necessary."

"Why? Because we need the money?" Thankfully, he didn't add, *because we're getting a divorce.*

"Partially."

"Because we don't." He grinned. "The movie rights to my book on Hunter Christiansen have been sold, Kat. Six figures."

I blinked. What normal theatergoer would see a biography on the crusty former chairman of the Federal Reserve? And what studio would pay six figures for it? "You're kidding."

"I'm not. Hollywood's hot for Hunter. And I gotta say, it's nice to have money for once."

"I wouldn't know."

"But you might know about this." He reached in his back pocket and unfolded a glossy photo of a house I knew well. It was in Rocky River's old historic section, at least two hundred years old, with stone walls and four fireplaces.

"That's the old Mansfield place," I said, practically drooling. "I love that house."

"Do you?" His eyes twinkled. "Good. Because I bought it."

I didn't dare breathe.

He added, "For you."

"What?" My throat felt tight. "You bought it for me to live in? Alone?" It was an awful thought, me rambling around in that big old house.

"No, not alone. With *me*." He slid his hand over. "If that's okay."

All I could do was stare at that hand. It didn't seem real. Not his hand. Not this moment in our kitchen with this fantastic house in front of us.

Not him asking if he could stay with me. I didn't dare hope or presume. The possibility was too fantastic. The likelihood that I'd misunderstood too devastating.

"Griff . . ."

"I'm so sorry I overreacted like that, Kat. It was just that there's something about Liam that . . ."

I threw an arm around him and kissed him. Hard. "I don't work for Liam anymore."

"I know. He told me." Griff played with my hair. "He called last week and came over to my office. We kind of cleared the air."

Oh, to have been a fly on the wall that day.

"So I'm assuming yes on the house . . . because I put in an offer."

"That's too bad." I went to the drawer in the kitchen where we kept the take-out menus until we quit doing take-out since it was too expensive. "Because I put in an offer, too."

I handed him the printout from the Internet. Griff leaned over and studied it like it was a rare piece of parchment.

"What *is* this?"

"It's sixteen acres in Vermont. Woods. Mountains. End of a dirt road. No running water. No electricity. I bought it for you because this is what *you* want."

"With what money?"

I shrugged. "Kind of amazing what you can scrape together when you put your mind to it. At least enough for a deposit." No point in telling him now that it was the money I'd saved on contingency, for a divorce.

"The Penny Pinchers. You blow me away. I . . ." He took another glance at the paper, this time picking it up and laughing. "So now we have to choose between the house you love and the seclusion I crave. It reminds me of that O. Henry short story."

"'The Gift of the Magi.'" I pushed the two photos positioned side-by-side. "Except not even the Gift of the Magi are free."

"Nothing's free, Kat." Griff kissed my neck. "Not even love. Sometimes that costs most of all."

Maybe, I thought to myself. *But not nearly as much as a divorce.*

TOP FIFTEEN DOs
AND DON'Ts

THE PENNY PINCHERS CLUB

1) DON'T go grocery shopping with your husband.
2) DO vacuum the back and underside of your refrigerator once a month and disconnect the icemaker if it hasn't already stopped working.
3) DO share high-speed Internet with your next-door neighbors (with their permission).
4) DON'T buy a durable item when it's brand-new (except for mattresses, swimsuits, and underwear). Shop for used items at flea markets, thrift stores, or yard sales.
5) DO knit quick and easy hats and socks from unraveled sweaters.
6) DON'T buy gas in the afternoon on warm days. Buy it in the early morning, when it's colder—and thicker—in the ground, to get more bang for your buck. Also, always keep your tank more than half full.
7) DO place all "phantom" appliances—TVs, DVRs (total energy hogs), stereos, and

microwaves—on power strips that are easily turned off at night. Replace all bulbs in the house with five-kilowatt CFLs—compact fluorescent lights.

8) DON'T pay for curbside trash service; you'll save $600 a year by recycling and composting instead. Shoot for one bag of trash a week to be taken to the local dump.

9) DON'T pay for expensive name-brand cleaning products. Remove shower mildew with a mixture of water and bleach for pennies instead of spending $4 for mildew-removing products.

10) DON'T wash dishes by hand. Use the dishwasher instead, but use only one half of a dishwashing detergent tablet per load.

11) DO store batteries in the refrigerator. They last longer there.

12) DON'T watch TV. TV creates artificial wants.

13) DO save empty plastic liners from cereal boxes to use later as free waxed paper. Also, they make excellent lunch bags.

14) DO shop the warehouse stores with a frugal girlfriend and split up bulk buys.

15) DON'T get divorced if you can help it. Saving your marriage can save your IRA.

ACKNOWLEDGMENTS

Like many of us, I'm the daughter of parents who grew up in the Depression and who tried to teach me how to shop for groceries, clip coupons, save leftovers, find the best deals, and, most important, save money. Did I listen? Hah! Therefore, I owe much of this book to them. And all I can say is that I, like most Americans, am finally learning their generation's lesson the hard way.

From a more practical point, there were several websites and blogs I visited that offered excellent budgeting tips: betterbudgeting.com, frugal-families.com, usesupermarketcoupons. blogspot.com, and couponmom.com to name a few. The Web is filled with hundreds of resources and coupons and upcoming store fliers and I relied on them to show me the way.

In addition, I owe a huge debt of a different sort to my editor at Dutton, Erika Imranyi, who patiently guided this book back on track with her smart, insightful comments, to my former editor, Julie Doughty, who applauded the idea, and to Dutton publisher Brian Tart for being his usual supportive self. My agent, Heather Schroder, as always, cheered me on.

Finally, I picked up many tips from our fantastic backbloggers at The Lipstick Chronicles (thelipstickchronicles.typepad.com), where I blog with Nancy Martin, Elaine Viets, Kathy Sweeney, Harley Jane Kozak, Michele Martinez, and Lisa Daily. That blog is a wealth of fun and information. But mostly fun. Stop on by.

Also, thank you, Charlie, Anna, and Sam, for respecting my closed office door. Fred, not so much.

I never get tired hearing from readers. Please email me at writesarah@aol.com or contact me through sarahstrohmeyer.com. You never know— I just might have a lead on a good deal.

Thanks for reading!

Center Point Publishing
600 Brooks Road ● PO Box 1
Thorndike ME 04986-0001 USA

(207) 568-3717

US & Canada:
1 800 929-9108
www.centerpointlargeprint.com